MW00912633

THE IDENTICAL CORPSE

by
David F
Winchester

Pittsburgh, PA

ISBN 1-56315-266-5

Paperback Fiction
©Copyright 2000 David F Winchester
All rights reserved
First Printing—2000
Library of Congress #99-66933

Request for information should be addressed to:

SterlingHouse Publisher, Inc.
The Sterling Building
440 Friday Road
Pittsburgh, PA 15209
www.sterlinghousepublisher.com

Cover Design: Michelle S. Vennare—SterlingHouse Publisher
Typesetting: Teresa M. Parkman

This publication includes images from Adobe Illustrator which is protected
by the copyright laws of the U.S., Canada, and elsewhere.

All rights reserved. No part of this publication may be reproduced, stored in
a retrieval system, or transmitted in any form or by any means—electronic,
mechanical, photocopy, recording or any other, except for brief quotations
in printed reviews—without prior permission of the publisher.

This is a work of Fiction. Names, characters, places, and incidents either
are the product of the author's imagination or are used fictitiously.
Any resemblance to actual events or persons, living or dead is
entirely coincidental.

Printed in Canada

CHAPTER 1

It was 5:30 a.m. Sunday, May 3, 1987. Bonnie Cole's phone rang. As she picked up the receiver, she heard Mike Dailey say, "I'll pick up the morning paper and be there in about 30 minutes."

Twenty-seven minutes later, showered, with what little make-up she wore properly in place, and dressed in her favorite pink suit, she answered the soft knock on the door. When she opened it, she liked what she saw. A tall, well-built man with a touch of gray at the temples, Mike still carried his 55 years with style. Dressed casually today in preparation for their lengthy drive, his white shirt, brown trousers and jaunty tan hat surrounded him with an aura of quiet confidence.

She watched Mike pick up her cases and leave. As she slipped on the pink jacket that matched her skirt, she thought, *I'll never see 36 years young again. I suppose I have a few cracks and crevices to prove it, but I'm not dead yet, and obviously neither is he.* Actually, she looked younger than her admitted age. Small boned, she stood five feet three inches, and her soft-brown hair just topped her shoulders. A casual observer might guess her to be a secretary, cosmetic saleslady, or a retail clerk, but no one would think of her as a criminal defense attorney, and a very good one, until they could see and hear her in the court room. She had earned the reputation as one of the best, and clients call her from all parts of the country. Today she and Mike, her private investigator, were on their way home, to Elton, Oregon, from Fargo, North Dakota.

As she slipped in the front seat beside him, she asked, "What's the name of this place?"

"It must be River City, as we stayed in the River Motel. What's your schedule like? Have you any clients in big trouble right now?"

Although his question struck her as odd, Bonnie answered at once. "For the first time in a long time, my slate is clean. The Fargo case lasted so long and took so much of my time that I couldn't accept anything else."

He glanced at her. "What would you have done if the jury had found young Steven guilty?"

"The very thought is scary! Steven was only 15-years-old, as you know, and that overbearing jerk of a father of his was trying to pin his own crime on Steven. Imagine, the father choked his two-year-old son to death and then tried to blame it on Steven. Sometimes I wonder about people!"

"The world has all kinds, but it's the only one we have, and we have to live in it," was Mike's only reply.

Being a careful driver herself, she had always appreciated those same traits in Mike, but today it seemed that he drove faster and with a little less concern. *Somethings on his mind, I wonder what it is?* She kept her thoughts to herself.

"We've been gone a long time, and I know you're anxious to get home. Since we're only 60 miles out of Windcove, Idaho, lets go by and say 'hello' to Art Wilms and his father, Donald. I haven't seen them in three years."

"I'm positive Elton, Oregon can get along without us for another few days. You're the driver." She slid lower in the seat. "Let's go."

They drove on a couple of miles. Bonnie saw a sign that pointed to Windcove, Idaho, and Mike left the main highway.

"We're on our way. How large a town is Windcove?" she asked.

"I really don't know. It's grown so fast. I think Donald Wilms' mining operation helped increase it more than the local people realize."

"Then the Wilms, as the old saying goes, are the big shots of Windcove?"

"That I can't say. The way I heard the story, soon after Donald and Marie were married, her folks died very suddenly, leaving her a large estate, all in cash. Donald saw an ad in the Phoenix News, 'Mine and mountain for sale,' which intrigued him. Donald and Marie packed the same day and moved to Windcove. He bought the mountain, with all the mineral rights, and changed the name to Wilms' Mountain. He discovered the richest vein of gold ever found in the state of Idaho. He operated the mine for about 45 years. Donald has all the money he'll ever need, so he sealed the mine and retired five years ago," Mike said.

He drove through the main part of town. Soon Bonnie spotted the majestic Snake River ahead. "I've never seen the Snake up close before. One doesn't really get the feel when you see it from a plane."

"I've seen this river when it was on a rampage, and believe me, it's not a pretty sight." Mike turned away from her and rolled down the window as he pulled into a service station. "Art owns this Ford dealership and garage," Mike said as the attendant walked over. "Fill her up. Is Art around?"

"No. Really I don't expect to see him today. Sunday's usually the slowest day of the week, so Art stays away," the attendant said.

"How is Art's father doing?"

Bonnie noticed the attendant had a beautiful smile when he said, "He's the same old guy. How long have you known him?"

"I met Donald about 40 years ago. Thanks for the service. If Art should call, please tell him Mike's in town." The attendant nodded, and Mike turned to Bonnie. "I hope Art is home." He drove back to 'D' street and made a right. Shortly after that, he pulled into a double driveway along side a large, two story white house, with roses and more roses.

"Art is no poor or average working fellow and live in a house like this," she said.

"No, his mother died when he was a small boy, and Donald tried to make it up to him. He worships Art, and spends as much time as he can with him." A large Doberman bolted out with the longest, white teeth showing below a snarling upper lip. "I hope she remembers you. Otherwise she might not let us get out of this driveway," Bonnie said.

Mike stuck his head out the window and called, "Come here, Millie."

Bonnie felt relieved when the white teeth disappeared and her short tail began to wag. "She remembers you." At the same moment, Bonnie saw a handsome man come forward with an outstretched hand. "Mike Dailey, what are you doing in town?"

"We came by to see you," Mike grabbed the offered hand and added, "meet my friend, Bonnie Cole."

Art held out a welcome hand. "You're both mighty welcome. Come on in. Today is Dad's birthday, and I'm fixing a box to take to the mountain. With you two along, it will make a real party, and he'll be thrilled to death to see you."

"How old is Donald?" Mike asked.

"This is his 75th," Art said and held the backdoor open for Bonnie. Inside, she saw a spotless kitchen. She had to smile when she saw the small basket with food enough for 20 people spread on the counter.

"Have a seat," Art said and motioned for Bonnie and Mike to sit at the breakfast table, which overlooked the house next door with more roses, and a beautiful bird bath that Bonnie guessed every bird in town had decided to bathe in at the same time. Art quickly served hot cups of coffee and a plate of assorted doughnuts. He chattered away and continued to pack the basket.

During the next hour, Mike and Art reminisced about the past. Bonnie listened, enjoying the warm friendship between the two. Art was so interested in their conversation. When the phone rang, he seemed almost disinclined to answer, but did move slowly toward it, his mouth, however, moving faster than his feet. He picked it up, nonchalantly, on the fourth ring.

It would have been impossible not to hear. Bonnie and Mike

glanced in horror at each other as they listened to the wailing, almost like a small child.

"Dad! What's wrong?" Art screamed into the phone and was immediately alerted and obviously frightened. Another cry for help, and Art responded. "Hold on, Dad. Just hold on. We're on our way."

As Art reeled around with the phone still in his hand, Bonnie heard a weak voice. "Please hurry, Son, hurry," and then what sounded as if someone slammed the receiver.

Bonnie and Mike were already at the back door when Art said, "Let's get out of here. Dad is either hurt or sick."

"Take my car," Mike said and opened the car door. "Shall I stop at the garage?"

"Yes." As Mike stopped, Art stuck his head out the window and yelled, "Jim, get in, Dad's in trouble." In answer to Art's frantic command, a man dressed in greasy coveralls and a grease rag in his hang jumped in the back seat. "What's wrong?" he asked. "We don't know. Dad is either hurt or sick," Art said.

As Jim wiped the grease off his hands, he said, "I've got to put fuel in the helicopter." The landing field was only about a mile from the garage, and as soon as Mike stopped, Jim jumped out and went on a run to fuel the helicopter, while Mike put the car in an empty hangar. Bonnie watched Art as he ran in circles or hopped on one foot then the other. It was then she realized that she had better keep her cool, just in case this was an emergency.

Within minutes, they climbed in the helicopter and took off. It was about three miles to Donald's house. Soon, Bonnie saw a large white house with trees and what looked like shrubs from the air, setting in a beautiful spot on the side of the mountain. Jim circled for the landing.

The helicopter had barely touched the ground when Art leaped out. "There's no smoke," he said and pointed to the chimney. "Dad would have had a fire."

Bonnie noticed it had rained heavily the night before and everything was soaking wet. The four of them ran to the house and stepped onto a covered porch. "Dad's motorcycle isn't here." Art might have said more, but they came face to face with what had been the back door. Someone had kicked it in, and the hinges were only partially holding the door. Both men pulled their guns, and the four ran up the three steps. Bonnie saw a large yellow and white collie stretched out on the floor. "Oh Snapper," Art said, but he and Mike kept on going. Bonnie saw an old-fashioned iron skillet on the floor and the kitchen reeked of burnt eggs and bacon.

She followed Art and Mike as they rushed toward the living room.

On her way, she noticed a couple of huge wet blood tracks showing someone headed toward the outside.

This horrified Bonnie, but Art and Mike were so anxious to get to the living room, apparently neither one noticed the bloody tracks. Bonnie saw a couple of odd, looking shoe heels. She removed her small camera from her jacket pocket and hurriedly snapped a couple of pictures, even though she was shaking so badly that returning the camera to her pocket was a chore. After a deep breath, she followed Art and Mike into the living room. Art's anguished cry brought her to the doorway in a hurry, and she stared at the body of Art's father, a white-haired elderly man tied in a rocker. His head was bent forward and his teeth and gold fillings were scattered on the rug in front of him. She saw blood dripping from his left hand. Someone had cut off his little finger and part of the side of his hand. *Why or how could anyone have so much hatred for someone that they would do such a thing?* she thought.

Someone had tied his arms around the back of the chair. It made her shudder when she saw blood dripping from his left hand onto the rug. Again, she got her camera and took pictures of his butchered left hand. Then she saw his legs cinched so tight to the front of the rocker that she knew he had very little, if any, circulation in his feet. All she could think about was how his legs and arms must have hurt. Again, she gazed at the bent-over head. She noticed swelling on the right side of his head, and the left side had bled so much that blood had run off his head, down his face and neck onto his white shirt and tie. *I've seen some horrible sights in my life, but nothing like this,* she thought. She took her camera and snapped more pictures. The longer Bonnie stared at Art's dad, the worse she felt. She put her handkerchief over her mouth and ran as fast as she could through the kitchen and out the hole in the wall where a door once hung. She got as far as the bank east of the house. With every heave, she thought her stomach would come too. While she waited for her stomach to quiet, she saw where someone had dumped a bouquet of wilted flowers over the bank, and she felt what she guessed was a warm, rough tongue lick her arm. Never in her life had she experienced anything like this. She turned her head and came face to face with a huge elk, with his antlers on both sides of her head. She screamed and ran for the house.

Mike rushed out with his gun. "That's Bronco, he won't hurt anyone. All he wanted was for you to pet him. Are you all right?"

Bonnie nodded. "I'll be okay," she knew after so much throwing-up, her breath could choke a horse. "Do you have a stick of gum?"

"Sure," Mike said, as he slipped a half of a package in her pocket.

"Thanks Mike. I must help Art. He needs us now," she said and returned to the living room. She saw Art kneeling in front of his dad. His head resting against his father's body. Art's cries were almost more than she could bear. She leaned over, gently put her arm around his neck, and put her face against his. "What can I do to help?" she whispered.

She felt him press his face close to hers and try to talk. Bonnie nodded. "We must call the sheriff. What's the number?"

Art rattled off a number. "Just ask for Bob Ingram. Tell him to bring the helicopter and Dr. Phillips."

Bonnie stood, cleared her throat, then looked around for the telephone. When she called, a lady answered, and she asked, "Is Sheriff Ingram there? This is an emergency."

While she waited for the sheriff to answer, she turned and eyed Art. He had laid his head back against his dad's body, and she heard him whisper, "Oh! Dad if you could only tell me who did this." Bonnie swallowed her tears. *I must keep my cool and help him anyway I can.*

Soon, she heard a man's voice. "Sheriff Ingram, how can I help you?" he said.

"Sheriff, I'm Bonnie Cole. Art Wilms asked me to call. He wanted me to tell you to come to Donald's house on the mountain at once, bring the coroner and your helicopter." Bonnie sensed fear in Bob's voice. "Not Donald?" he whispered.

"Yes. Someone brutally murdered him. Please—I know you won't mention this to anyone until you see the condition things are in." All this time, Bonnie was struggling to keep her composure.

"Is anyone else there?"

"Art, Mike Dailey, Jim and I are all here." As Bonnie hung up the phone, she noticed Art's face had lost its redness. It could mean he was going into shock.

"Behind that metal door in the kitchen is an electric heater." He pointed toward the east wall. "Let's turn it on. I'm sure that won't be against their rules," Art said.

Bonnie noticed if she kept her voice under control it seemed to help Art. *Really, it's not that cold in here. He must get warm.* She slid the door open and pressed the 'on' button. Then she remembered the green and white afghan on the arm of the davenport in the living room. She slid the host chair from the end of the dining room table, and Art sat as Bonnie covered him with the comforter. She turned back to the table, her professional mind picking up vibes. The table held a beautiful one place setting of fine china, an oldfashioned large handled silver knife, fork and two teaspoons. She saw a fresh linen napkin in the plate and a silver cream and sugar placed on the fancy mat. In the middle of the table, on a fancy doily, set a potted baby white rose covered with bloom. Art's father must have been a meticulous person. She knew Art had accepted the first terrible blow when he said, "Dad must have been ready for breakfast when a stranger kicked the door in, and whoever did this had to be a stranger, otherwise Snapper would have stayed on her rug."

Bonnie nodded. "What time did your dad usually eat breakfast?"

"Around 9:00 a.m. He was as punctual as the hands on funny-face through the week. Sundays, he slept in." Art smiled as he pointed to the odd clock on the wall. "That's what I've always called his clock."

She glanced at the large clock, ticking away, on the east wall, and half-smiled in relief as she heard the sound of the helicopter. Help was here.

Art laid his head against her and whispered, "I'll soon leave Dad's mountain with him for the last time."

She felt a closeness to this man whom she had met such a short time ago, and held his face against hers. She felt his hot tears as they ran off her face onto his white shirt. *If I could only say or do something that would make it easier for him.* At that moment, the sunlight disappeared from the hole in the wall where it had reflected into the kitchen and the doorway was full of men.

Art coughed and said, "Bob, meet Bonnie Cole and Mike Dailey."

"You're the lady who called?" Bob asked as he shook hands with Mike. Bonnie nodded. "This is our coroner, Dr. Phillips."

Bonnie greeted them. She watched Dr. Phillips stoop and lift Snapper's head. One officer removed some blood and what she thought was food, from around the collie's teeth. As soon as they examined Snapper, the doctor laid the dog's head back on the floor and lovingly petted her, then walked to the middle of the kitchen.

"Whoever did this must have taken your dad by surprise," Bob said.

"I think you're right," Mike said and pointed to the chair someone had pulled away from the table. "It's obvious this is where the son-of-a-bitch broke Donald's right arm."

They all walked into the living room, and Bonnie watched their reactions when they saw the body. The coroner seemed concerned with Donald's head, and she wondered why.

An hour had gone by since the sheriff arrived. Bonnie had watched them take fingerprints, pictures and gather the things they needed.

"Donald looks so uncomfortable," she said and looked at Dr. Phillips.

"He was my old friend. I've known him for 50 years. I'll release him." The doctor clipped the heavy twine. When Donald's arms and legs relaxed, a change came over Art's face.

"Thanks, doctor," Art said, and Dr. Phillips nodded.

She noticed when Donald's feet and legs were on the rug, the crease in his dark blue pants showed, and his black oxford's glistened in the sunlight. "He was a proud, handsome man."

"Good Lord, what they must have put Donald through." Bob hesitated. "Donald's rings and watch are gone," he said. Then he turned to the forensic team. "Do you have all the pictures-and-so-forth you need in this room?"

"Yes, we're through in here," the officer said, and as they began to pack up their gear, it was clear they were anxious to leave.

"I'll go with Dad. Mike, please finish for me."

"We will, my friend," Mike said and squeezed Art's shoulder.

As the officers laid Donald on the stretcher, she took another good look at his head. It was then she noticed the left side of his skull. *Ye Gods, somebody had crushed his head, from the looks of the marks, they must have used the cut glass vase that I saw on the rug,* she thought. The officers loaded Donald into the helicopter. Bob, Art, and one officer climbed in. Bonnie stood in the sunlight and watched the helicopter as it lifted and soared over the tall trees, on its way to town.

"Art's right, this is Donald's last trip off the mountain, and what a sad way to leave," she said. Mike nodded and wiped the tears away.

CHAPTER 2

"Mike, you promised Art we'd take care of things. Where do we start?" Jim asked. They were free to stay, for Art had told the sheriff enough about their professional background that he was comfortable leaving them. "Art's lucky to have friends like you," was all Jim said.

"Let's cover the doors and windows with plywood," Mike said.

While Mike, Jim and the officer cover the windows and doors on the house, I'll look around, she thought. With her camera in hand, she walked to the east side of the cellar, where earlier in the day she had noticed tracks in the mud. She took pictures of the tracks along with some trash that lay off to the side. Bonnie picked up a styrofoam cup, bag, some egg shells and a wrapper, which looked like it could have had a sandwich in it. She took pictures of the motorcycle tracks both up and down along the cellar. It surprised Bonnie to see several heel tracks that matched the ones she saw in the kitchen earlier. Behind the cellar, were two deep holes, and she assumed he had parked the motorcycle there for sometime. Whoever made all the tracks behind the cellar, must have been nervous or excited and couldn't stop pacing. From the two sets of tracks up and down along the side of the cellar, Bonnie knew the stranger had gone in the house, came out and went back behind the cellar. Later, he returned to the house. BUT WHY? She looked at the tracks again. I would guess someone or something scared him off, she whispered to herself.

By now Bonnie's sandals had wet mud all over them and her feet felt wet and cold. She glanced at them and shrugged. Getting muddy or being uncomfortable went with the territory! She returned to the house, wanting more pictures of the chair and rug, and now that she was free to do so, she wanted to take pictures of the bedroom. Inside, she saw Donald's dresser drawers dumped on the floor, and a stack of cardboard boxes crushed. She found wet mud in the closet, as if someone had hidden there, and she wondered why. After she had all the pictures she wanted, she again went outside, this time to the old shed nearby. An old motorcycle lay in the far corner. She wondered instantly whose motorcycle it might be, and her trained mind and eyes noted the cycle tracks along side. The tread was not the same as those on the tracks near the cellar.

"That's Tom Finch's cycle," Jim said, as he drove in the last nail.

"Who's Tom Finch?" Bonnie asked. Again, she wondered why she should care about that motorcycle and the owner.

"He's a fellow who does odd jobs around town," Jim said.

"Have you heard anyone complain or get angry with Donald Wilms?" she asked.

"No, Donald had helped almost everybody in this town from time to time," Jim said.

As they walked toward Art's helicopter, Mike looked her over casually. "Just like a kid, somebody couldn't stay on the sidewalk."

She glanced at her muddy white sandals, grinned, and looked at Mike. "I was so interested in what I was doing. The mud didn't matter." At that moment, she remembered how happy she felt at the opportunity to meet Mike's friends. She stopped and eyed the house. Shook her head and said, "I'll remember this day as long as I live."

Mike held her arm. "We've done all we can here. Let's go to Art's and be there when he gets home."

Mike is worried about his old friend. And she realized that she, too, was concerned about this man she considered her newest friend.

The four boarded the helicopter. Jim started the motor, and as they flew above the tall trees, the only sound was the helicopter's motor. No one spoke. Each seemed to be in a world of his own. At the hangar, they got in Mike's car and Jim spoke for the first time. "Let me off at the garage, please, if you will."

After Jim and the officer got out, Mike said, "Remember when I helped you out of the helicopter, did you see those coyotes run past the house?"

"NO! I wonder if they could smell the blood?" Bonnie shuddered at the thought. She remembered how cold and damp the kitchen felt. "Perhaps those coyotes would have stopped just inside the door with Snapper, but in time, one of them would have ventured into the living room."

"Yes, I think they were afraid to go inside, but eventually the smell of blood would have drawn them in. Then all of those meat-eaters would have slipped in," Mike said.

"Oh dear, what we might have seen." She glanced at Mike and whispered, "Evidently, Art didn't see them."

"I don't think he did. I suggest we say nothing."

"I agree. It makes me sick just to think about it."

On the way to Art's place, Mike said, "Before we left the mountain, you said we must have a talk. What was on your mind?"

"Go back to the phone call Art received from Donald. He said he hurt so badly and begged Art to hurry," she said.

Mike glanced at Bonnie. "Yes, what about it?"

"I saw blood on the phone. That tells me Donald had to walk from the rocker to that telephone. How did he do it?"

"Wait a minute," he said. "If Donald could walk around, why did he sit in that chair and never put up any resistance?"

"That's one point of view. Now suppose whoever beat him and broke his arm, tied him to the rocker. How did Donald get loose to make that call?"

Mike frowned at Bonnie. "I can't answer your question."

Mike pulled into Art's driveway, and she temporarily forgot that subject. As Bonnie walked toward the house, she saw the door was open. Millie stood in the doorway, with her head down and she was acting very strange. When Mike opened the screen door, the dog put her head against Bonnie's sleeve and sniffed the blood on it. Millie's big sad brown eyes gazed up at her. All of the time, she kept making a mournful sound. Bonnie laid her hand on the side of the dog's face and pressed the dog's head tighter against her. Bonnie eyed Mike and whispered, "Millie senses a death and knows from the smell of our clothes that it's Donald." She held the dog's face gently between her hands and said, "Yes Millie." The big dog jerked her head away, changed from a mournful sound to an out and out cry, and dropped on her rug. Bonnie stooped and petted the sad dog.

She noticed the lunch that Art was packing earlier in the day was still on the counter, which included a three-tier white cake with 75 blue candles.

Just then, Art called out, "I'm in the office."

As Mike and Bonnie entered, Art stood. She noticed the blood had disappeared from his hair and face. He had changed out of his stained and bloody clothes and now wore brown trousers with a tan sport shirt. As Bonnie sat in the chair across from him, she asked, "What can I do to help?"

Art looked at Bonnie, and his big soft blue eyes, which she had admired earlier in the day, were swollen, red and set in black circles. "Nothing I can think of now," he said and leaned back in the chair and folded his arms across his chest. "Today, my life changed forever." He stared toward the kitchen. "That dog has whined like that since I got home."

"When we arrived, she sniffed at the blood on the sleeve of Bonnie's jacket. Millie knows," Mike said.

"She seldom follows me, unless dad was away for a long time, but today she's stayed at my heels."

"She's confused and can't understand what is going on. Do you allow her to come in here?" Bonnie asked.

"Oh yes, she has the run of the house."

"Millie, come here." The big dog came on the run. She laid her head in Bonnie's lap and her big brown eyes stared up with tears running across her face onto Bonnie's skirt. Bonnie rested her arm around the dog's neck, the dog nestled closer to Bonnie, and soon the sad cries stopped.

"You've made a friend for life," Art said and smiled at Bonnie. He went on to say, "Sometime ago, Dad said, when it was his time to go, he wanted me to move Mother and bury them side by side in the local cemetery."

"Would you like me to stay for a few days? I could answer your phone or anything else that you need taken care of while you fellows are away." Bonnie wasn't sure why she made the offer; it was just something that seemed right, and she knew it was something she wanted to do.

"I'd be most grateful. Right now it looks like the funeral will be Thursday afternoon. I've only three days to make all the arrangements, and I can use all the help I can get," Art said.

For the next three days, Bonnie answered the phone. She answered questions from friends and the many people of all ages who had known Donald. She prepared meals and kept an endless pot of coffee available. She seldom saw Art or Mike except at meal time.

On Thursday morning, something woke Bonnie from a sound sleep. She could hear someone in the kitchen. She bounced out of bed, dressed, and joined Art. "Good Morning."

"The same to you. I'll get you a cup of coffee," he said, as he motioned for her to join him.

"Sit still. I've learned my way around your kitchen." She opened the cupboard door, got a cup, and faced Art. He wore a black suit, white shirt, black tie, and his black hat was pushed back on his head. Bonnie sat across the table from him. *He's a handsome fellow, but looks nothing like his dad.*

"I'm going to sit with Dad until it's time for him to go. This is the last time I'll have a chance to talk face to face with him and I've so much to tell him," he said. His eyes lingered on his father's house next door. As he turned to face her, he said, "I've reserved three chairs. I'd like you and Mike to be with me."

"We'll be honored." *I feel like I've known this man all of my life.*

Art continued. "I've put six white roses tied with pink ribbon on Mom's casket from Dad, and six red roses, tied with white ribbon on Dad's casket from Mom. I cut them from Dad's baby-roses on the mountain." Art paused for a moment. "Ask Mike to park as close to the roadway as possible. After the sermon, I want to leave as quick as I can. I know people are concerned but I can't shake hands with everyone." He rubbed his hands together and shook his head. "I just can't do it."

Just the idea of what's ahead of him today is almost more than he can accept. Bonnie wanted to cry when she said, "I know how you feel. With what you've gone through the last few days, surely the crowd will understand."

"I hope so! I may grab hold of you and run for dear life."

"If you do, I'll know why and run as fast as I can to keep up."

He got up, stooped, put his arm around her neck, and kissed her on the cheek. "Thank you for being here. You and Mike are the best friends anyone could ask for." Then he rushed out.

Bonnie saw him drive away in the pickup. She wondered what she would do if something like this happened to her dad.

CHAPTER 3

Friday morning, the day after the funeral, Bonnie was certain Mike would want to help his friend. *I'll stick around a couple of days, then leave for home,* she thought. As she sauntered into the kitchen, she could hear Art and Mike in the office. The door was open. "Are ladies allowed?" she asked.

"Of course you're welcome," Art said. He stood and reached for the coffee pot. His hand trembled so much, she knew the hot brew could never hit the cup. She squeezed his hand, smiled and poured herself a cup.

As she glanced up to thank him, the grief and sorrow she saw in the soft blue eyes staring back, startled her. What was he thinking at that moment?

"Sunday, while we waited for the sheriff, I found an envelope in Dad's desk marked, 'personal,' " Art said and shrugged his shoulders. "Inside was a note from Dad. It read that if something should happen before he got the courage to explain to me about his life, I would find everything in a letter. The instructions in the back of his wristwatch would tell me where to find it."

"Did he ever say anything, or show any signs that made you wonder?" She had studied Art's habits enough to know when he crossed his legs and wove his fingers around the back of his curly head, he didn't want anyone to disturb him. She jotted down a few notes that she wanted to question Art about and drank the last of her coffee.

Art started to move around in his chair. He leaned forward and laid his arms on the desk. "Well, Dad's with Mother. To answer your question, yes, I remember Mother had passed away some time before. I must have been seven- or eight-years-old, had a bad day in school. The teacher set me on a tall stool in the corner, with a pointed cap on my head. She left me there until it was time to go home. When I came out of the building, Dad was there on his big red motorcycle. At first, I thought the teacher had called him, instead he said, 'Get on son, Daddy's home for the weekend.' I'll never forget. Dad made oyster stew for dinner with those little round crackers."

It amused Bonnie when Art held up his right hand and made a little round circle between his thumb and his finger.

He continued. "Dad knew oyster stew was my favorite dish. I can remember that I sat there stirring the oysters around and around in the milk. He asked me what was wrong. I wanted to tell him that I missed Mom something fierce, but I was afraid to say it because I didn't want him to cry, and I knew he might. So I kept my feelings inside and stirred the oysters. He gently squeezed my hand and said, "When I was your age, I went to bed many a night without a bite. A slice of bread or a raw potato would have tasted good. I want so much more than that for you.' That's the only time I remember my dad mentioning his childhood."

Mike said, "If we can't find Donald's watch, you may never know."

Bonnie noticed Art's expression change, and his voice showed Mike's remark frightened him when he said, "We'll just have to find it." Art put his hands on the desk and he pushed upward. After he stood, he stumbled a bit, unable to get his balance.

I don't think he's slept a wink in four days, thought Bonnie.

"Art, did you hear any unusual noises last night?" Mike asked.

"Not that I remember."

Mike tarried, then said, "Let's go through your dad's house."

The three sauntered across the driveway. Art and Bonnie climbed the steps to unlock the kitchen door, and Mike walked around the corner of the house. Bonnie was admiring the beautiful white roses climbing profusely around the porch when she heard Mike's call. "Hey, come here!"

Bonnie and Art hurried down the steps and around the corner of the house only to see Mike by the basement door, or what used to be a basement door. Someone had smashed it. Stray dogs had used the basement for their playhouse and a couple were still there. Mike let a yell out of him and kicked the door casing. Art hurriedly put his arm around Bonnie's waist and got them out of the way of the dogs. Two of the large dogs appeared ready to attack Millie, and Bonnie thought she was in the middle of a dog fight. Instead, Millie lunged at one of the dogs, barked furiously and stood her ground. The attacking dogs backed off.

Looking down into the basement, Bonnie could see broken jars of fruit, vegetables, and dill pickles on the basement floor. The smell of dog-dung made her sick. *How will Art ever get this place and the one on the mountain back in order?* Then the thought hit her, "What if the intruders left the doors into the house open and these dogs have had the run of the main floor?" she asked. Art ran and unlocked the kitchen door. Millie, with the hair on her back straight up, darted by Bonnie and Art. Millie sniffed in every nook and corner.

Someone had gone through the house, the same as they had the house on the mountain. Art opened the top dresser drawer. "As far as I can tell, the only things they took were Dad's two guns along with his shells. Whoever searched the house must have gone out the front door," Art said. He locked the door and picked up the mail off the floor. Bonnie waited while the men nailed a four by eight sheet of half-inch plywood over the basement door.

"That should do it," Art said and they strolled back to Art's place. As Art unlocked his kitchen door, Bonnie heard the grandfather clock in the hall strike ten times. *Already the day is almost half gone!*

Art leaned back in the big brown leather chair in the office. Bonnie had become familiar enough with Art's habits to know he would put his feet on the corner of the desk. She sat across and faced Art and Mike who sat at the end of the desk.

"Art, what was your childhood like?" she asked.

"My parents were married five years before I was born, and I was five when mother died. Dad said she had cancer of the spine and was terribly ill for about six months. Honestly, I remember very little about my mother. Dad was a wonderful father and friend," Art said and momentarily, he gazed at his father's picture.

"Your dad had a helluva life," Mike said.

"Yes. He never got over Mother's illness. More than that, about a year before Mother died, Dad got hurt in the mine. He lost one kidney as well as his manhood. He was lucky he could still go to the bathroom," Art said.

Mike frowned and said, "I never knew that."

Art nodded and dropped his feet to the floor, again he leaned forward and rested his arms on the desk pad. "Let's go to the mountain tomorrow or the next day. Maybe we'll see something the sheriff's men overlooked," he said.

Bonnie wondered if she could ever go in that house again. Just remembering what she had seen was almost more than she could bear.

The next morning, Bonnie was still worrying about the house on the mountain as Art drove to the garage. When they arrived, they all ambled into the garage, and after Art introduced Bonnie and Mike to his office and shop managers, they went into Art's office. Art motioned for them to sit, as he lowered his 175 pounds into the big red chair. "Come in," he answered as someone knocked on the door.

Bonnie expected to see Wanda, but instead Bob Ingram bolted in as if he owned the place. From the look on Art's face, Bonnie knew Bob was the last person Art wanted to see. *I hardly know this man, but still I mistrust him.*

"Hi Bob. Have a seat."

Bob shut the office door and took the last chair.

"Have you found out anything that might help?" Art asked.

Bonnie noticed Bob had a funny way of twisting his hair on the top of his head. Then he'd run his fingers through his hair to straighten it.

"We did find some fingerprints in the kitchen that we can't identify. Can you think of anyone who might have been in Donald's house on the mountain in the last few days?" Bob asked.

Bonnie's intuition, finely tuned from years in law work, turned on. *I feel Bob is here to lay one on Art, but why?*

"I haven't the faintest idea. I talked with Dad on Wednesday and promised I'd see him Sunday. We were to celebrate his 75th birthday," Art said.

Bonnie studied Bob Ingram. *I'm not sure about him. I feel as though he'd lie to me just as easily as he'd look at me.*

"Sunday, while we waited for Jim, a motorcycle exactly like Dad's skidded into the station. The owner filled it with gas," Art said.

Bob's eyes widened. "Why didn't you tell me this before?"

"With all I've had on my mind, you're lucky I thought of it now."

"We brought Tom Finch in this morning," Bob said.

"Tom! Why?" Art asked bewildered.

"To question him."

Art raised his voice. "He'd never hurt my dad. I'll admit Tom is a near-do-well, but murder! That's not his way. Besides, we attended school together. As far as I know, he never got into any serious trouble."

"He was at Donald's house Friday. His fingerprints were on the murder weapon. You know Tom is unpredictable. If he's on a binge, he can get mad over the least little thing. You and I know he always needs money," Bob said.

"Bob! Tom liked Dad. He'd go to the mountain to see him. While he was there, he'd do small jobs. Tom often ate there. Besides, Tom wouldn't have a reason to murder Dad," Art said.

Art's tone of voice sounds like he's positive that Tom would never harm his father. At least Art believes that to be true, Bonnie thought.

"I've heard a rumor that Donald had shoe boxes full of money hidden around the place," Bob said.

"Dad was never that foolish."

It's irritating Art to think Bob would make such a remark. Bonnie's well-trained mind was in full swing.

"Donald's house is in such a mess. I'd say the killer was after those boxes," Bob said.

"As many times as Tom has cleaned Dad's house, he'd know every closet and corner of the place," Art said.

Bonnie knew she should stay out of the conversation but she couldn't resist throwing in a comment. "Bob, your own words should tell you Tom didn't do it."

"Like I said, Tom is unpredictable."

"How come you didn't search Donald's house in town the day of the murder?" Bonnie asked. Once again, she knew her comments weren't welcome, but clearly Art was struggling to hold onto his temper and she wanted desperately to help him any way she could.

"She's right, somebody took Dad's three guns and shells, and you know Tom wouldn't steal his guns," Art said.

"Art Wilms, you and your little lady can argue all you want. Tom is in jail to stay," Bob said and slammed the door behind him.

Art obviously continued to control his anger and finally said quietly to Bonnie, "I've got to stop at the bank." He picked up his briefcase and together they said goodbye to Wanda.

The three of them entered the bank together. Bonnie and Mike waited on a bench by the large window that overlooked the street, and Bonnie thought about Tom.

Finally, she asked, "Mike, how do you feel about Tom Finch and wasn't that his motorcycle we saw in the shed?" There was no reply and no indication that he heard her question. She asked again, "Mike, how do you feel about Tom?"

Mike scratched his head and shook it as if trying to bring himself back to the present. After a sigh, he said, "Tom is a man with problems he can't solve, but I don't think he killed Donald."

Art joined them and they left together, but she suddenly found that she had to hurry to keep up with Art and Mike. "What's the rush?" she asked.

Art whirled around and waited for her to catch him. "Sorry, short stuff! I guess I have my mind on Tom."

"I'd like to ask you a question. Please don't think I want to butt in. That's the last thing I want to do. But would Tom resent my asking him a few questions?"

Art chuckled for a few seconds. "He has a temper, but he never hurt anyone. When Tom loses it, he's the one who gets hurt." Art hesitated. "I know Bob is wrong. There's more here than meets the eye. See, Bob has a thing for Tom's wife—it's pretty well-known. And I'm positive that it has occurred to Bob that if he had Tom out of the way, he'd have her all for himself."

"Uh huh, there's an underhanded scheme that just crept in." She faced Art. "You believe in Tom and think Bob has dished him a plate of crap?" Bonnie asked.

"Yes I do. I noticed a change in Tom sometime ago. Lately, he drinks more than he ever did. He has a son whom he idolizes and he used to talk about him constantly. But I've noticed the last few weeks, he seldom mentions him."

Bonnie looked at Art. "From the way you've described Tom and the hateful way Bob said, 'Tom is in jail and going to stay there' I'd like to talk with Tom. Can you arrange it?"

"Oh Bonnie, if you will help Tom, I'll be in your debt for the rest of my life," Art said and squeezed her arm.

"From the way you uphold Tom, I'd like to meet him. Let's go right away."

"Great, I'll go to the mountain in the morning and then we'll plan to see Tom the next day. If that doesn't work for Bob, we'll just go see Tom tomorrow!" They walked to the pickup, all of them conscious of the clear air and delightfully warm afternoon. When they entered the house, Bonnie heard the air conditioner running and the cool office felt inviting.

Art picked up the phone and punched a number from memory. "We're going to the mountain in the morning. Can you go with us?...Okay, meet us at the garage about 9:00 a.m."

Ever since Art mentioned going to the mountain, she'd tried to think of a good excuse to stay home. She bid the guys a goodnight and went promptly to bed. But there was no sleep, and after six hours of restless turning, she glanced at the little gold clock on the dresser. *It's 5:00 a.m. Oh heck, I'm going to get up.*

In a few minutes, she was up and wearing a casual outfit she felt suitable for the day—an orchid and white blouse with a purple skirt and white sandals. Leisurely, she walked into the kitchen, made a pot of coffee, and took the pot with her to Art's office.

An hour later, Art came in. "You're at work early. Is this the way lawyers do things?" he asked.

Bonnie closed her books, rested her head on the cushion of the chair. By this time, Art had a cup of coffee, but before he could seat himself, someone knocked on the kitchen door.

"I wonder who that could be at this hour?" Bonnie asked.

Art shook his head and hurried to the door.

Bonnie could hear Bob. "I saw your truck on the driveway, and knew I'd get a hot cup of coffee."

Bob the sponger, Bonnie thought, *I'll bet he's in line for anything that's free.*

Art and Bob approached the desk. As they sat, Art asked, "Is Tom still in jail?"

"Yeah, his prints are on the murder weapon."

"Tom's prints were on the vase?" Art asked in a loud voice.

"Yes, just as plain as the ones you just put on the cup you have in your hand," Bob said.

Art put his cup on the tray, bent forward, and laid his head in his hands. Bonnie noticed Art stare at her from time to time. She wondered why. It was almost as if he were sending her a silent message, but it didn't come through to her.

"We're on our way to the mountain. Would you and Mike like to go along?" Art asked her.

"I think not. We have too much to do," Bonnie replied.

"Very well. I'll see you when we get back," Art said.

Art and Bob were within shouting distance when the telephone rang. It startled Bonnie. As she lifted the receiver, Mike snapped on the speaker.

"Bonnie Cole speaking."

She heard a woman's voice. "Bonnie, this is Grace Wilder, Art's friend from way back. Clay and I would like to talk with you and Mike as soon as possible. Can you have lunch with us around 2:00 p.m.?"

"Sounds wonderful. Sure, we'll be there. See you about two." Bonnie shut the phone off and stared at Mike. "It's obvious she wants to talk with us, but why?"

"It must be about Art or Donald. Are we getting ourselves into something that's none of our business?" he asked.

"I don't know. From the way Grace spoke, she is most anxious to talk with us. It's fine with me, but these are Art's friends. I'm pleased, of course, that they all seem to accept us, but it's up to you. Is it okay that I said we'd be there?" Mike nodded his head in firm agreement.

Bonnie and Mike spent the morning reviewing every aspect of Tom's case. Mike looked at his watch. "It's 1:30 p.m. we've worked longer than I thought. We better get on our way, it's 25 miles to, The Diner."

Mike locked the kitchen door. "Let's take my car," Mike said, as he set her briefcase behind the front seat and got under the wheel. As she made herself comfortable in the seat beside him, he asked, "Are you intending to stay on this case?"

"Whether we like it or not, if there's a case, we're in it. Art has made it clear that he wants us to do so." She looked anxiously at Mike and hoped he'd say something.

"When Grace called, did you have a strange feeling?"

"She surprised me. Truly I don't know how I felt. It appears we've got into something she doesn't want Art to know about."

Mike mumbled something to himself. His eyes were on the road, and he never answered. When they walked in The Diner, Grace said, "Just go on through the kitchen." As they made their way, Bonnie saw an open door marked 'private' and could see Clay stretched out on the davenport. When Bonnie and Mike came in, he raised up very slowly, wiggled his feet and then grabbed his walker. He had spent years in a wheelchair, but it seemed to Bonnie that he made a show of the effort it took to stand.

She stood quietly and watched Mike push Clay's wheelchair closer. Mike reached out his hand. "Would you like some help?" he asked.

"Oh, I stumble around. Eventually, I get where I want to go," Clay said. "As a matter of fact, I'm close to taking a few steps."

She kept her eyes on Mike as he steadied Clay into the wheelchair. She noticed Mike had a good grip on Clay's arm and once again, the thought reared its head that Clay was letting Mike lift him. *Hummm.*

"Didn't Clay ask you to have a chair?" Grace asked, and closed the door into the kitchen.

"They've been too busy," Bonnie said, as she sat beside Grace and placed her recorder, pad and pen on the table.

"Well Grace, you go ahead, because this has been on your mind for a long time," Clay said.

At the time, Bonnie wondered about the tone of his short-and-to-the-point remark.

"Clay hasn't been anxious for me to talk with you," Grace began. "He doesn't think this has anything to do with Donald's murder. I'm not so sure."

It didn't really surprise Bonnie that this had to do with Donald's murder but nevertheless she asked: "This has something to do with Donald?"

"Maybe! Have you met Zeeta?" Grace asked.

When Grace said Zeeta, Bonnie wasn't sure why, but her mind sapped to attention. In a soft, relaxed voice, she said, "No. I haven't. Who's Zeeta?"

"She's a woman here in town that Art is sweet on," Clay said, with a silly grin on his face.

Bonnie noticed that Grace ignored and completely disregarded Clay's remark, but went on to say. "Zeeta moved here about a year or a year-and-a-half ago. She has two kids, a boy about 12. The girl is a year younger. These kids only go to school half of the time. The rest of their day is spent roaming the street. Some of the stores have refused to let them in because they've caught them stealing,"

Grace said.

Bonnie felt trouble. *I wonder how much Art knows about this?* Then back to realty, she asked, "Is this one of those cases where the mother just can't handle her kids? And is there a father in the picture?"

"There isn't a father, and I don't think she can see the problem. There's an old widower who lives east of town. Zeeta and the kids shacked-up with him for several months. One afternoon, he brought her and the kids in here. They just sat down when the kids began wandering around. It didn't take Clay long to tell her and those kids to sit down or they'd have to leave. When the widower told them to sit down and stay in their seats, they stayed," Grace said and turned in her chair facing Bonnie. "What made me so concerned was Donald being so worried. He was here one evening about a month ago. He wanted to know if we had seen those kids. Then he told us that Art brought her along with the kids to the mountain to see him. He said he was never so glad to see company leave as he was that day." Grace hesitated, glimpsed at Clay, then continued. "Zeeta Cockran is five feet tall, a little on the chunky side. She has black hair and eyes. Believe me, when she gets mad, those eyes SNAP."

Before Grace could say another word, Clay said, "Her laugh is more like a hyena than a person."

Bonnie looked at Clay, laughed, then said, "I'm sorry. I never expected a remark like that from you."

If Grace heard the remark, she never let on and simply kept on talking. "Art brought her here one night. I think they had been drinking before they arrived. At first, they were quiet, but evasive, like a couple might act on their first date. Art ordered a whiskey-sour. She had a dry-martini. I served their drinks. One of the girls—and she's a real good waitress—asked if they would like to order." Grace hesitated, as though she couldn't make up her mind whether to go on, or shut her mouth. Finally, she continued. "Suddenly Zeeta stood and shouted at the waitress. 'You little snot-nose, who said we wanted to order?' At that moment, every customer stopped eating and naturally stared at Art's table. The waitress apologized. But she did say, 'We are a diner and most people want to eat,' " Grace said.

"Art is such a gentleman. What did he do?" Bonnie asked.

"Art is a gentleman. He talked quietly to Zeeta and told her to sit down and not to make a fool of herself. He was really nice to the waitress, smiled at her and told her they'd have the chicken with all the trimmings."

"Zeeta must have liked that," Mike said.

"She yelled. 'I don't want chicken'."

"You could have heard a pin drop. Everyone was looking at them, and even though he kept his voice low, everyone heard Art tell her that she had said she wanted chicken, and now she was going to eat it!"

"It was awful. I was behind the counter, but I didn't go out. It happened so fast. Later our waitress told me that Zeeta tipped Art's drink over on the tablecloth, then did the same with hers. She slapped Art in the face. The waitress set some dishes on the counter, and she told me that Zeeta gave her a look that would have killed if it could."

Grace paused in her story and gave Clay an unusual glance, which made Bonnie wonder. It was almost as if to say, this my story and I'm going to tell it all!

"I was at the till when they left. Art handed me a $20 bill. He whispered, 'I'm so sorry' and walked out. Honestly Bonnie, I felt so sorry for Art." Grace hesitated, then went on with her story. "The night Donald visited us, he said he told Art if he married Zeeta, he would sell his house in town. From what he said, I got the idea he meant to leave," Grace said.

Grace's remark surprised Bonnie. "Donald intended to leave Windcove?" Bonnie asked.

"Oh! That's not all. I thought from the little things he said, he intended to change his will. He didn't put it in plain words, but he hinted," Grace said.

Bonnie sat unable to speak. Her eyes turned from Grace to Clay.

"Bonnie, have you lost your voice?" Mike asked.

She faced Mike. "I think, for the first time in my life, I can't think of a thing to say," she said and squeezed Grace's arm.

Grace flinched. It was at that moment that Bonnie noticed a huge black and blue spot on her arm. "How did you hurt your arm?" Bonnie asked.

"I tried to help Clay into his wheelchair and he slipped and squeezed my arm too hard." Grace smiled quietly as she spoke.

"If Art should see us on our way to town, or asked if we have talked, do you mind if we tell him we were here?" Bonnie asked.

"Of course not. Are you going to help him get through all of this?" Grace asked.

"We haven't discussed a thing to date," Bonnie said, and as she did, she looked toward several beautiful wood carvings on a nearby table. "Those are lovely!"

"Oh, Clay makes those," Grace said proudly.

"The first time you're at the house, I'll show you my workshop," Clay said.

"I'd love to see it."

"Thanks so much for the delicious lunch," Mike said as he rose, indicating they should be on their way. In the manner of a couple who had worked together for many years, Bonnie had thrown a look in his direction minutes earlier and he picked up the clue with ease.

They bid the Wilders goodbye and found their way through the restaurant and out to the car. On their way to town, Bonnie said, "Mike, I wish you would find out what the town folks think of Zeeta."

"It's odd. Art hasn't mentioned Zeeta to me," Mike said as they got out of the car. "I really find it hard to believe he's serious about her."

"Evidently, we'll have to mention Zeeta in order to get Art's side of the story."

As they walked in the kitchen, Art called from the office. "I'm in here." In the office, Bonnie noticed Art had his legs across the corner of the desk as usual. He had his hands around the back of his head. On the desk, Bonnie saw three bottles of beer.

"Have a seat." Art started to pour a glass of beer. He stopped, held the glass in one hand, the bottle in the other, and said, "I knew you two would be in soon. I waited because I don't like to drink alone." After he served Bonnie and Mike, he had a sip. Then he took his legs off the corner of the desk and faced Bonnie. "I must tell you what we saw on the mountain today."

"Don't tell me there's another problem. We have more now than we can handle," she said. She dropped her pen on the pad in front of her and pushed her chair away from the desk. She slowly leaned back. After she took another sip, she asked, "What could you have seen today that wasn't there the Sunday we were?"

"This thing gets more complicated every day," Art said.

Mike leaned forward, put his arms on the edge of the desk, and said, "My shoulders are broad, go ahead. Let's have it."

Bonnie had heard Mike make that statement many times before, and it usually meant he'd prepared himself for serious trouble.

"As we landed, a guard came running up the path east of the house. Bob remarked, 'I wonder what's happened now.' The guard told us that an hour before we arrived, they found two male bodies hidden in the brush along the path. Bob had never seen them before, neither had I. However, I'm sure they're brothers, they look alike. With black hair, their eyebrows are just as black; also, they're the same height," Art said.

He hesitated momentarily. "Both were shot in the back of the head. The only thing the guard could tell us was that they found tracks on the path where an animal or someone had dragged them across. Like

I said, they found them in the brush," Art said.

Bonnie sighed. "Someone dragged them, like one might drag an animal?"

"That's right," Art said. "The coroner said they had been dead for several days."

"Did the coroner think they were shot Sunday morning before the attacker got to your father?" Bonnie asked.

"Bob thinks so. He wondered if this killer might be the fellow that walked in on Dad," Art said.

"Were there any signs that someone had tried to get in the place since we were there?" Bonnie asked.

"No, the guard said nobody's been near," Art said. He set his glass on the desk and peered over his eyeglasses at Bonnie. "Will you two stay until this thing calms down?"

"From what I've seen, you're in for a long haul," Mike said.

Mike's statement surprised Bonnie. "Are you sure?" she asked and stared at Mike.

"Never more sure in my life," Mike said.

"We'll have to do it by the book, Art. We can't back off because we're friends. We'll dig into your personal life, as well as Donald's." Bonnie felt it had to be said early on, if they were to become involved.

Art nodded. "I don't think we have anything to hide." He wiggled in his chair and continued. "I don't think there's a lawyer within a 100-miles who could solve this mess. That's why I know I need you two on my side," Art said.

"Bonnie? Shall we? We can't just leave now." Mike's voice was pained and serious.

"You're right. So let's get to work," she said, then smiled at Art.

"Thanks, I've been afraid to ask, for fear you'd say no. Use this room for your office. You can have the keys to both doors," Art said.

"That won't be necessary, but I would like to keep my records locked in a safe place," Bonnie said.

Art showed Bonnie the combination to the safe. He started to remove his papers.

"I won't need all that space, so leave your records there," she said.

Art handed Bonnie two keys. "These are for the inside compartments. If I need anything, I'll ask." The phone rang. Art pressed the switch on the speaker. He answered as though his mind was elsewhere. "Hello."

Bonnie recognized the voice. "Hello Son, is everything all right?"

"Yes Grace. I'm just tired," Art said.

"Some local people seem to think the bartender at the Cross Roads attacked Donald. Billy Pile is positive he's your man," Grace said.

"We better look into that. Thanks for telling me. Tell Clay 'Hello'," Art said.

"I will, good luck," Grace said.

"Every Friday evening, Billy spends some time at the Cross Roads Bar," Art said.

Bonnie looked up from her work and watched Art for a second. "What kind of a fellow is Billy Pile?"

"He's a big Irishman with a fat face. And boy oh boy! Does that man have a temper! But after he grew up, he got along well with Dad," Art said.

"Let's go to the Cross Roads Bar tomorrow evening. Maybe we'll be lucky and talk with this Mr. Pile," she said.

CHAPTER 4

About 5:00 p.m. Friday, Art held the swinging door open into the Cross Roads Bar for Mike and Bonnie. Art suggested a table in plain sight of the front door. After they seated themselves, the waiter asked for their order.

"Three whiskey sours. What do I ask for to get a plate like you served the table on my right?" Art asked.

"We call that a snack tray," she said. "Would you like one?"

"Please." In the next breath, Art said, "Excuse me." He stood and walked over to the bar and sat on a stool alongside a large, well-dressed man.

"He makes Art look like a midget," she whispered. Then she felt herself almost choke when the stranger emptied his glass in one big gulp. He followed Art to their table. As they approached, Bonnie thought, *Art said Billy was large, but this fellow is as big as an elephant. He does have the appearance of a well-to-do business man.*

Everyone got acquainted, and Art explained who Mike and Bonnie were and how they happened to be in town. Bonnie started the conversation. "I understand you were here the Friday evening before Donald died?"

"Yes, I was. But let's not talk here. Suppose all of us get together where we can talk without a crowd," Billy said.

"How about my place about 10:00 a.m.?" Art asked.

"That will be fine with me," Billy said.

"See you then," Art said, as he handed Billy a note. "This is my address."

The next morning about 9:45 Bonnie heard the front doorbell ring. On their way to the living room, Art said, "That must be Billy." Art opened the front door. "Good morning, come on in."

As Billy entered, the grace and ease with which he walked impressed Bonnie. For a big man, he appeared light on his feet. Bonnie and Mike greeted him, and Billy sat in the large blue floral rocker across the room from them. When Billy crossed his legs, Bonnie noticed they stretched his brown trousers to the limit. *He must push the scales to 300*, Bonnie thought as she set out her recorder with a questioning look at Billy. "Do you have any objections?" she asked.

"Nope, cause whatever I say today is public information," Billy said.

"We're interested in what happened at the Cross Roads on the Friday evening before Donald died."

Billy waved his right hand toward Bonnie. "You may have heard.

The fat fellow who sat at the bar told us about the old man on the mountain who has lots of money stored in boxes," Billy said.

"Do you know the fat fellow's name?" she asked.

Billy raised his head and said, "I'm sorry. I've seen him in the Cross Roads bar several times before." He stopped briefly. "Come to think of it, he might be a salesman, because he isn't a steady customer," Billy said.

"I understand someone was with him. Before that night, had you ever seen the little no-good—at least that's how some have described him—who sat beside the fat fellow?" Mike asked.

"The heavy set fellow called him 'Charles' and that was the first time I'd seen him. He must have been hard up for cash, as I saw the heavy set fellow buy him a couple of beers and later on a hamburger," Billy said.

"Who was asking most of the questions?" Bonnie asked.

"The bartender, Dizzy, that was what the waitress called him, he seemed the most interested in the story the fat fellow told. The little guy who was on the stool next to the fat fellow asked some questions, but Dizzy seemed most interested in what the fat man said." Billy nervously wiggled in the chair.

"How long has Dizzy worked at the Cross Roads?" Bonnie asked.

Billy hesitated, changed his position in the rocker. "About a month or so, I'd say."

"Did you know the small fellow?" Mike asked.

Billy rubbed his chin and rolled his eyes toward the front door. Shook his head. "I'd never seen him before."

"Could Dizzy have been the one who hurt Dad?" Art asked.

"I'm sure he did," Billy said. "I'm sure of it. He was really interested in what the fat fellow said." Billy rocked back and forth several times. "Come to think of it, he was interested in everything the other men talked about."

Bonnie hoped to draw Billy out when she asked, "Donald must have been a terrible sight?"

"I can't say, since they never opened the casket at the funeral," Billy said. He glanced at his watch. "I must go. I promised my friends I'd meet them around noon at the bowling alley." He got to his feet.

Bonnie stood and held her hand out to him. "Thank you for coming and answering my questions. None of this is easy, and I appreciate your help."

Billy smiled at her, and in a very gentle voice said, "If I think of anything else, I'll call you."

"Thanks, I'd appreciate that," she said.

Art accompanied him to the front door. Billy was on his way out when Art said, "Thanks for coming and good luck with your bowling."

"Thanks. Art, I'm truly sorry for what happened," Billy said.

Art locked the door, and they returned to the office. While her tape rewound, she glanced at Art's feet and then at Mike's. "You know, Billy wears the largest shoes I've ever seen." She stirred through her snapshots until she found the one with the tracks of blood on Donald's kitchen floor. "I don't see any resemblance between Billy's shoes and these."

"Did you hear anything that we haven't heard before?" Art asked.

"No! But I wonder about the fat fellow that he talked about. If he's a stranger in this area, how did he know so much about Donald?" Bonnie asked.

"That's odd, I can't recall anyone who fits Billy's description of the fat man," Art said.

"He must live in small quarters, like a camper or a small trailer. When I mentioned Donald, I hoped Billy might help us. I wonder why he was slow with his answers and very careful how he worded them."

The telephone ringing got Bonnie's attention.

"Hello," Art said. "You found what?...Okay, if you find anything else, please let me know. Thanks." Art hung up the phone. "That was Bob. He found a shirt in Tom's garbage can with Dad's blood on it. Also, Dad's blood is on the vase. This proves the killer hit Dad on the head with it."

Mike interrupted. "Do you mean the heavy vase that Bob has as evidence?"

That must have been the cut-glass vase I saw on the floor. "Whoever took the vase dumped the water and the flowers on the rug at the end of the table," Bonnie said.

"That's the one. I saw it on the floor in the living room. That vase had Tom's fingerprints on it," Art said.

"The sheriff will have to charge Tom with murder now," Bonnie said, but she didn't express her real concern: *A vase is an odd murder weapon.*

"I don't believe he did it," Art said.

Bonnie stared at Art. "Why are you so sure?"

"Tom always seemed to go out of his way to visit with Dad."

"Sometimes, men especially, will go out of their way to coverup something," Mike said.

"Art, I'd like to know, why you are so sure Tom is innocent?" she asked.

She liked the tone of Art's voice when he said, "I'm not really. But

I've known Tom all my life."

"I must go and talk with Tom," Bonnie said, "you're so sure he didn't hurt your dad. Do you want to come along?"

"Oh yes. I don't want to miss this," Art said.

At the jail, Art said, "We'd like to see Tom Finch."

"You're his attorney?" the jailer asked with a devilish look in his eyes.

"You know I'm not a lawyer," Art said, "but Miss Cole is a defense attorney."

"Very well." The jailer called over the intercom. "Bring Tom Finch to room three." He looked at Art. "Down the hall."

In the room, Bonnie set her recorder on the table and with her pencil in her hand, she laid a pad in front of her. She watched an officer bring in a middle-aged fellow, clean shaven, with his brown hair neatly combed, and jail clothes that typically didn't fit. She looked at his sad face, and it was then she remembered Art telling her the two of them had gone to school together. But this man looked 20 years older than Art, and she wondered if the current crisis was the only reason.

"Tom, this is Bonnie Cole. She's here to help you," Art said.

Tom held out his hand. "Miss Cole."

Bonnie interrupted. "Just call me Bonnie." She knew instantly that she liked this man and could see why Art trusted him so completely.

Tom sat at the end of the table. "If any man ever needed help, I do," he said, in a childlike manner. "The sheriff read off a string of things I'm suppose to be guilty of. Honestly, I don't understand a lot of what he said!"

"For the time being, let's forget the sheriff. I want to know about you. Tell me what happened last weekend on the mountain," Bonnie said gently and smiled at him.

Before Tom could answer, Art asked, "You changed about four years ago. What caused it?"

Tom wove his fingers together and gracefully placed them on the nape of his neck. Bonnie watched his eyes roll from side to side, but he never looked up. In a sad, low voice, he said, "I have a son 11-years-old. I've adored that little fellow since the day he was born. Four years ago, the wife's father was ill. Her mother called for us to come. While we were there, Ernie fell and cut an artery in his right arm." Tom dropped his hands from his neck, hastily ran his fingers through his hair, and struggled to keep the tears in tact. "By the time we got him to the hospital, he had bled so much, the doctor gave him a transfusion." Tom got on his feet and rushed to the east wall, put his hands flat on the wall, and laid his face on his arms. She noticed his shoulders were bent, and his body shook. After she stopped her recorder, she walked over and put her hand on his shoulder. "What is it? Please come back and tell me," she said softly.

Tom's head was bent, and he slipped onto his chair. Barely above a whisper, he said, "When the doctor tested my blood, he said that I couldn't be Ernie's father. Later, I demanded an answer from my wife. She said..." That was as far as he got when he turned sideways on his chair and covered his face with his hands.

Bonnie sat quietly and waited for Tom to get his composure. In a few seconds, he cleared his throat, faced her, and said, "Ernie belongs to Bob Ingram."

The tears got the better of him and ran down his cheeks in sheets. "Oh, no" was Bonnie's only comment.

Slowly, Tom nodded. "That's when I began drinking more." He leaned forward and put his arms on the table. In a voice barely above a whisper, he continued. "About two weeks ago, the doctor informed me Ernie has AIDS."

It was all she could do to hold back the tears as Bonnie listened to the sad story.

"Why didn't you say something to Dad or me?" Art asked.

"What was there to say? I know Ernie can't live long and when he goes, I'll go soon after," he said as he rubbed his hands together and stared at the table.

"I'm so sorry," Bonnie said and squeezed Tom's fist that lay on the table. After a few seconds of silence, she softly asked, "Were you at Donald's house on May 3rd?"

Tom straightened up in his chair, raised his head, and swallowed a couple of times. Then he wiped his face and hands with a paper napkin and said, "Yes, I was."

Bonnie's heart missed a beat. She looked first at Art, then Mike, and at that moment, she wanted to run out of the room.

"I must explain," Tom said.

"Well, I wish you would," she said.

Tom had gathered his emotions. He spoke clearly and to the point. "This is a long story! The previous Friday, I went to the mountain. I've always been able to talk with Donald. I was glad he was cleaning house. It gave me a chance to keep busy while I told him my troubles. We dusted, vacuumed, and mopped every room in the house. We finished about 2:00 p.m. I had gone outside to chop some wood when Donald called for help. I found him hanging onto a chair and as white as a sheet. He had cut his right hand badly!" Tom frowned. "Blood was on everything."

"How did you get blood on your shirt?" Bonnie asked.

"I grabbed him. I thought he would faint. Between the two of us, with a lot of effort on my part, he half fell onto a chair. I got the bottle of alcohol and the wash basin. When I poured that alcohol on his hand, it must have burned like fire. He threw his arm up and flipped blood all over my shirt. He said he had been trying to pry two frozen steaks apart. He had the knife in his left hand."

"What did you do then?" Mike asked.

"I wrapped Donald's hand and threw the steaks in the garbage. Then I got a pan of water and a rag. I cleaned the blood off the counter and mopped the kitchen floor for the second time that day," Tom said.

"How did your fingerprints get on the murder weapon?" she asked.

After a sigh, Tom said, "Donald asked me to throw out the flowers that were in the glass vase. I dumped them over the bank east of the house. I cut a dozen pink baby roses, filled the vase with water and set it back on the table in the front room." Again, he ran his fingers through his hair. "Then I chopped enough wood to fill the wood-box in the kitchen and the one on the back porch, and after that, I filled the trough with water for the deer." Bonnie made a mental note that confirmed his statements. She had seen the wilted flowers on the bank.

"Donald and I had a bowl of bean soup, a piece of cake, and coffee. Donald gave me $20 and followed me out. My motorcycle wouldn't start. He told me to use the one in the shed. He said it needed some exercise."

"What are your feelings toward Donald Wilms?" she asked.

Tom's eyes met hers. With an odd expression on his face, he said, "I don't understand."

"Was he really special to you, or was he just another person who needed help from time to time?"

"I loved Donald. He was easy to visit with. He gave me good advice." Tom looked at Bonnie. "I didn't always follow it." He paused briefly. In a very soft loving voice, he said, "Bonnie, you could tell Donald your secrets, knowing it wouldn't go any further. Does that answer your question?"

"Yes, it certainly does. Then what did you do?"

"I pushed my cycle into the shed, climbed on the big red one and rode down the west side of the mountain. It was about 7:00 p.m. when I went into the Cross Roads Bar. The place was packed. I think the end stool was the last seat in the place. By 9:00 p.m. I felt my drinks and knew it was time to get out of there."

Again, Tom laced his fingers together in front of him on the table and rested his sad eyes on them. "In that two hours, all I heard was how much money the old white-haired man had that lived on the mountain."

Bonnie noticed Art straightened up and his eyes opened wide. "Did you think they had Dad in mind?" Art asked in an anxious voice.

"Not at that time. How I wish I had," Tom said and looked at Art out of a pair of red swollen eyes. Then the same pair of red sad eyes met Bonnie's. She felt like he knew he needed help and would appreciate her assistance.

"What did you do Saturday?" she asked.

"I promised to be at the Windcove Grocery Store to stock shelves. We quit about 7:00 p.m. with the understanding I'd return at 10:30 a.m. Sunday. Saturday night I was really tired and down in the dumps and I really tied one on. I awoke Sunday morning about 8:30 a.m. stretched out on my garage floor. I was stiff and sore with a head as big as a three-gallon barrel. I think that was really the first time I realized that crazy bunch at the Cross Roads were talking about Donald.

"I straddled the red cycle and headed for Wilms' Mountain. I rode up the west side of the mountain and put Donald's cycle in the shed. When I came out, I heard two shots that I think came from the east. I couldn't tell if the sounds were on the east path to the creek or the adjoining mountain. I wish now that I had hurried in the house and told Donald, but instead, I climbed on Donald's cycle and rode down the west side of the mountain as fast as I dared."

"What time did you hear the shots?"

"It was about 9:30 a.m.," Tom said.

"It amazes me you didn't have an accident, that path is steep," Art said.

"When I got to the highway, I was going way too fast to turn up the grade. The only thing I could do was go toward the bridge and face the traffic."

"You could have killed someone," Mike said.

Tom fixed his eyes on Mike. "I know that now, but what else could I do. The worst of it is Julie Foster, a local cop, was on the bridge. She gave me a ticket for reckless driving."

Afraid of Tom's answer, Bonnie asked, "Have you still got the ticket?"

"I put it in my pocket. It could be in my room," Tom said.

Again, afraid of what her answer might be, she asked, "Did you tell Officer Foster about the gun shots?"

"No. I still had the shirt on with Donald's blood stains on it. I hurried home, changed, and worked at the grocery until 2:00 p.m. From there, I went to the Zukor Building and helped clean carpets until 6:00 p.m.," Tom said. He dropped his hands in his lap, heaved a big sigh, as if he felt good someone knew what he had gone through the last few months.

"I imagine the way you work it comes in streaks," she said and asked another question. "What time did you get the ticket?"

"Around 10:15 a.m.," Tom said.

"Tom, I want you to promise, after Mike and I get you out of here, you'll quit drinking and take care of that boy of yours. In his condition, he won't be with you long."

"That's what Donald said, and I promised him."

"Well, I can't think of anything else." Her eyes switched from Mike to Art, and she hoped they would say something rather than shake their heads.

She got to her feet. "Thanks, Tom, for being so candid. See you tomorrow."

Outside the jail, Mike said, "Well Bonnie, you found another fellow who needs help."

"I certainly have," she said, as she hurried along between the two men toward the pickup. "Something tells me Tom is, as the old saying goes, caught with his pants around his ankles and doesn't know how to pull them up. I must go to the grocery store and have a talk with the owner and some of the help. Do you fellows want to go along?"

"Have you ever driven a pickup?" Art asked.

"A few times," she said, hoping it wasn't a stick shift.

"Unless you need us, take the rig. Mike and I have some other business," Art said.

"Thanks," Bonnie said, as she slid under the wheel. Unfortunately, it was a stick, but she quickly remembered enough about stick driving and within minutes, she arrived at Windcove's Grocery. As she entered, she expected an oldfashioned, dumpy place, with obsolete merchandise. To her surprise, the Weeks Grocery was an up-to-date store. She stepped up to the first cash-register and asked, "Is Mr. Weeks in?"

A middle-aged, well-dressed man said, "I'm John Weeks. How can I help you?"

"I'm Bonnie Cole, a defense attorney."

"Oh yes, the big city lawyer," Weeks said in a teasing way. Bonnie realized this little town wasn't taking her seriously and probably never would.

Weeks smiled and said, "This town isn't that large." His face brightened. "I suppose you want to know about Tom Finch?"

Bonnie stood abash. "How did you know?"

"A customer told me. He seemed surprised a stranger would take the time to stop and help Tom," Weeks said. "Now, how can I help you?"

She grinned. "I understand Tom helped stock groceries on Saturday and Sunday?"

"He did. Tom got to work late Sunday morning."

"Do you have a time clock?"

"It's by the side entrance. I see to it that everyone punches in when they get to work and again when they leave."

"May I see Tom's time card for Sunday morning, May 3rd?"

A lady interrupted them to ask John the location of a couple of items. After he answered her question, he said, "Sorry, lets you and me go upstairs." He motioned to the rear of the store.

Upstairs in the office, Bonnie saw a lady working on payroll cards, and John introduced Bonnie to the bookkeeper. "This is my wife, Effie. She'll be glad to help," he said and disappeared out of sight down the stairs.

Bonnie sat in the chair at the end of the desk. "I'm from Elton, Oregon. I met Tom Finch this morning. He seems very honest and open. I'm sure you know that the sheriff has him in jail on a murder charge. Tom has no idea what the sheriff has accused him of, or why, and I'd appreciate any information you have that will help me prove he's innocent."

Effie gave Bonnie a copy of Tom's time card. "He was on time Saturday and only ten minutes late Sunday morning. We try to be fair with all our employees and when any of our help comes in a few minutes late, and they're not in the habit of it, we pay no attention."

Tom was only ten minutes late. Bonnie felt this case might be easier to solve than she had anticipated. She looked at Effie, smiled and said, "Bob made it sound like Tom was an hour or two late for work. Thanks for your help. I'm sure this information will help Tom."

Effie grinned and said, "I hope so."

"Did Tom leave anytime during the forenoon?" Bonnie asked.

"Not that I know of, but we can ask the two fellows who worked with him."

On the main floor, Effie spoke with one of the clerks in the grocery section who told her both Carl and Jean were in the tool department. Bonnie and Effie caught up with them in aisle 14 and both of them were confident that Tom never left the store on Sunday.

Bonnie thanked John and Effie for their help. On her way to the police station, she thought how kind that the Weeks appeared to be and how much they seemed to like Tom. She wondered if they were that considerate of all their employees.

At the main desk, she said, "I'm Bonnie Cole, Tom Finch's lawyer. I talked with him about an hour ago, and he said Officer Julie Foster gave him a ticket Sunday morning for reckless driving. Could I get a copy of that ticket?"

Another officer approached the counter. "May I ask why a copy of that particular ticket?"

"Certainly. The sheriff has charged Tom Finch with murder. I'm establishing exact times of his whereabouts. In this way, I believe I can prove him innocent."

The officer disappeared and in a few minutes returned and handed Bonnie a copy of the ticket. "I've known Tom all my life. I'm glad someone cares."

Bonnie smiled. "Thanks. Wish me luck," she said and departed. On her way to the pickup, she remembered how angry Bob Ingram was, and also his sharp angry voice when he told Art that 'Tom Finch was in jail and he would see to it that he stayed there.' She unlocked the door to the pickup on the driver's side, climbed in under the wheel, and started the motor. She forgot she was driving a pickup instead of her car and slipped it in reverse before she put her foot on the gas. The beautiful white truck leaped and jumped away from the curb into the street. A loud horn blasted, and she heard an irritated voice that yelled, "Lady, if you can't drive that thing, leave it at the curb."

She took her foot off the gas pedal, and the truck eased to the curb. As she laid her head on the steering wheel, she heard Art when he whistled. She slowly leaned back in the seat and stared through the windshield. Art and Mike were in front of the truck and both wore wide grins. Obviously they were enjoying her performance.

She moved to the middle of the seat and Art took the wheel as Mike slid in on the passenger side.

"Did I ruin your truck?" she asked.

"No! Of course you didn't hurt it. What happened? Did you get confused?" Art asked.

"Not exactly, I was trying to solve Tom's case and drive a gearshift at the same time. I guess I can only do one thing at a time!"

Art smiled, then he glanced at her and asked, "Is Tom in trouble?"

"I think Tom's all right, but how will Bob Ingram take this?"

"Perhaps, as he usually does, he'll blow off steam and make a fool of himself," Art said.

When they arrived at Art's house, they crossed the walkway to the back door. Inside, Art placed three bottles of beer and three iced glasses on a tray. In the office, Bonnie sat across the desk from Art, and while everything was fresh in her mind, she jotted down a few notes, then laid her pen on the desk. She picked up her cold glass of beer and leaned against the pillow on the back of the chair. "Art, how far is it from the north side of the bridge to Tom's house?"

Art hesitated for a second. "I'd say two miles and a quarter or a half. I'll get the exact mileage if it's important."

"How long would that take on a motorcycle?" she asked.

"Five minutes, if traffic isn't too heavy."

"Tom got a ticket at 10:15 a.m. and arrived at the grocery at 10:40 a.m. In the mean time, bear in mind, he stopped by his home to change his shirt," Bonnie said.

"Mike, we better measure the mileage Tom traveled," Art said.

While Art and Mike were out, Bonnie started the recorder, leaned back, closed her eyes, and shut out the world. She gave her undivided attention to Tom's troubles. The recorder snapped off. *I don't think Art has any more respect for the sheriff than I do.*

Soon, two amused fellows filled the empty chairs.

"You must have had a fun trip," Bonnie said.

"We figure Tom had two and half miles to go. We included five minutes to change his shirt. It's a couple of miles to the store. Two minutes to park his cycle and get in the store, ready for work. Maybe I've rushed things a bit," Art said.

"We could add 10 or 20 minutes, it wouldn't make any difference. I want to have all the answers before we talk to the district attorney," Bonnie said. She jotted down a couple more notes and then lifted her glass to her lips to wet a very dry throat. "Who's the district attorney and what's he like?"

"Lyle Frulik, he's fair but strict. He follows the law to the letter — black or white, no gray or middle ground," was Art's reply.

"It's after 5:00 p.m., and too late to talk with him today."

"Do you have enough evidence to get Tom out of this?" Art asked.

"I don't think Tom has to worry. Let's see the district attorney in the morning."

CHAPTER 5

The following morning. Bonnie packed her briefcase, set it by the door, and rushed to touch up her face. She wondered if Bob would give her a rough time over this? *I would rather get along with him; however, if he wants to make this an issue, I can too.*

Art opened the door into Frulik's office, and stepped aside for Bonnie and Mike to enter. Inside, introductions were brief: "Lyle, meet my friends, Bonnie Cole and Mike Dailey."

Bonnie explained to the district attorney what she had learned. Then she showed him Tom's ticket, as well as his time card.

After Frulik studied all the data she had, his expression changed. "You've convinced me. It looks as if we have the wrong man in jail."

Frulik called Bob Ingram. "Why do you have Tom Finch in jail?" It seemed to Bonnie that the district attorney had only time enough to put the phone back when Bob rushed in. He waved his arms and jabbered in a way Bonnie would expect a crazy man to act.

Frulik raised his hand. "Just a minute, I agree with Miss Cole. Tom Finch is not guilty," he said.

"The hell he's not," Bob shouted.

"Well, I've dropped the charges. I'll release him today," Frulik said.

"Mr. Frulik, would you two like to settle this in private?" Bonnie asked.

"No, honestly I'd like you to hear this. Bob and I have had several disagreements lately."

"It's no wonder you and I disagree from all the dumb things you've done. What's more, Tom put $20 on the bar Friday night and drank until all hours," Bob said.

Bonnie's intuition went into overdrive: *Bob won't listen. He never heard a word the district attorney said.*

"What does $20 have to do with this?" Frulik asked.

I'm not sure it matters. From what I've heard, I don't think Tom can do anything Bob would approve of.

"Tom drank so much Saturday night he could hardly stand up. Donald's motorcycle and jewelry are gone," Bob said.

Frulik had a ruler in his hand. He slapped the metal desk so hard that the sound reverberated across the room.

"Sit down, Ingram," Frulik shouted. "You've done this to me before and I'm sick and tired of it. In fact, one time we were in court, you made us look like idiots."

Bonnie eyed Bob, who stood behind the straight chair with both of his hands gripping the top of the chair. She wondered if he intended to take a swing at Frulik.

Bob tried to get in a word, but Frulik had the floor, and Bonnie was sure he intended to keep it. "Listen to this report." Frulik played the tape of Tom telling about what he had done for Donald. He omitted the part about Tom's son. He showed Bob the ticket and Tom's time card. "There's no way we can hold him. Tom couldn't have killed Donald Wilms or the Ryan Brothers. These witnesses placed him at work by 10:40 a.m."

"He was only 10 minutes late," Bonnie said.

Bob snapped at her. "Lady, if you had kept your nose out of Windcove business, we'd all be better off."

"Sheriff, you'd send an innocent man to prison, perhaps for life, because of your personal problems?" Bonnie asked in disgust.

"Our town would be better off," Bob said again and slammed the office door as he went out.

Frulik stared at the closed door. Finally, he said, "I'll make copies of your report." In a few minutes, Frulik handed Bonnie her original report. As they got up to leave, Frulik held out his hand. "Thanks. I assure you Tom will be free soon."

As the three climbed into the pickup, Art was pensive. "Well Bonnie, you're on Bob's list."

"I've studied that man, but I don't understand him. Have you ever had any trouble with him?" Bonnie asked and eyed Art.

"We've had a few name calling sessions," Art said.

She laughed at Art's remark. "It surprised me when Bob ordered me to stay out of Windcove business. That's the last thing I intended, to interfere in anyone's business."

"Don't let it bother you. You're exactly what he needs, because he tries to run this town. You've made a lot of friends here," Art said.

"I certainly hope so. I've met some lovely people," she said.

At Art's house, Bonnie reached into the fridge for a bottle of pop as the men went into the office. Through the half-opened door, she heard Art when he said, "I hope I didn't hurt her feelings."

"I don't think so. She's so deep in thought. Soon she'll ask me question after question," Mike told Art.

He knows me better than I know myself, she thought and sauntered onto the back porch. She sat on the top step in the moonlight with Millie beside her. Her thoughts turned to Tom's description of how Donald had cut his right hand. Also, Tom said what a thoughtful, kind person Donald was. Her mind drifted back to the white curly haired man she saw that Sunday tied in a chair. *Like Mike said, 'If he was able to get up, why did he sit there and take such a beating?' If someone cinched him in so tight, how did he get to the telephone? I've asked myself these questions 50 times.*

She finished her can of pop and went to her room, pulled on the long Tee nighty she often wore to bed and picked up a book. Sleep might be a long time in coming.

CHAPTER 6

She woke the next morning feeling groggy. What day was it? Monday? Tuesday? The newspaper on the floor, still scattered from the night before, read Monday, May 25th. While her sleep-clogged mind was still concluding that this must be Tuesday, May 26th, the clouds parted, and brilliant sunlight filled the room.

A limb on the big fir tree raked noisily against the screen on the west window, and she flinched as she folded the paper and put it in the rack. As she lowered the west window, she noted the unusual calm and quiet. Even the air had a peculiar smell. Then a low rumble of thunder sounded off in the distance. A storm, probably a bad one, was not far off.

Dressed for the day, she happily sauntered down the hall and pushed open the kitchen door. With a friendly hello all around, Art slid over on the bench to give her room to join them.

"We're going to the garage. Want to come along?" he asked.

"Sure, I'm free today." While Art locked the door, Bonnie stepped out on the walk and stared at the sky. "I've never seen such wicked looking clouds in my life," she said and ran for the truck. Before she got in, raindrops hit her in the face. By the time they got to the garage, what had begun moments before as random drops had increased to a downpour. They filed into the shop where Jim greeted them.

"From the looks of those clouds in the northeast, we're in for an awful storm. I must help the fellows get the new cars inside," Jim said and hurried out of sight.

What sounded like an explosion to Bonnie was an awesome clap of thunder. As Bonnie and Art stood in the show room looking out the large window onto Main Street, she saw a power pole fall across the street, and sparks were shooting in every direction. As the show room lights went out, Art said, "That hit took our transformer out." A blinding flash of lightning hit the big tree across the street, and the thunder vibrated the building.

The rain was coming down in spurts. Almost as if a zipper had held the water for as long as it could then give way and the water poured out. Art grabbed Bonnie's hand, sensing her uneasiness as she whispered, "I've never seen a storm like this in my life. Do you get them often?"

"We get one like this about every three years," Art said. He pointed out the window. "The building across the street used to be a drive-in restaurant, and that tree just missed it. But it did hit the power line across the highway, which will back traffic up for miles."

For the next few minutes, the flashes of lightening and the thunder were continuous, and the downed power lines shot sparks in every direction.

In a flash of lightning, she saw a man on the other side of the street. Evidently, Art saw the same stranger, humped over, and on his way up the street in the rain. "My God! That's Dad," Art yelled. "What's he doing out in this storm?" Art jerked Bonnie as he started for the service station, then he stopped, shook his head, and dropped on the bench by the window. He rested his elbows on his knees and slowly put his head in his hands. "Dad died almost a month ago; have I gone mad?" he asked and raised his head.

Bonnie watched him cautiously as his eyes darted to the window. A second later, Bonnie did the same and saw the same man in the tan raincoat. She glimpsed at Art. "That can't be your dad, Art. You know your Mother and Dad are together now."

"Did I hear someone call out?" Mike asked, as he stood alongside the bench Art was sitting on.

"I think I've lost the two peas I had in my head. I saw Dad running up the other side of the street," Art said.

"I think you've lost your mind if you tell me Donald is out in this storm," Mike said.

Art moved to the south window and stared up the street. During another flash of lightening and a crack of thunder that again shook the rafters, Art let out a yell. "Mike, look quick! Who can that be, if it's not my dad?"

After the third flash of lightening, Mike said, "He's wearing the same type clothes as Donald. He runs like Donald. From here, he looks like him. I think we're all hallucinating."

Another flash of lightning almost blinded Bonnie the second time. After her eyes adjusted, she said, "The man has disappeared." Art and Mike said the pedestrian looked and acted like Donald. The thought crossed her mind that perhaps another problem, heretofore unthought of, might be rearing its head. *Was someone deliberately pretending to be Donald? Why? To hurt Art? Why?*

Mike walked over by Bonnie and whispered, "So help me that fellow running up the other side of the street acted and dressed like Donald? What do you suppose it all means?"

"I haven't the faintest idea, but we can be assured there's a lot more to this than we realize." Her own words frightened her.

After the storm subsided, the lights flickered. "Well, Jim got the generator on," Art said.

Art depends on Jim more than he realizes. "How long has Jim worked for you?" she asked.

"He and I go way back. When dad hauled ore from the mine to the river with mules, he bought 100 acres from Main Street." Art pointed to the street in front of the garage. "His land extended west along the river and 10 blocks along the south side of town. Dad built a small garage on the back of this lot and stored his trucks in front. The way I heard the story, Jim sauntered into the garage one sunny day and hit Dad up for a job. He said he could repair the trucks for less money and has kept them on the job every day. Jim was married with a one-year-old baby boy, and he was only 16-years-old! He needed a job in the worst way!"

"Then Jim and your dad go way back?" she asked.

"Oh yes. Dad never knew what happened, but Jim and his son had a falling out and his son ran away. I was still in school. After his son left, Jim took me under his wing," Art said.

Bonnie watched Mike get out of his chair and slowly walk over in front of the big window that overlooked the magnificent Snake River. Mike turned and stared at Art. In his inquisitive, nosy way of getting information, Mike asked, "Art Wilms, can you sit there and tell me Jim Rams is 64-years-old, only 11 years younger than Donald?"

"That's a fact. He talked Dad into building this place. He told Dad he'd make a business man out of me if it was the last thing he ever did." Art laughed. "He's taught me a lot." Small talk continued for several minutes when the phone rang. It wasn't difficult to hear Bob's roaring voice even before Art could get the receiver to his ear.

"Just a minute, Mike and Bonnie are here. I'll turn on the speaker." Art reached over and pushed the button. "Go ahead."

"I got a call from the Denver police. They have arrested a Charles Robbins for drunk driving. Charles was riding a stolen motorcycle with Idaho plates registered to a Donald Wilms," Bob said. "I told the detective we wanted to question him about the murder of Donald Wilms."

"Did the Denver police find a wristwatch?" Art asked.

"I don't know," Bob said. "I've faxed all the fingerprints we found in your dad's house to Denver. I'll let you know what they have as soon as they send word." Art hung up the receiver. Bonnie noticed Art's hands were trembling. He stared at her. His face was pale, and he acted almost as if he were afraid or unwilling to accept Bob's story.

"Did we see Dad's motorcycle Sunday afternoon?" Mike asked.

"Only one way for you to find out," Bonnie said. All this time, she had wondered if she should suggest Art see a doctor. Soon, Art was in control of his emotions and he tossed his pencil on the desk and leaned back in the chair. With his fingers curved, making a halo over the top of his head, he scanned the ceiling for a moment, then sat up and his feet hit the floor. "Let's fuel the plane and fly to Denver," Art said. "I'll explain to Bob what we intend to do."

He can lose it and put himself back together faster than anyone I've ever seen, Bonnie thought. "Will you be gone long?"

"We better go prepared to stay two or three days," Art said.

"Let's leave the first of the week and in the meantime make a few plans," Mike said.

Before they left the garage, Art called Jim and asked him to fuel the plane and plan to leave early for Denver.

Monday morning, Mike and Art bid Bonnie goodbye on their way to the airport. She poured herself a cup of coffee, picked up the morning paper, and settled comfortably at the breakfast table. *Maybe I'll have a few days of peace and quiet.* She had no more than released the thought of peace and quiet when someone tried to open the kitchen door.

As Bonnie started to get up, a friendly voice called out, "Relax Honey. I'm the housekeeper. Call me Sadie. I think everybody in town knows your name." She helped herself to a cup of coffee and sat across the table from Bonnie.

"Do you know who killed Donald?" Sadie asked.

"I haven't an idea. Have you heard anything?" Bonnie asked.

"Some think Art might have done it."

"Why would anyone think that?"

"I don't know," Sadie said. She sighed, then laughed in a silly way for a few seconds. "What a show Zeeta put on in Weeks Grocery about a month ago. It seems Zeeta thinks she'll marry Art. She shouted at him, 'After we're married, I'll buy the groceries, and you won't have to bother'. I don't know why buying the groceries was important, but I guess it was."

Sadie had a sip of coffee. "Donald laughed and told Zeeta she was out of her mind if she thought she would ever get that son of his to the altar."

Sadie continued with her story. "Zeeta had a large strawberry milkshake in her hand. She screamed at Donald, 'Old man! What Art and I do is none of your business.' She threw that shake in Donald's face. It splashed all over the front of his suit and on his white shoes.

"I was busy in the fancy glass section and I asked Mr. Wilms if he'd like to come to the back of the store. Between the two of us, we got his suit and oxford's presentable. He washed his face while I cleaned his white hat."

"What did Mr. Weeks do?" Bonnie asked.

"He apologized to Mr. Wilms and said there's trouble every time she comes in the store. He ordered Zeeta out. When she didn't leave, he escorted her to the door and shouted, 'Don't ever come back.' On the way, she kicked over the janitor's mop bucket in front of the cash registers. It splashed on an old lady's feet and legs," Sadie said.

"I never had the pleasure of meeting Mr. Wilms. Everywhere I go, I hear good things about him," Bonnie said.

"Donald Wilms was very polite and kind to everyone. The next week, Art paid me double for cleaning this place. He said that was for being so kind to his father."

Bonnie noticed Sadie push herself up from the table like a well-over-60-year-old might. She poured Bonnie another cup of coffee and filled hers. "With that woman loose, I wouldn't stay in this house alone if I were you," Sadie said.

"Why would she bother me?"

"One day, I was here alone when she slipped in. After she searched the entire place, she realized I was the housekeeper, and she seemed satisfied. I don't think Art has any idea what he has gotten himself into. She has a key to this place." Sadie paused. After a small chuckle, she said, "Someone heard Zeeta say that Art has a new girlfriend. That could mean trouble." Sadie rolled her eyes toward Bonnie.

"Me," Bonnie said. Her eyes popped wide open. "I had no idea such a rumor was going around." She hesitated then asked, "How do you know she could walk in on me?"

"Because one day she walked in on me. She didn't know, to begin with, that I was the housekeeper. Hard to say how she would have reacted if I had been someone else."

Bonnie stood. "I must get to work. Thanks for the information" She moved toward the office.

Sadie kept on with her line of gossip. "I've seen enough women ready to start to bud and Zeeta's bud is about ready to bloom. She may claim it belongs to Art."

"Are you telling me Zeeta is pregnant?" Bonnie asked.

"No question about it. People laugh at me. Every time a bud gets far enough along to want to bloom, a woman starts to swell."

Bonnie wondered what she should do? Her thoughts were going round and round so fast they were overlapping. *The way Mike talked, they could be in Denver two or three days, and I'll be in this house alone.* She could hear Sadie still rattling on and on about Zeeta. *Doesn't she ever shut up?*

"You won't need to bother the office or my room," Bonnie said.

"Which one is yours?"

"The front bedroom on this floor."

Soon Bonnie could hear the vacuum cleaner running. She knew Sadie was upstairs. She closed the door to the office and called the police station. After she told the officer her problem, he said he couldn't do a thing unless Bob Ingram approved.

Bonnie thanked the officer. Then she called the airport; luckily, the Wilms' plane was still there. Art answered the phone.

"Bonnie, what's wrong?" Art asked.

"Sadie tells me Zeeta is out to get me. Will Bob send an officer to stay here while you're gone?" Bonnie asked.

She heard Bob's voice on the phone.

"I'll send Officer Julie Foster. She's the best officer we have on the force. I'm sure no one will bother you with her there."

"Thanks, Bob. Tell Mike to do us proud. You gentlemen have a good flight," Bonnie said.

As soon as Officer Foster arrived, she assured Bonnie she would stay until the men returned from Denver.

When the vacuum started, Julie jumped.

"That's the housekeeper. We must be very careful what we say while she's here. She's a big blabber mouth." Bonnie liked Julie Foster, and with an officer in the house, she felt better.

CHAPTER 7

Mike was more than a little concerned when Bonnie did not answer his call. As he stood with the receiver in his hand, he heard the phone ring. *I shouldn't have left her alone. Maybe I better call a cab and go back?* At that moment, the phone clicked. Mike heard Bonnie when she answered. "Are you all right and is Julie Foster there? Will she stay with you till we get back?"

"Yes to all three questions," she said.

"We'll be back as soon as we can. Just be careful." After Bonnie hung up, he still felt concerned about leaving her alone. "Bob, will Officer Foster stay with Bonnie until we return?" Mike asked.

"Yes, we've had calls before about Zeeta. From other women. Each time Foster has protected them," Bob said.

He heard Jim when he revved up the big motors. "Sounds like we're ready to take off," Mike said. He wiggled in the seat until he was comfortable.

"Who knows what this trip will uncover," Art said and plunked in the seat beside Mike.

After they landed in Denver, Jim stayed with the plane. Art, Mike and Bob found their way through the airport to a cab stand.

"Our lucky day," Art said, as they got in a cab that had seen its best 10 years ago.

"Police station please," Mike said.

As the driver pulled to the curb, Art said, "Wait for us."

Inside the station, Mike asked the sergeant at the front desk. "Who's the detective investigating the Charles Robbins case?"

The sergeant touched a couple of buttons on the computer and said, "That's Jack Cummings. He's on the second floor."

"Thank you," Mike said.

Art, Bob and Mike met Jack. Mike explained the reason they were in Denver. Then he asked, "Can we question Charles Robbins?"

"I don't know why not," Jack said. "I'll have him brought to an interrogation room." In the hall, Jack pointed to the door on his right and said, "Wait in there. It shouldn't be long."

Before Bob and Mike went in, Mike said, "Art, maybe you shouldn't be in here. We'll join you later?"

Art hesitated. "Well, all right," he said.

Mike wondered if Art wanted to see the man who robbed his dad or did he want to beat the stuffing out of him? He closed the door and sized up the barren room. *Four chairs and a table. I've forgotten how many hours I've spent in rooms like this.*

The officer showed up with Charles Robbins. Mike changed his position in his chair and looked at a small man with dirty clothes, three sizes too big. He hadn't shaved in four or five days. Charles had wads of dirty long black hair, decorated with over grown lice, and trimmed around the edges with flaky dandruff. But he looked confident and not at all concerned about being questioned.

Mike disliked him immediately. *I'll bet he hasn't shampooed his hair since his mother washed it. He's so sure of himself. I'll take that smug grin off his face.*

Following a knock on the door, it was opened by an officer who was followed closely by a well-dressed man. "I'm Phil Harris, Charles' lawyer. You weren't going to question my client without counsel?"

"Of course not." Mike stood and stepped around to the other side of the table, studied Charles, then he asked, "What were you doing in the Wilms' home on Sunday, May 3rd?"

"Who is Wilms?" Charles asked.

When Charles opened his mouth, Mike noticed a green film covered what few teeth he had. His breath reminded Mike of riding in a buggy behind a gassy horse. "Donald Wilms is the elderly man who you attacked and robbed in his home on Wilms Mountain."

Charles glared at Phil and said, "This bunch is crazier than a drunk skunk. I ain't never saw a Wilms Mountain."

"How did your fingerprints get on Donald Wilms' door and on the glass vase?" Mike asked. He noticed Charles was restless. He fidgeted in his chair and dug at his fingernails, which were already bleeding. "You stole his wristwatch along with three diamond rings. What did you do with them?"

"It shows how smart you idiots are. The stupid rings were plain glass, just glass," Charles said. "The other night I was in a poker game. The devils were crooked. They beat me out of the rings and watch, and every cent I had including the motorcycle," Charles added. He slumped as though he couldn't look at Mike.

"Charles Robbins, you're a liar. The police have Donald Wilms' motorcycle that you were riding when they arrested you." Mike shook his head at Charles' lawyer.

"What was the name of the fellow who won the jewelry?" Bob asked.

"Only one of you ask the questions," Phil said.

"All right," Mike said. "Who was the guy in the poker game?"

Charles' beady little green eyes glared at them. He laughed in a silly way. "You ain't never gonna find any of that bunch. Nobody goes by their real names. He called himself Lee Steele."

"What does Lee Steele look like?" Mike asked.

Again Charles lifted his face. Mike noticed this time he gawked at the ceiling avoiding everyone in the room. Mike's eyes rested on Bob for a second and Mike realized Charles' performance didn't fool him either. "I don't believe a word this punk has said. Bob, why don't you call the district attorney in Windcove. Have him extradite Charles on three counts of first degree murder."

Mike noticed Charles' eyes opened wide and Charles stared at Mike. That scared Charles.

"I'll make that call right now," Bob said and stood.

After Charles started mumbling, Phil said, "Be quiet."

Mike noticed his last remark brought Phil Harris to life.

"Don't say another word." Phil glared at Mike. "You didn't say a thing about murder. I thought you were charging my client with theft," Phil said.

"You didn't ask what he was being charged with."

"Donald Wilms, the man who owned the motorcycle, was beaten to death, and two others were shot in the back of the head. Charles' fingerprints were on the murder weapon that puts him at the scene," Mike said. "Your client had his chance. He sat there, called us names and made smart remarks. When this thief decides to tell us what he knows, we'll take the time to listen," Mike said and started to leave.

The officer removed Charles from the room.

As Bob slid his chair against the table to leave, Mike said, "Let's find Detective Cummings." Down the hall, Mike pushed on the door to the detective's office. Out of 20 desks, Mike saw Jack at one in the rear, and they made their way carefully to his desk.

"Do you have an address for Charles Robbins?" Mike asked.

"I thought you might want to see it. He has a room on the other side of town," Jack said, as he held up a paper. "I have a search warrant."

The three men took Jack's car. They had ridden about five miles when Jack turned off the main arterial onto a narrow dirt street. Mike saw small dilapidated houses on both sides. The farther Jack drove, the rougher the ride. Mike counted 15 kids in two blocks. He couldn't handle it any more so he stopped counting.

After four more blocks, Jack turned into a driveway, which was actually a lane with weeds a foot high. Mike frowned as he looked at the place. *No one has painted this house in 50 years.* Someone had boarded up a few of the windows. The screen door swayed and banged in the wind. *I knew Robbins would have a room in a dump, but this is worse than I imagined,* Mike's thoughts continued.

Jack knocked on the old weather-beaten door. Someone opened it a couple of inches. Mike saw the chain on the door and heard a woman's voice as she yelled, "What the hell do you want now?" But when she had peered through the crack and could see them, she calmed down a bit. "Yeah? What do you want?"

"We have a warrant to search Charles Robbins' room," Jack said.

After she unhooked the chain, they stepped inside and Mike saw the largest woman he had ever seen. He guessed she would weigh 400 pounds or more. It was all she could do to walk around the room and *the stench in this place would make a dog sick*, Mike thought.

"Upstairs, second-door on the right. I'm telling you fellows, I don't want any fooling around," she snapped.

"We won't be any longer than necessary. How long has Charles Robbins lived here?" Jack asked.

"He rented the room five days ago," she said. The woman offered Jack the key and took the search warrant from Jack.

Mike cringed when he saw her dirty hands and wondered how Jack could even handle the key. The three of them climbed the dirty, squeaky old stairs and Jack pushed on the door. The hinges were so rusty the door squeaked and only opened about halfway. None of the doors had any doorknobs, but there were deep scratches around where the knobs had been. Mike assumed someone had stolen the knobs. Inside, Mike noticed Charles' room was about 15 square feet, with one little, cracked, dirty window, and no shade or curtain. The floor was so dirty that they left tracks as they walked across the floor. Many of the floor boards squeaked.

Jack handed Mike and Bob each a pair of gloves and both of them nodded their thanks. The bed looked like an old sow had had a litter of pigs in it. He tipped up the mattress and peered through a set of old bent-down coil-springs and saw dust and gobs of lint on the floor. Mike examined the rusty metal bed posts. He noticed a string hanging on the side of one of them. He held onto the string as he twisted the cap. When it popped loose, he pulled out a small plastic bag. "Look here," Mike said, as he stood holding up the bag. "I think this is cocaine."

"I'll bet you're right. I'll add a charge of possession against Robbins," Jack said.

Mike hurried across the floor to the dilapidated old dresser. He tugged on an old broken drawer until it let loose and he discovered it was empty. In the next drawer, he found some dirty underwear and holes that Charles probably called socks. Mike gripped both handles on the third drawer. He wiggled, jerked, uttered a few swear words, and finally it snapped open. Inside, he found some dirty shirts and a pair of pants. Under the shirts, he collected some rings, along with a tie clasp, a wristwatch, and a gold pen and pencil set with Donald Wilms' name engraved on them. Mike picked up the pen set and said, "I guess this will prove Robbins was in Wilms' house."

He ransacked the bottom dresser drawer and found more filthy clothes. Mike saw a dirty white shirt rolled up in the far corner of the drawer. He held onto the tip of the collar, flipped the shirt enough to straighten it. On one sleeve was a big spot of what Mike felt was blood. He held the shirt up and said, "Look at this."

Bob whirled around and asked, "Is that blood on the sleeve?"

"I think so," Jack said, as he held up a plastic bag for Mike to put the shirt in. "I'll send it to the laboratory."

To be sure, Mike stirred through all the jewelry he found among Charles' possessions. He said, "Donald's favorite ring isn't here."

"The one Donald always wore on his little finger. I believe it was a present from his wife," Bob said.

"You're right. Maybe Robbins lost it in the poker game." Mike looked around the room. "I think this does it."

Downstairs, Mike, Bob and Jack thanked the woman and walked out to the police car. "I've seen messes, but nothing like this," Mike said.

"Are you holding Robbins?" Bob asked.

How Bob would like to get this fellow in Windcove and accuse him of killing Donald, Mike thought.

"All we have on him is drunk driving, possession of cocaine and stolen merchandise. If you can make murder charges stick, as far as I'm concerned, you fellows can have him," Jack said.

At the police station, Mike said, "May I have a few minutes alone with Charles?"

"His lawyer might be hard to find," Jack said, and let Mike know he agreed with what he wanted to do.

Mike opened the door into the same interrogation room. The officer brought Charles in and said, "I've got to give these papers to the sergeant at the front desk. I'll be right back." He shut the door.

"Hey, you can't leave me in here alone with him," Charles yelled.

Mike pointed to the chair and shouted, "Sit down." Charles sat in a hurry. Mike charged over in front of him. With an attitude of disgust and impatience, he said, "I'll get right to the point. Charles Robbins you sat here this morning and fed us one lie after another. Your remarks were anything but wise."

Charles slumped down in the chair, scratched his head, and with his mouth hanging open, he stared at the flakes of dandruff on the table. Mike assumed he looked at the dandruff and lice because there wasn't anything else to look at.

"Mister, I'm going to ask you four questions. I better get four logical answers, or I'll beat the crap out of you. I don't have to follow the rules like these other men," Mike said. "Question number one: What did you do with the third ring you stole?" *He doesn't appear half as big as he did before,* Mike thought as he glared at Charles.

Charles squirmed around in his chair. Then lifted his pale, greenish brown eyes toward the ceiling. He lowered them, gaped at Mike, then at his dirty fingers, which he had been digging on since he scratched his head. After another pause, Charles said, "I done lost the watch in a poker game to Lee Steele. That's a name he goes by." He shook his head and continued. "I don't know nothin else."

"I found Donald Wilms' watch in your dresser drawer. Again I'm asking you. What does Steele look like?" Mike asked.

"He has long red hair, freckles, about as tall as me. I ain't sure, but I think he has a scar on his face."

"Question number two," Mike said. "Why did you kill Donald Wilms?"

"I ain't never killed nobody. When I got to the house, someone had bumped off a dog inside the kitchen door. In the livin room, I found an old man roped to a chair with a lump on his head. I needed money, man. I stole his change, two rings, and a watch."

"What did you do then?"

"I got out of there. I tried startin my cycle. The thing had runned out of gas. I shoved it over the bank and climbed on the beauty sittin on the porch. That's the truth, man. I swear," Charles said.

Mike eyed Charles. *I don't know why, but I believe him.* Mike paced the floor for a minute. He stopped and studied Charles. *He shows he's beginning to think that he could be in serious trouble,* Mike thought. "As sure as I know the sun will set tonight, you've lied to me again. So you better start talking," Mike said. Again, he saw a frightened man trying to keep from rolling his eyes at him. Charles ran his fingers through his long dirty hair. Mike cringed, as Charles crushed the lice that fell on the table. Mike shoved the table into Charles and yelled, "I want to hear some truth, not next week, but right now." Mike leaned forward, hit the table with his fist. Charles had exhausted Mike's patience, and from the expression on Charles' face, Mike thought Charles was beginning to realize it.

Beads of perspiration showed on Charles' forehead. He gasped for breath and said, "I got off the highway at the bridge, bucked the narrow path to where it runned up the hill. I saw the river path didn't go no more."

Mike heard a knock on the door. Phil charged in and said, "Why is my client in here without benefit of counsel?"

"If I want to talk to this punk, I'll talk to him," Mike said and picked up his briefcase to leave.

"I'll tell your commanding officer about this. What's your badge number?" Phil asked.

"Tell anyone you want. I don't work here." At the door, Mike said, "If I were you, I'd have my client sprayed for lice." Mike walked out and closed the door. In the hall, he felt like he had lice all over him. He scratched his arm. *These little devils are all hungry,* he thought.

On the way to Jack's office, Mike joined Art and Bob and the three of them soon found chairs at Jack's desk.

"Let's listen to the tape we made this morning," Mike said and took the tape from his briefcase.

Jack lifted his recorder out of the drawer. "Good idea," he said and put Mike's tape in the recorder.

After the tape finished, Mike said, "I have a tendency to believe him."

"So do I," Art said, and in the same breath, he asked, "Are we taking Robbins to Windcove?"

"I'm sure they'll send Robbins to Windcove one of these days. In the meantime, let's go home," Mike said.

Bob agreed. They thanked Jack for his help and found their way back to their cab.

As Mike boarded Art's plane for Windcove, he was glad Donald's personal things would soon be back in his local town; however, to be going home without any concrete information saddened him deeply.

CHAPTER 8

Tuesday morning, the sound of the percolator woke Bonnie. She slipped on a summery print and added a dab of lipstick.

Walking into the kitchen, she found Officer Foster, who handed her a cup of coffee. "Like a slice of toast?"she asked.

"Sounds good. I'm not used to this kind of service," Bonnie said.

Foster pushed the button on the toaster. "Did you hear Art and Mike come home about 4:00 a.m.?"

Bonnie knew her mouth dropped open. Doubting her own ears, she asked, "What time did you say they got home?"

"About 4:00 a.m. It was so early, I laid down again and went to sleep. You're safe now, and my family will be up by the time I get home," Foster said.

"Thanks for everything. The first day you're free, let's have lunch."

"I'll remember and thanks for asking," Julie said and departed.

Bonnie took her cup of coffee into the office. She was making notes and reminiscing about the officer's remarks as well as the housekeepers statements. She wondered what they were going to do with Zeeta.

"Good morning! You're deep in thought," Mike said.

Bonnie jumped. "I didn't hear you come in. How did things go?"

"Let me get my breakfast," Mike said disappearing into the kitchen. Soon he returned with his cup and lowered himself into the chair. "That was quite a trip to complete in 24 hours."

"How do you like Charles?" Bonnie asked.

Mike frowned at Bonnie, shook his head, and in a half-laughing, silly voice, he blurted out, "I'm playing an old record. It's not how I like him. It's what we're going to do with him? He's a sloven excuse of a man with no education."

"You have me guessing. Do you believe him?" she asked.

"I hoped you wouldn't ask that question. Frankly, I don't want to answer," Mike said.

"Why? I feel like you are keeping something from me. What is it?" she asked.

Mike set his cup on the desk, rested his weight on his feet. While moving around the desk, he crammed his hands into his pant's pockets. With a long face, he stared at Bonnie. She noticed his face was drawn, and he showed the trip had exhausted him.

He bent over, rested his hands on the desk. His weary eyes met Bonnie's. In a sad, discouraged voice, hardly above a whisper, he said,

"Darn it, you're going to want to help this creature."

Bonnie knew she hurt Mike at times. "What can I do when people need help?"

"Some of these characters never so much as say thank you. Once in a while, please, just once in a while, shut your eyes, and I'll lead you away," he said and smiled.

She knew Mike was right. *Some do take advantage of me,* she thought. "Let's listen to your tapes."

Mike hesitated, scratched his chest, but that wasn't good enough, because he unbuttoned his shirt and scratched again. Then he said, "Every time I think about Charles Robbins, I itch." He got a stack of tapes from his briefcase. Bonnie's thought process snapped into place. *He doesn't seem anxious or want me to hear what went on in Denver.*

After two big sips of coffee, Mike slipped a cartridge in the recorder. Then he said, "A Mr. Harris showed up and insisted he was Charles' lawyer. It surprised me Charles had such good representation." He started the tape. One after another went into the machine.

At times, Bonnie wanted to ask Mike to forget the rest of the interrogation. When the last tape stopped, Bonnie said, "You said he had no education, but I didn't realize his speech was so atrocious."

"You haven't heard anything yet. Wait until he gets in a conversation and gets all the unused machinery wound up," Mike said.

"How does Bob Ingram feel toward this fellow?" Bonnie asked.

"Bob wants to get him in Windcove as soon as possible and hang him," Mike said.

"Did you believe Charles when he said, 'I ain't never killed nobody'?"

"Yes I did. Why I don't know, but I want to believe that little weak soul." Mike threw his hands up and shook his head. "Bonnie, this man is about five feet tall. I'd guess he's about 24-years-old, but he looks 30. I doubt if he will weigh a 120 pounds and that includes his dirty clothes. He does have a lot of one thing."

"What's that?" Bonnie asked anxiously.

Mike laughed. "Head lice," he said and laughed some more. "Every time he scratched his head, which was often, he'd smash the lice that fell on the table." Mike wrinkled his face, shrugged his shoulders, and scratched his head. "I itch every time I think about him."

Art walked in. Bonnie noticed his face was drawn and he sank into the chair across the desk from her. She looked as Mike. "I hope you didn't bring any lice with you. At the present time, Charles' case can rest. We must decide what to do with Zeeta Cockran." To her astonishment, neither man said a word. Art reached for his cup of coffee. He emptied the cup in one swallow. He tried for a second, but got a mouth full of air. Bonnie hoped Art would open up and enlighten her. After waiting for an answer, she said, "Art, I don't like to keep bringing up this subject, but I must know. What about Zeeta?"

Art removed his legs from the corner of the desk, leaned forward and laid his arms on the desk. His big blue eyes looked her in the face and in a soft voice, he said, "I met Zeeta during my last year of college. She was engaged to a friend of a friend of mine. They must have gotten married, because she has two kids. I had forgotten about her until she moved here."

"Zeeta is telling everyone around town that you are her sweetheart. She makes it sound like you're getting married soon," Bonnie said.

He shook his head and said, "Oh no! I happened to see her at Weeks Grocery last January. I suggested we go for dinner and talk over old college days. That was the last time I saw her until she drove in for gas. I waited on her and mentioned the dinner we were going to have. That night I picked her up; she was home by 10:00 p.m. We talked about things that happened while we were in college. She was very much like her old self, and we did have a lot of memories. She said that she had gotten a divorce. We laughed about the professors we had, as well as other things, but with no intentions, at least on my part, of going any place. When we arrived at her place, I took her to the porch, and she asked me in.

"I thanked her, but said I had to be going. Then I got in my rig and drove to the Cross Roads Bar. Why I went in there is more than I know. I felt like, if I ever needed proof of my whereabouts that evening, the Cross Roads was the best place in town to meet someone you know. Sure enough, Carey and Janice Kelly were celebrating their 10th wedding anniversary and invited me to join their crowd."

"I see. You did take her to The Diner," Bonnie said.

"Yes, I did, but just how that happened is still a mystery to me. It just sort of fell into place. See, Dad and I and Dr. Crugar had stopped at the Cross Roads Bar for a drink and she was there. Dad and I had planned to have dinner at The Diner. I don't remember the conversation, but somehow Dr. Crugar said, 'Young fellow, you take the young lady to The Diner and your Dad will have dinner with the wife and me'. I drove Zeeta to The Diner for dinner."

Bonnie waited; she hoped Art would go on. Finally, he asked, "Have you talked with Grace or Clay?"

"Yes, we have," Bonnie said.

"That night was a disgrace. I've never been so ashamed in my life. I saw the meanest, most cruel, hateful person I've ever seen. I had never seen her like that before." Art said, barely above a whisper. He choked and swallowed a couple of times. "The last time I saw Zeeta was on a Sunday in February. I was in the truck on my way to the helicopter. Dad was expecting me. Zeeta drove in with the kids. I tried to tell her I was on my way out. About that time, the kid started begging he wanted to go along, because he had never ridden in a helicopter. She joined the kid. 'Since we've never been in a helicopter, I think that's the least you could do.' Like a fool, I took them. Those kids made Dad so nervous. I've always thought she told Dad that we were planning on getting married soon. When I got her and those two kids home and in her car, I swore never again."

He stood and rushed into the kitchen. Soon he returned with the coffee pot. After he filled their cups, he continued. "Later, Dad said if I married that bitch, he would sell his house. He gave me the impression that I might never hear from him again. How she got a key to this place is more than I know. I never gave it to her."

"Your housekeeper said some rumors are flying around town that Zeeta wants me out of the way. She thinks I'm coming between the two of you."

"Did you ever go to bed with her?" Mike asked.

"Absolutely not. If rumors are correct, since she moved to Windcove, she's been with most every playboy in this area, and she shacked up with an old widower for several months. The story I hear is that he's crazy about her." Art rolled his chair away from the desk and stared at Bonnie. "I'm telling you one thing, Bonnie Cole. You're not staying alone in this house again. If Mike and I have to go anywhere, we're taking you with us."

This took Bonnie by surprise. "That's the last thing I'll have time for," she said.

Art spoke up. "Nobody can get along with Zeeta. She's a little pit-bull." He winked at Bonnie. "But sometimes, it's tempting."

Mike rolled his eyes toward the ceiling. Then he said disgustedly. "Oh brother! There's an old saying, 'Love is blind,' but I never realized until now, it's deaf, dumb and stupid."

Bonnie noticed it tickled Art when Mike took his remark seriously.

"That old widower, would he kill for her?" Mike asked.

"Some of the men at the garage seem to think so," Art said.

"From where I sit, you're walking on a suspension bridge that's made out of wet tissue paper," Mike said.

Art gazed at Mike for a moment. Slowly, Art got out of his chair, walked across the floor, turned and said, "I must go to work." He shut the door on his way out.

Six hours later, Bonnie closed the books in front of her and piled them on the corner of the desk. She stood and slowly walked across the floor to the north window. The big night light on the garage lit the driveway and the north side of the yard as bright as a sunny day. She closed the drapes, moved back to Art's big leather chair, laid her arms on the back and faced Mike.

"What's wrong, you look so worried?" he asked.

"I've watched Art. If he doesn't get some rest, he'll have a nervous breakdown." She rubbed her hands over the smooth leather on the back of the chair. "The worst of my job is prying into other people's personal affairs, but we must investigate Zeeta. Will you go all the way, find out why she is so determined to marry Art and wants Donald out of the way?"

"Sure. Do you want me to go the limit regardless of how far I have to travel or how long it takes?"

"It's obvious Art has no interest in her. Before this is over, she'll try and pin something on him, and we better be prepared."

"I gotcha. Since Art has the information, have you wondered why he hasn't looked into Donald's past?" Mike asked.

"Honestly, I think he's afraid and putting it off as long as he can. I wonder if I wouldn't do the same thing?"

"He'll surprise us one of these days. If I were in his shoes, I might go through the papers, but never let anyone know about it." Mike jotted down a few notes in his little green book. He glanced at her with those big brown eyes. "I haven't told you, but ever since Art told you about the letter, I've dreaded for him to tell me the story. He said his dad always packed a gun. I saw two loaded guns both in the kitchen and in his bedrooms."

"Did he live in fear of somebody?" Bonnie shrugged her shoulders.

"I remember a few times when him and I were fishing, the conversation would lapse. I'd notice Donald's eyes drift toward the heavens. You know me. I'm always questioning anything unusual. When Donald's thoughts wandered, his eyes showed fear or sadness. I was never sure which."

"Did you ever ask?"

"No, but many times I've wished he'd said something."

"Maybe one of these days you'll get your answer," she said as she removed her arms from the chair. "Let's call it a day." As Mike started to climb the stairs, she whispered, "Goodnight and pleasant dreams."

He smiled and moved on up the stairs. At the top, he called, "Bonnie, those west windows are so low anyone could crawl in. Why don't you sleep up here in the room next to Art's? I really think you should."

"Well, okay, but Art will get a surprise if he hears a noise in the room next door," she said.

CHAPTER 9

Bonnie heard the little clock she brought with her the night before when it softly chimed seven times. *It's 7:00 a.m. Millie isn't on her rug so someone must be up.* Off came the light quilt and her legs swung over the side of the bed. The cool breeze, which was gently blowing in the open window, felt refreshing. *I could relax here for the rest of the day. Now that Art has the note from his dad's wristwatch, I wonder when he will find the courage to look into his dad's past.*

Her feet touched the floor. She ran downstairs, and in no time, she was in a warm shower that felt so comforting. Soon in her plaid gingham dress and white sandals, she was ready for a new day. Try as she would, she couldn't get Art off her mind.

She pushed the swinging door into the kitchen and expected to see Art or Mike, but the warm room was empty. The smell of fresh coffee tickled her nose and she carried a cup as she softly knocked on the office door.

"Come in," Art called out.

Bonnie noticed Art's desk had papers strewn from one end to the other. "Have you any answers?"

Art swivelled around in his chair, looked at Bonnie and said, "The note in the watch explained how everything he should have told me was in the back of Mom and Dad's picture. Dad's real name was Donald Rigby. After he moved to Florida, he changed his name to Wilms. Later, he and Mother married."

Bonnie sat across from Art. She noticed Art was very nervous. He waved his arms and talked so fast, he reminded her of an auctioneer. "Art, are you in any condition to go over this again?"

"Yes," Art said. He slammed the desk drawer and jumped to his feet. He kicked the waste paper basket across the room spilling its contents in ever direction. He started kicking the loose papers on the floor. One landed in Bonnie's lap and two or three on top of the desk.

Bonnie felt sorry for Art. Still, she wanted to laugh. *If I only had a camera,* she thought.

Art gazed at Bonnie. Then he said, "Sorry." He slapped the desk with his right hand. "Darned if I know who I am or what I'm doing." He dropped back into his chair, rolled his eyes toward the window and said, "Before we can go on, the two of you have to know the whole story."

Bonnie heard Mike when he spoke softly. "Did Donald say why they skipped out?"

"Yes! When Dad was born, he was the youngest of triplets. Arnold was the oldest and mentally ill. Ronald became a playboy, landing in the pen in Thomaston, Maine." Art jumped up. While he paced the floor, he slowly started talking again. "My Dad, Donald, was the ambitious one. He graduated from college with a degree in engineering. After graduation, he wanted to see his mother before moving on. When he came home, he met Marie, my mother. She had promised to marry Arnold, the crazy one. Donald and Marie fell in love at first sight. One month after Dad got home, Marie visited friends in New Orleans. Dad skipped out to Florida and changed his name to Wilms. Mother changed her name from Cameron to Wells, and they married in Phoenix, Arizona in 1937," Art said.

What would it be like to think I was in love with a man, and find out I was really in love with his identical twin brother? Bonnie thought. "How did Arnold like this?" she asked.

"He didn't. Like I said, Arnold was a nut and a hot head. He swore that when he found Donald, he would kill him."

"I wonder if that was Arnold we saw walking up the street?"

"It had to be Arnold or Ronald. Because, like you said Bonnie, Dad is with Mother now."

Art stood and crammed his hands in his pant's pocket. "When I think about this mess, I wonder who I am and what's ahead. Thank God I'm not married or have any kids. How could I explain all of this to a family?" Art asked. Mike shook his head. Art continued. "I can't understand it myself. Who are the Rigbys? How much family do I have?" Art waved his arms in the air. Again he paced the floor.

In a soft caring voice, she said, "We'll have to find out."

Art quit pacing, leaned on the desk again with his eyes staring straight ahead, as if they were frozen, and his voice sounded far away. "I know now why Dad kept a loaded gun in the kitchen on the mountain, besides in the kitchen drawer over here." Art pointed to the house next door. "Dad always packed a loaded gun."

"Did you ever ask Donald why?"

"Yes! Dad said he saw so many rattlesnakes around the mine."

Bonnie tried to put herself in Donald's place. She wondered how he felt, and what a person could do, living year after year, with such a problem hanging over them like Donald had. "Donald spent 50 years of his life expecting Arnold to show. He knew, if and when Arnold did, he'd have to kill him."

"Why do you suppose he kept all this from me?"

"Being a parent, maybe he didn't want you to worry about him and I imagine, he was afraid he might have to shoot his own brother."

"Dad had clippings taken from an Augusta paper about Ashland, Maine. My Uncle Ronald was in the state penitentiary in Maine. The court convicted him of being an accomplice in a bank robbery during which they killed a guard," Art said. He sank into the chair, leaned forward, placed his elbows on the desk, and laid his face in his hands. His head moved from one side to the other. "I don't know Bonnie. I just don't know," he muttered.

"We better go to Maine. There we can get the facts."

Again, Art traipsed back and forth across the floor for what seemed like an hour to Bonnie. "Let's put these papers in the safe and say nothing," Art said.

"With that look-a-like running around town, you're going to have to tell Bob Ingram."

"Tell Bob Ingram." Art stopped and grabbed the edge of the desk. "Bonnie, by noon, he'd have Dad on the 10-most-wanted list."

Mike started carefully picking up the papers. When he found the picture of Donald and Marie taken the day they married, he said, "Your mother was a beautiful woman. How much you look like her." He handed the picture to Bonnie.

"You do look like your mother," she said.

"That's what Dad used to say. Many times when I hugged him, tears would fill his eyes. 'You hug just like your mother,'" Art said. He leaned on the end of the desk while Bonnie and Mike finished gathering up the newspaper items that Donald had saved.

In the kitchen, Art set three bottles of pop out of the refrigerator. "In his letter, Dad said that when he was a child, his parents were very poor. They were lucky to have something to eat and warm clothes," Art said.

"Let's find out more about Ronald and his associates," Bonnie said.

"Have we got to get into all of that?" Art asked.

"I can't see any other way. Right now, we're at the bottom. There's no way to go but up," she said.

CHAPTER 10

A couple of days had passed. Talking about Art's family had been set aside for the time being. The following morning during breakfast, Art said, "This is usually one of our busiest days of the week. Let's go to the garage and help out, if necessary."

Since she knew nothing about a garage, she said, "This is all new to me. I've never so much as filled my car with gas." When Art drove in, she noticed cars in line behind the pumps, and the men were going on a run. Art elected Bonnie as the cashier. As she stood behind the till in the warm morning breeze, she greeted one customer after another. *This is fun.* The thought had hardly registered in her mind when a well-dressed man slowly approached. *He looks exactly like the man I saw tied in a chair on the mountain,* she thought.

In a voice that sounded like Art's, the stranger stared past her and asked, "Are you Art Wilms?"

"I am."

The stranger held out his hand. "I'm Ronald Rigby. I'd like to ask you some questions."

Bonnie was trying to listen to the stranger and make change at the same time.

"Well, Mister Rigby, I have a few for you. Let's go to my office, there we can talk in private." Art called. "Rick, will you take the till?" He turned to Bonnie. "Come with us, please. Let's go to my office and hear what this fellow has to say."

In the office, Art introduced Ronald to Mike, and insisted Bonnie sit in the chair behind the desk.

When Ronald sat, Bonnie saw the old man with his head bent forward and a face so swollen she thought it would burst. His teeth and gold fillings scattered on the rug in front of him. She felt she was seeing things. She noticed Art never stopped walking until he got to the large north window. He stood with his hands in his pockets and gazed outside, as if he had never seen the place before.

"Art, would you like for me to talk with Mr. Rigby?" Mike asked.

Never moving, Art said, "I certainly would."

Turning to the Mr. Rigby, Art explained: "Bonnie is an attorney and a good friend. She can speak for me."

"When were you released from prison?" Mike asked, in an easygoing manner as if that were a normal question.

The stranger seemed surprised that Mike knew he had been in prison. The white-haired man's eyes moved toward Bonnie, then Art.

He wiggled around in his chair, as if he wasn't comfortable. Finally, he faced Mike and said, "I got out six months ago."

This sounds more like a fairy tale than reality, Bonnie thought, as she sat in the large swivel chair and wished she were any place, but in this office across from an ex-convict.

"Are you on parole?"

This time Bonnie noticed the stranger expected Mike to question him. He answered more like a student. "Nope, my record was good, and they released me early."

"Where is Arnold living?" Mike asked.

"Arnold is supposed to be in the Augusta sanitarium, but I understand he escaped six months ago. As far as I know, he's still on the run."

"Is he still determined to harm Donald?" Mike asked.

Bonnie noticed Mike's question threw Ronald off guard. His eyes flashed with anger and he rubbed his hands together, as if he would like to strangle Mike for having asked that question.

"Arnold hasn't changed his mind. He's just as angry with Donald as he was years ago," Ronald said.

It surprised Bonnie when Mike didn't ask another question. All she had heard lately was how Arnold wanted to kill Donald. Could this be Arnold and he beat Donald to death? she wondered.

A mechanic started an air-wrench outside the window. Ronald leaped to his feet. On his way to the door, he ran into Mike's chair and almost knocked Mike over. He acted like somebody had given him an electric shock. *Honestly, he acts like a madman. Perhaps 40 long years behind bars could do this to a person.* Nevertheless, the stranger frightened her. She wondered if the fellow who sat across from her was Arnold, if so, would he try to kill them. She felt afraid to move and scared to look at Ronald.

Soon Ronald returned to his chair. "This place has funny sounding tools," he said.

She noticed Mike never let on that he had even heard the comment. He continued just as if nothing had happened. "How did your father make a living?"

"He didn't, many times we had no heat or food in the house. Old Perce would sit on his dead butt complaining while Mother did laundry. We boys delivered the clothes then we'd go to the grocery store and buy as much food as we could. The old man would raise hell when he didn't get a bottle," Ronald said.

"Sounds as if your father was a typical drunkard," Mike said.

"Yes, he was. We never knew what the Old Man might do. On one particular day, I guess we boys were about six-years-old, Perce was on a rampage and for no reason that I know of, he grabbed Arnold and threw him into a four-wire barbed fence. It tore Arnold's right hip all to pieces. He still packs the scars," Ronald said.

Cold chills raced up and down Bonnie's spine at the thought.

"Would you like to ask me any more questions?" Ronald asked.

"I have a few more. Why did they send Arnold to a sanitarium?" Mike asked

"A half-lit guy bumped into Arnold, in a bar one night, spilling Arnold's drink. From the story I got, Arnold was so mad, he almost beat the man to death," Ronald said.

"Where is your partner that helped rob the bank?"

In a loud voice, he asked, "How did you hear about that?"

"I can't remember," Mike said.

"A rat in the prison killed him," Ronald answered in the same loud angry voice.

"Did your mother ever hear from Donald?" Mike asked.

Bonnie could tell this question seemed to calm Ronald. In a normal voice he said, "Not that I know of. However, I'm positive the money that Mother received came from Donald. The postmark was Florida." Ronald paused temporarily and then said, "Donald tried to tell me my ways were wrong, but I couldn't see it." He scratched his head and went on to say. "When the three of us were born, we were so much alike our mother put name tags on us," Ronald said and rolled his eyes toward Art. "You don't look a bit like us."

By this time, Art had taken a chair beside Bonnie. Art smiled. "I resemble my mother."

Bonnie noticed when Art made that comment, the most cruel, mean expression crossed Ronald's face. Again he leaped to his feet, slapped the desk with both hands, and shouted, "You should have been my son." He stopped for a second, then stuttered and stammered. Finally, he said, "I meant to say Arnold's son." He dropped into the chair, rocked back and forth, as if he needed time to control his temper.

Bonnie kept watching Mike, he never flinched, but from the way he was sitting, she wondered if he were prepared to draw his gun at any moment.

Finally, Ronald asked, "What year is it?"

"Nineteen-eight-seven," Mike said.

Bonnie noticed Ronald's head jerk. She wondered if he were having some kind of a spell, then she realized it's a habit of his. *Why does this crazy nut keep staring at me? I hope he doesn't think I'm Marie.*

"What is Arnold like?" Mike asked.

"He's a mean bastard. He used to drink a lot and would have made a poor husband. He'd have abused Marie, the same as Dad did Mother," Ronald said.

"Did your mother ever try to find Donald?" Mike asked.

"Like I said, the only clue she could find was the postmark on the envelopes with the money in them from a small town in Florida. Mother could never trace it beyond that point," Ronald said.

Bonnie noticed most of the time Art had his eyes closed. When Mike asked Ronald where he was staying, Art's eyes popped open.

"I have a room in a small boarding house in Sugar City," Ronald said. He stood, bid them goodbye and closed the door.

"Who do you think he is?" she asked.

"I have no idea. I'm certain of one thing, from his looks, he's your relative," Mike said and eyed Art.

"Yes Mike. This fellow has to be either Ronald or Arnold. He did say Arnold escaped from the sanitarium and is still at large," Art said.

"I had a lot more questions. When you said you resembled your mother, he acted so queer I was afraid to ask anything else," Mike said.

"Remember you're talking about my relatives." Art laughed and looked at Mike. "I have to admit, he did act queer at times. Did you see his eyes, when he said Arnold would have been as mean to Marie, as Perce was to my grandmother?" Art asked.

"Yes! At times he acted frightened and afraid someone was after him," Mike said.

"I've never been in such a predicament. I know he isn't Dad, but to sit across this desk from a stranger that looks and acts exactly like dad is more than I can tolerate. When Ronald leaned over the desk, leered at me and yelled, 'You should be my son', I almost fainted," Art said.

"You almost fainted. Move over," Bonnie said. "Honestly, I've never felt so scared in my life."

"Yes, I was afraid of him," Mike said. He leaned forward and put his elbows on his legs. Then he wove his fingers together, rested his chin on the back of his hands and studied the floor. When Mike raised his head, he frowned. "At times Ronald truly acted like a madman."

Art rubbed his hands together. In a voice louder than usual, he said, "I don't know what to think."

"I suggest we call the penitentiary. See what the warden can tell us about Ronald. Then call the sanitarium in Augusta, Maine and get his doctor to enlighten us," Bonnie said.

"We'll plan on that, for the present, let's go home and forget it," Art said.

Back at Art's house, Bonnie eased into the chair behind the desk. She remembered Art when he said, 'Let's go home and forget it'. *I don't think we can do that,* she thought. "I believe, we're going to find there's someone involved in Donald's murder that none of us suspect," she said.

Bonnie expected an answer or at least a suggestion. When neither man said a word, she went on. "I must find out if Charles Robbins is in the Windcove jail." She laid a quarter in front of Mike. "Are you a gambling man?"

"Depends on what I'm gambling on," Mike said.

"Heads, we go talk with Charles, tails, I go alone. He has no idea what the sheriff is trying to pin on him and Bob Ingram is hoping to find someone to blame for Donald's murder. That isn't the only reason I want to talk with him."

"I'd like to know what other reason you have to talk to him?" Art asked.

"Charles saw Donald, maybe 30 or 40 minutes, before we did. Perhaps he can enlighten me on some odd things I saw that Sunday," she said.

"Bob would have bagged Tom if he could have figured a way," Art said.

"My first experience with criminal law was 11 years ago while I worked for Kerr and Kerr in Portland, Oregon. Fresh out of school with no experience, I had no idea how many different ways the law works. The wife, of a young man who was on trial for murder, asked Earl Kerr if he would help her husband.

"I read the man's statement. To this day, I'd say he was innocent, but the public defender's office appointed an inexperienced lawyer and he lost the case," she said.

"What happened to her husband?" Art asked.

"The young man received a life sentence. A month later, he hung himself. I was in the courtroom when they pronounced his sentence and I'll see his face as long as I live." Her thoughts drifted back to that day in court. "If I'd have understood the law then, like I do today, I'd have tried to free that man. I'll never understand why Kerr and Kerr didn't help him. I said at the time, if I ever came in contact with another case like that, I'd try to help. After listening to the tapes, I don't think Charles Robbins can kill anyone."

Mike's head swayed back and forth like the pendulum on the grandfather clock in the hall. He reached for the quarter. "I'll do the flipping."

Art laughed. "You better examine that piece of silver. It might have heads on both sides."

Mike flipped. "Heads, it is. Let's go. Do remember this hoodlum is loaded with lice and we better sit at the end of the table," Mike said.

Mike drove to the jail. In the interrogation room, she remembered what Mike had said about the lice, and it amused her when he placed two chairs at one end of the table and one at the other. The officer brought Charles in. She noticed his clothes were clean. He had washed and combed his hair. He can't be more than 22-years-old. She did notice he thought he had all the answers when he said, "How come that CRAB is in here?"

"Charles Robbins, I'm Bonnie Cole. Mike and I are here to help. Do you understand the trouble you're in?" she asked, as she set her recorder on the table.

"I ain't in any trouble. The cops have thrown me in jail before for stealin."

"Young man, stealing is the least of your problems. The sheriff is accusing you of killing three men," Bonnie said.

"Miss Cole, I ain't never killed nobody," Charles said in a self-assured voice.

It's sad for him to be so sure of himself when he knows so little, she thought. "That's beside the point. The police arrest many people who spend time in prison," Bonnie said.

"I ain't never known a person that went to prison."

"Why did you go to Wilms' Mountain?"

"I ain't never seen a Wilms' Mountain," Charles retorted.

"Charles, unless you tell me the truth, I can't help," Bonnie snapped.

"This lady is here to try to get you out of this mess. If you're not smart enough to realize that and give her all the help she needs, you'll rot in prison. The Denver police found Donald Wilms' jewelry in your room. Also, you stole Mr. Wilms' motorcycle. The Denver police have it. Surely, you can see that proves you were in the Wilms' home," Mike said.

"When are these idiots gonna let me out of this rats nest?" Charles asked.

"Charles Robbins, you haven't heard a word I've said." She pointed a finger at him. "You're the idiot, your bail hearing is set for Monday morning. The judge will hold you over for trial," she said.

"Will you be there?" Charles asked.

"You have lied or refused to answer my questions. I have no reason to talk with you again," Bonnie said and put her things away.

"Please come to the hearing and see how I do?" Charles said.

"Charles Robbins, I'm certain the judge will hold you, without bail," she said, put her recorder in her case and walked out.

On their way to the car, she said, "Mike, I just can't let Bob Ingram send that know-it-all to prison."

"I know Bonnie," he said and helped her in the front seat.

Monday, Bonnie, Art and Mike waited in the courtroom for Charles' hearing. They listened to a couple other cases before the bailiff brought Charles in.

Frulik, the district attorney, stood and said, "Your honor, the accused, Charles Robbins, is charged with three counts of first degree murder."

Bonnie came forward.

"Miss Cole, why are you here?" Judge Rowland asked.

"I'll represent the defendant," she said.

In the same voice, he said, "Very well."

The district attorney's eyes rested on her for a moment, then he shook his head.

"Your honor, the defendant pleads not guilty, waives time, complete reading of the charges, and wishes to proceed directly to the matter of bail," Bonnie said.

"Mr. Robbins has no ties in the community. Flight to avoid prosecution would be no problem. He's a drifter with no permanent address. Therefore, we request bail be denied," Frulik said.

"We realize that, your honor. However, we do request a reasonable bail," Bonnie said.

Judge Rowland's eyes narrowed. He tarried for a moment, then he said, "Because the charges are so serious, I agree with the district attorney. Bail is denied." The judge flipped through the book that he had in front of him. Soon, he said, "The preliminary hearing will be Monday, July 13th."

Frulik and Bonnie both agreed on the date. The bailiff escorted Charles from the courtroom.

As they were leaving, Mike said, "I wonder how Charles feels, he was so sure he would get out of this."

"Bonnie, you set the judge back about 40 knots," Art said.

"I've never surprised a judge before when I entered the courtroom." Bonnie got a newspaper from the stand. The first article caught her attention. "There's a rumor that someone saw Donald Wilms roaming the streets. Also, some people say Donald is still alive. Why would anyone tell such a ridiculous tale about your dad when everyone knows someone murdered him."

"The local paper always makes an issue of anything the Wilms' do," Art said.

The three returned to Art's house and Art excused himself. Mike and Bonnie went into the office and settled comfortably in their chairs for another overall discussion.

"Before we start let's have a snack," Mike said and excused himself. Soon, he returned with two beers, a bowl of nuts and a plate with most everything in the kitchen on it. Mike poured a glass of beer and set a plate of goodies, on the desk, in front of her. After serving himself, he sat crosswise in the big chair with his knees draped over one arm and the small of his back propped against the other. The ring of the glasses echoed through the office.

"Thank you. This was a wonderful idea." After a sip of beer and a cheese pop, she asked, "What did the warden say about Ronald?"

"The warden, Cy Jones, said that because of good behavior, they released Ronald six months earlier and he had no idea where Ronald had gone, or what he was doing." Mike popped a couple of nuts in his mouth, wiggled around in his chair and continued. "Maybe that was Ronald that came in the garage but he didn't act like a normal person." Mike turned around in his chair, put his left leg on top of his right knee and swivelled his chair so he was facing her. "Frankly, I was scared to death of the fellow in Art's office. According to Dr. Hegge, Arnold is still at large and at times Arnold is a raving maniac. Dr. Hegge said, he's seen the times it would take three or four of their aids to keep him in hand. When he is having one of those spells, he might kill anything or anyone that gets in his way. When Art said he looked like his mother, and if that was Arnold and Art's remark had of struck the right chord, he might have jumped on that desk and tried to kill all of us. Had that happened, the only thing I could have done was shoot him."

"Oh Mike, for the rest of your life you'd felt like you shot Donald," she said.

"I know. I've thought about that a 100 times and each time I get more terrified." Mike said.

"How did you make out with Zeeta?"

He put his foot on the floor, leaned forward, and laid his arms on the desk. "She's a wild-one. Her folks said by the time she was 12-years-old, they had to keep all money, jewelry, silverware and anything else that was saleable out of her reach."

"What would one do with a child like that?"

"I don't know. Her father shook his head. Honestly Bonnie, he's very sad and lonely. I know he hated to tell me what Zeeta had done." After a moment of silence, Mike said, "The old fellow said that when she couldn't find a thing around the house to sell, she began slipping into our room and she'd go through my pant's pockets. He said, She got away with it a couple of times, before we caught onto what was happening. On her 14th birthday, she ran away. Two years later she slipped in one night and for a while stayed close to home. He told me that two men came to the door and asked about her. They never heard whether she knew that the men were looking for her. She just disappeared. Some four-years later, they learned she was in college, that she had two kids and living in Windcove Idaho."

"Have you told Art any of this?"

"Nope! He has enough to worry about," Mike said.

The next day, Bonnie noticed Art was nervous and his easy-going disposition had exploded into a short tempered hot head.

I'll let that red pepper stew along in his own juice, she thought. The phone rang, and Art showed he had no intentions of answering it.

"You better pick up that receiver," Mike said.

"If you're so interested, you answer it," Art snapped.

Mike never let on like he heard Art. He put his briefcase on the desk, calmly lifted the receiver to his ear, turned on the speaker and said, "Good Morning, Mike Dailey speaking."

A slow husky voice said, "This is Dr. Hegge. Yesterday I promised to let you know if and when we heard anything about Arnold Rigby. It's my understanding, an officer is on his way to the sanitarium with a Rigby. If this is Arnold Rigby, and he's securely back in our institution, you can talk with him all you like."

"Thanks doctor, we appreciate your kindness," Mike said.

"I'll get back with you as soon as my staff gives me the good news," and the doctor hung up.

"Where did they find him?" Art asked.

"Dr. Hegge informed me yesterday the Minneapolis police arrested a queer acting stranger who fits Arnold's description," Mike said.

"Why didn't you tell me?" Art asked, very short and curt.

"Because you have been beside yourself for the last week. Bonnie and I have kept our mouths shut for fear you'd snap our heads off," Mike replied.

"I'm so sorry, I didn't realize," Art said. He put his head on the pillow of his chair. "This last six-weeks has taken its toll."

"I suggest you get Dr. Crugar to prescribe something that will calm your nerves. Furthermore, let me take care of this phone. You've been trying to handle Bob Ingram and another dozen things all by yourself. Bonnie and I are used to this kind of turmoil, and we're not as close to this as you are, my friend. If this is Arnold, I'm sure we're in for some surprises. When we talked to Ronald, I felt he knew a lot more than he let on," Mike said.

"That day at the garage was some test of human nerves," Bonnie said.

"My housekeeper is coming today so we should be careful, what we say. She's nosy and repeats all she hears in her version," Art said.

"I found that out," Bonnie said and grinned.

Mike had changed places with Art and Bonnie sat facing Mike. With an impish smile on her face, she said, "Yes Mr. Dailey, what would you like for me to do for you today?"

The phone rang. "Saved by the bell," Mike said. He switched on the speaker and lifted the receiver. Before he could say a word, Dr. Hegge said in an excited voice. "We have your man. Arnold is back safe and sound, but I'm afraid he's not very happy."

"You're sure it's Arnold?"

"No doubt about it," doctor said.

"Thanks for the call. We'll see you tomorrow," Mike said.

Three hours later, Art, Bonnie, and Mike were getting on a plane.

Art showed her to the seat next to the window then sat beside her.

The flight attendant came by and smiled at Art. "Hello Aggie. Meet my friend Bonnie Cole," he said.

"Good to meet you," Aggie said.

Bonnie smiled at her. "Thank you. I'm glad to meet you."

Mike sank into the seat in front of them next to the window.

When the plane took-off, Bonnie grabbed Art's arm and held on. "It always makes me nervous when we take off," she said.

Art squeezed her hand and asked, "How about when we land?"

"Oh, I'm worse when we start down."

Art laughed. "If you get too nervous just sit on my lap."

She knew he was watching her but she never let on—just peered out the window.

It was late when the cab arrived at the hotel in Augusta, Maine. After Art registered, he said, "Let's go to our rooms and freshen up for dinner."

After dinner, they said a goodnight and agreed to have breakfast about 8:00 a.m.

Bonnie spent a restless night. All she could think about was the sanitarium. She was tired when the alarm went off, but nevertheless she welcomed its sound. She dressed, ready to meet Art and Mike in the dining room for breakfast.

After they finished eating, Art called the car rental agency. He asked to have a car brought to the hotel. They were outside in the morning sunshine when Art asked, "Has either of you ever called on anyone in a sanitarium?"

"Not me," Bonnie said.

"I interviewed a fellow they were holding in the asylum. I knew he didn't belong there," Mike said.

Bonnie noticed a new Cadillac pulled to the curb. The driver laid the keys in Art's hand. Art, Bonnie, and Mike climbed into the front seat. "Well, asylum it is," Art said and stepped on the gas. "The desk clerk said turn left onto the freeway four-blocks south of here."

Bonnie saw a large sign: Sanitarium next right. Art selected the next off ramp. He parked in the visitors section. Bonnie felt weak. *What have I gotten myself into?* As they moved along up the wide walk to the front steps, Bonnie's actions showed she wasn't eager to enter. Twice she stooped and smelled the gorgeous red roses that gracefully showed off their beauty in the warm breeze. Then she followed Art and Mike into the sanitarium.

"Who do you want to see?" the guard asked.

"Dr. Hegge," Art said.

The guard called in. He told the receptionist Art Wilms and his friends to see Dr. Hegge. The receptionist called over the speaker. "Send them in, Dr. Hegge knows they're coming."

As Art, Bonnie, and Mike entered, an aide said, "Mr. Wilms?" Art smiled. "This way please."

They followed her down a long hall, through a wide, steel-covered sliding door. "Dr. Hegge is in conference room three," the nurse said.

They passed two doors. Art knocked. Bonnie heard a voice say "Come in."

Bonnie recognized Dr. Hegge's voice. Inside, she saw a larger man than she expected to see, with gray hair, and his eyes were glassy and protruding. When he smiled, a mouth full of snow white teeth showed.

"Dr. Hegge, I'd like to introduce Bonnie Cole. She's an attorney. We want her to sit in with us today," Art said.

The doctor smiled and said, "Please have a chair." Art pulled a chair for Bonnie. She noticed the doctor stood until she had taken her seat. Then he slowly eased into his oversized black chair. "I said as little as possible on the phone yesterday because of strange ears around here."

"I understand. Thanks for calling," Mike said.

"We're in an odd position with Mr. Rigby. He wants us to believe he's Ronald, but we're positive Arnold is the man they brought in. I think I told you he has some bad scars on his right hip," Dr. Hegge said.

"Yes, I remember," Art said.

"The would-be Ronald is Arnold because he has the same scars, and in a fit of temper he admitted he killed Ronald and took his identification."

"So we're dealing with Arnold. Is he really as crazy and dangerous as they say?" Bonnie asked.

"He's suffering from intermittent explosive disorder. A person with this problem is very unpredictable. He shows no signs of aggressiveness between episodes. Then he may lose control, at which time he could become very angry, even to the point of murder. Of course, drinking so much cheap whiskey in his younger days didn't help any," Dr. Hegge said.

"Since he's been in custody, how is he behaving?" Bonnie asked.

"He's mad and very bitter at the officers that arrested him. Arnold swears when he gets his hands on them, he'll cut them up and feed them to the hogs. When you see him, remember to pretend that you believe him to be Ronald, and don't let him fool you, this man is clever," Dr. Hegge said. An aide came in. "Please show these people to room 24."

Down the hall, they entered a room with a table Bonnie guessed to be four by ten feet fastened to the floor. Bonnie sat between Art and Mike along one side of the table. Soon one male aide sat alongside Mike and another on Art's right.

"Why are you here?" Art asked.

"We never know the strength of a mentally ill person. We don't want anyone to get hurt, and in this case, we're taking no chances," the aide said.

"From what Dr. Hegge said, and the way this aide describes Arnold, he must be a wild man, and we better be on our guard," she whispered to Mike.

The door at the end of the room opened. Bonnie noticed two very large, muscular, male aides had a strong hold of Arnold's arm's and stayed close to him. They brought him to the table directly across from them.

Art whispered to the aide on his right. "Should I keep quiet or greet him?"

"Greet him," he said.

Bonnie watched Art, as he slowly stood and held out his hand. "Good morning Ronald."

Arnold laid both hands flat on the table and stared at them. Soon he yelled, "Who the hell are you?" He rolled his eyes up until the pupils almost disappeared under the eyelids.

"Don't you remember coming into my garage recently?" Art asked.

It frightened Bonnie when Arnold sneered at Art. Then in a

hysterical manner Arnold screamed, "Damn you, Donald! What did you do with Marie? She was my girl." He lunged forward like a Brahma bull and pulled both aides to the end of the table. Again he shouted, "You ruined my life. I want to know where Marie is. I swore if I ever saw you again. I'd kill you." By this time, Arnold's whole body was shaking, and his face was red with anger. Bonnie guessed the aides would weigh 275-pounds each. It was all they could do to keep Arnold from getting to them.

"He's in a bad mood. He'll probably rave on like this for most of his waking hours," the aide said on Art's right. "I suggest you folks get out of here."

Art, Bonnie and Mike made a wild dash for the door that they had come through only minutes before. Bonnie kept holding back. She saw the four aides pilot Arnold out of the room. *That shot one aide gave him didn't slow him down a bit.*

"Come on Bonnie," Art said and grabbed her arm. "Please! Let's get as far away from this place as we can," he shouted and pulled Bonnie into the hall. Outside, she noticed Mike's face was pale, and he kept gripping her arm. The three hurried out the gate and quickly got in the car.

Art laid his arm on the top of the seat so he was facing Bonnie and Mike. "What do you think, are we in danger?" Art asked.

"That depends on how much trouble Arnold causes," Bonnie said. "Art, I'd like to ask you a question."

"Sure, go ahead," Art said.

Bonnie noticed when the aide that sat by Mike saw Arnold come through the door, his eyes showed he was frightened and it was obvious he dreaded what was ahead of them. "Are your nerves going to take this?" Bonnie asked.

"I believe, as crazy as Arnold is, he'll give us some help, if and when we can get him in a talkative mood. Besides Bonnie, to answer your question, I have to bear it."

Bonnie noticed Art was holding onto the steering wheel with both hands. He adjusted his position in the seat, thanked the guard at the gate, and they drove away.

Bonnie wondered why Art and Mike were so quiet. "Just as well relax, my friends. It looks like we'll be in Maine for sometime," she said.

"How about a sandwich before we go to the hotel?" Art asked.

"Art, you wanted to see where they buried your grandmother. Why don't the two of you find out? I'll stay at the hotel in case Dr. Hegge calls," Mike said.

"That's a great idea. Then as soon as we hear what Arnold has to say, we can get out of here," Art said.

After lunch, Bonnie knew, Mike was worried when he asked, "Art, what's wrong?"

Art laid his arms on the table in front of him, eyed Bonnie, then Mike, as if he wasn't sure how he should ask the question that worried him. "I was thinking about the way Arnold acted this morning. What could we have done if he had of gone on a rampage in the garage?"

"I don't think we could have handled him alone. If he had shown any sign he might attack us, all I could have done was shoot him," Mike said.

Art glanced at Bonnie and asked, "Are you sorry you're here?"

"I wouldn't have missed this trip for anything."

"Maybe you'll change your mind before we get home," Art said. He pushed his chair away from the table. "Shall we go to the hotel?"

Mike agreed and said, "Dr. Hegge might have called about Arnold."

At the hotel, the clerk said no one had called.

"Bonnie, let's find out what we can about the Rigby's tomorrow," Art said.

CHAPTER 11

The sun in Bonnie's eyes wakened her. *This is going to be a hot one. I hope we won't have to do a lot of running around.*

She dressed and touched up her face. *I promised to meet Art and Mike in the dining room at 8:00 a.m.* She slipped on her jacket, grabbed her purse, and hurried to the elevator.

Bonnie saw Art and Mike waiting in the dining room. As she got close to their table, she put her hand over her face.

"I'd think you would cover your face. We've waited for over an hour," Mike said and laughed.

"It's only 8:15 a.m.," she said.

After breakfast, Art and Bonnie decided to start looking for someone who could tell them about the Rigbys. They left the hotel, got in the car, and headed for the last known address Art had for his grandfather.

"Service station attendants usually know everything that's going on," Art said and drove through a small business section. He stopped at the first service station she saw.

A little old fellow sauntered over. Bonnie liked his big smile and his most pleasant voice when he asked, "What can I do for you folks on this beautiful morning?"

"Filler up," Art said as he climbed out of the car. "How long have you lived in this area?"

"Been here 60 years," the man said.

Terrific! We've found an old timer, Bonnie thought.

"The clerk at the grocery store said you know most everyone around here. Do you remember a family by the name of Rigby who had three boys?" Art asked.

Bonnie noticed Art's question aroused the old man's curiosity.

"Old Perce was a rough character and very hard to get along with. Always wanted $2.00 worth of merchandise for one. I don't think he got along with anybody in this town. If he did, I never heard of it," he said.

"Where did the Rigbys live?" Art asked.

"Their place burned 20 years ago. That section of town has new homes on it." The old man frowned at Art, then asked, "Why do you want to know?"

"I'm Perce Rigby's grandson," Art said.

Bonnie noticed Art's answer surprised the old fellow. He stared at Art then her. *I wonder if he thinks we're from outer space.* Bonnie sensed a change in his voice when he said, "Old Perce died a long time ago. The county buried him in the Augusta County section of the cemetery."

"Where are the Rigby boys?" Art asked.

"Don't know. I haven't seen the triplets for years."

Bonnie noticed that after Art told him he was Old Perce's grandson, the old fellow lost all interest in their conversation. *It's obvious the old fellow had no use for Perce Rigby.*

Art paid for the gas. He thanked the old fellow. As they drove away, Art said, "The owner of the station didn't think much of my grandfather."

Bonnie grinned. As fast as the grin appeared, it faded. "I believe the stranger in your garage told the truth about his childhood. I think he despised his father," she said.

"You could be right. I wonder if they buried all of the Rigbys here in Augusta. Let's go to the cemetery; maybe they can tell us," Art said.

In about 30 minutes, Art parked in front of the office. Inside, he asked, "Can you help us find where they buried Perce Rigby?"

A large black gentleman smiled. He slid a large book over and began leafing through the pages. Bonnie noticed Art's questions puzzled him. He sat up straight in his chair, gave Art and Bonnie the know-it-all look. Then he said, "The county paid for Mr. Perce Rigby's funeral almost 20 years ago."

"It's my understanding they buried Irene Rigby here," Art said. Again he fumbled through the records. After he turned several pages, back and forth two or three times, he said, "Yes, 10 years ago in the new section. Recently, we placed her oldest son beside her."

It shocked Bonnie when she heard that. "Did they bury Arnold Rigby beside his mother?" she asked and looked at Art.

"That's right."

"I wasn't prepared for that one. Can you show us where their graves are?" Art asked.

"My assistant just drove up in the truck. He'll be glad to help you," the man said. He handed Art a slip of paper with three numbers written on it.

"Thank you, sir," Art said.

When the young fellow saw the slip of paper, he said, "Follow me."

They drove along on a road with fancy tombstones on both sides. Bonnie said, "This is the new section. It must cost plenty for a lot here."

Art stopped behind the truck. They followed the truck driver about 50 feet up the grassy hillside where the driver pointed to a head stone. "I believe these are the graves you were asking about."

Bonnie noticed the wooden marker. "According to this, they buried Arnold here. Your grandmother must have kept track of him over the years."

"I am glad Mrs. Rigby has a lovely stone," Art said.

"All that's on Arnold's grave is a wooden marker with his name, date of birth and the date he passed away. I'll bet Ronald was right when he said Donald must have sent his mother money. From that headstone, he must have taken good care of her," she said.

As Art drove past the office, Bonnie saw the black fellow motion to them. When they stepped up to the counter, the man said, "The funeral home always takes a picture of every corpse before we bury them."

"I've never heard of such a thing," Bonnie said.

"We've done it ever since one old lady accused us of putting the wrong body in her husband's grave. We had to dig him up and prove to her we buried the right person. Would you like to see Mrs. Rigby and Arnold's pictures?"

"Yes, we would," Art said anxiously.

The man removed two pictures from the file gently laying them in front of Art.

"Oh Bonnie, you'll never believe this! If his suit were black instead of brown, I'd swear on a bible that he was Dad," Art said.

"You can have those if you like," the old fellow said.

"I never had the pleasure of meeting my grandmother. Thanks, you'll never know how much this picture means to me," Art said.

Bonnie laid her face against his arm and looked at the pictures. "Your grandmother was very pretty. Donald looked like her. Did he ever tell you what happened to them?"

"He told me they died before I was born," Art said as he put the pictures in his inner coat pocket. Art thanked the gentleman for his help.

Art opened the office door for Bonnie. On the way to the car, Bonnie asked, "Is there anything else that we should do or ask about?"

"Yes, we must find out who's in that grave beside Mrs. Rigby. After all the funny things Arnold has done, we may find out Ronald is in that grave," Art said, and at almost the same moment, Bonnie said, "Wonder if it might be an empty grave."

"Gee. I never thought about that. As clever as old Arnold is, he might pull a stunt like that. Dr. Hegge said Arnold had a bad scar on his hip, and he wondered how Arnold got hurt. Perhaps, I should have told the doctor about old Perce throwing Arnold into the barbed wire fence. Let's talk to the coroner."

Bonnie looked up the address in the phone book that she had brought from the hotel. After a 20 minute drive, Art turned into the parking lot, and they walked inside. After Art explained his predicament, the coroner said, "Let's see what we have."

In a few minutes, the coroner found the file. After he studied it, he said, "The body in that grave has a scar on the right shoulder from a bullet."

"Then that is Ronald Rigby beside his mother. How do we go about changing the name?" Art asked.

"That I can't help you with," the Coroner said.

"How did Ronald die?" Bonnie asked.

The coroner opened the file again and said, "A passerby found his body in a clump of trees along a country road. Person or persons unknown smothered him to death. In his pocket, we found a scribbled note with the name Arnold Rigby on it."

But of course Arnold did it, Bonnie thought.

"His real name is 'Ronald Rigby.' Arnold is his older brother."

"Try the Snow Funeral Parlor; more than likely they can help," the coroner said.

Art thanked him for his kindness, and they drove to the funeral parlor. Again, Art explained his problem.

Mr. Snow studied his records. "In your case, I can easily correct the name. All we had to go on was a small slip of paper with some poorly written letters on it."

"Would it be much trouble to match the stone on Mrs. Rigby's grave?" Art asked.

"No, of course not," he said.

"How long will it take, and how much do I owe you?"

"It should be in place by noon tomorrow. That will be $500, no charge for changing the name."

Art gave him a check and thanked him. "I think this will do it. Let's go to the hotel. Perhaps Mike has heard from Dr. Hegge."

CHAPTER 12

Another five days passed with no word from the sanitarium. Tuesday morning, while they were having breakfast, the waiter brought the telephone to Art's table. He talked for a few minutes. "That was the nurse, Arnold seems normal. As soon as we finish, let's get out there. Five days ago, when we saw Arnold he was a mess. The aide said he was having one of his bad days. I hope today will be a good one," Art said.

"I'll agree to that," Mike said.

When Art, Bonnie and Mike arrived at the sanitarium, an aide escorted them into the same room they were in a week ago. A male aide sat in the chair alongside Art, another aide took the chair beside Mike. Bonnie sat between Art and Mike.

Soon, a couple of male aides brought Arnold in. As far as Bonnie could tell, Arnold acted like any ordinary person. Bonnie noticed the longer Art sat the worse he looked. "Mike, ask the aide beside you if we could have a cup of coffee."

"Certainly." Mike gazed at Bonnie. "Are you all right?"

"I'm fine. But Art's in trouble," Bonnie whispered.

In a few minutes, the aide returned. Soon, a nurse brought Art a small cup of coffee and a little pill. "Take this with your coffee; I'm sure it will help," he said.

Art swallowed the pill then drank the lukewarm coffee. In a couple of minutes, Bonnie noticed he seemed to feel more relaxed, and Arnold's peculiarities didn't seem to bother him so much.

Bonnie saw the aide touched Art's arm and whisper. "Remember, Arnold wants us to think he is Ronald."

Art reached out a hand to the man sitting across the table and said, "Good morning, Ronald."

Apparently, for no reason that Bonnie could think of, Arnold made a visual examination of everybody around the table. Then he sat up straight in his chair, again for no reason, he studied Art. "You hope I'll tell you what happened at your dad's house. Don't you?" Arnold asked.

Bonnie felt Arnold wanted Art to beg for his answer.

"If you can help me, I'd appreciate it," Art said.

"Oh, I can help, but why should I? Donald stole my Marie," Arnold said. He leaned forward and stretched his arms on the table. With a sneer on his face, he glared at Mike and then at Bonnie.

Bonnie wanted to leave, but she knew the only way they would ever find out what happened to Donald was to stay and listen to this sick maniac.

"One of you owns a service station, right?" Arnold asked.

"Yes, I do, a Ford garage. We talked there some time ago," Art said.

Arnold stared at Art, but this time Bonnie noticed his expression had changed. The sneer on his face worried her. She wondered if he would turn into a wild man again.

"I loved Marie, why did that S.O.B. of a brother of mine kill her?" Arnold asked. Before Art could answer, Arnold went on talking about what happened in 1935.

"Let him talk," the aide on Art's right whispered.

"Donald talked Marie into running away with him. I swore the day she disappeared, if I ever saw Donald again, I'd kill him. That was in 1935, I spent two years looking for him. Well, it's 1937, that's two years," Arnold said.

Bonnie saw that the aide next to Arnold motioned for Art to be quiet. She laid her right arm on the table. Arnold hit the table with his right fist so hard she could feel it vibrate. Then Arnold glared at Bonnie and yelled, "Marie, how did you get in here?"

Bonnie knew, from Art's expression, he didn't know how to answer Arnold's question.

"I guess it's okay, as long as you're with him." He stared at Art with a wild, cold look, which made Bonnie wonder if Arnold wouldn't like to kill all of them.

"I found out Ronald was out of that dungeon. I wanted to talk to him, because I was sure he knew where Donald lived, but Ronald wouldn't tell me a thing. I hit him several times, but he still wouldn't talk. All I could do was kill him and go through his papers. I found an envelope with an Idaho postmark on it. Oh yes, I picked out the best clothes Ronald had. I removed the store tags from some of them. I'd never used an electric razor before. So you see, I traveled like a business man."

He straightened up in the chair, put his shoulders back, and glanced at everyone in the room.

I wonder if he expects someone to congratulate him, Bonnie thought.

"Oh, that wasn't all I found," Arnold said. "Ronald had a good suitcase. I filled it with his clothes, a shaving kit, also the best shaving lotion." A silly grin and a devious look lingered on Arnold's face. "I fooled 'em all. I'm using Ronald's name, and I put Arnold's name in Ronald's pocket. Those idiots buried Ronald with Arnold's name on the tombstone."

He laughed so boisterously that Bonnie wondered if whoever lay in that grave could hear him. Arnold pounded the table again as if he wanted to get everybody's attention, and said, "That's how I got the name of Ronald."

The longer Arnold talked and shouted, the more nervous it made Bonnie.

Finally, Art asked, "Did you find Donald's address in Ronald's papers?"

"Oh yes! That's why I headed west, because Donald lived on a mountain in Idaho. It wasn't long before I flagged a car. The driver was an old man, I'd say he was 70 some. He asked if I wanted a ride. When I told him yes, you're taking me to Idaho. That old fool pointed a gun at me and said, 'Oh no, I'm not.' If he had shot me, I wouldn't be here today. Would I?" Again, that loud silly laugh rang through the room.

That laugh would drive a saint crazy, Bonnie thought.

Arnold stopped the silly laugh and continued with his story. "I flagged an old woman in a big car, and before I said a word I climbed in the front seat. I told her I wanted to go to Idaho. She said she was only 10 miles from home. When I told her that I didn't give a damn where her home was, she was taking me to Idaho, she agreed." Arnold frowned. "I wonder if she thought I was crazy." He rubbed his chin. "That's why she didn't argue. If I had thought that, I'd have killed her." He frowned at Art and asked, "Why are you ogling my aide?"

Bonnie could see Art's face redden. She wondered what the attendants thought.

Art softly said, "I wasn't."

"Good," Arnold said with a hateful tone in his voice. He mussed up his hair and wiggled in his chair. "Where was I?"

"The old lady," the aide on Arnold's right said.

"Oh yes. I let her know that if she would ride along, keep her mouth shut, and pay the bills, I wouldn't hurt her. She said she had never been in Idaho. If I wouldn't do her any harm, she had enough cash to pay our way. I drove she paid the bills. At night, we would pull off in a lonely spot for some sleep. Usually, we'd be awake before daylight. I bid her goodbye in Boise." Arnold rubbed his chin. "Is that in Montana or Idaho?"

Art was about to answer, when again, Bonnie saw the aide frown.

"Oh well," Arnold said in an inane way. "I suppose she's home. She was a sweet old lady. I kinda hated to leave her." His eyes glowed, and he searched the room, just as if he expected to see her. "She gave me $50 to help me get to Windcove. The night I got into town, no one knew me because I had on a false beard and wig."

When Arnold was at the garage, he didn't have on a beard or wig,

Bonnie thought.

Arnold continued. "I went into a bar and sat at a tiny table in a far corner. The place was packed. The bartender was so interested in the conversation he forgot to tend to business. The girl on the floor waited for him to fill her orders. I must have waited 20 minutes for a glass of beer. I heard a fellow at the bar tell the bartender he knew an old white-haired man that lived on a mountain. The old fellow had lots of money hidden in boxes in his closet. I decided to wait outside until the bar closed. Soon, the bartender, the fat man, and the little fellow came out."

I'll bet the short man was Charles Robbins, Bonnie thought, as she glanced at Mike. Arnold stood and stretched his legs. *Arnold is tired. I hope he'll keep on with his story.*

"What happened when they got outside?" the aide asked.

"The fat fellow and the little guy went one way. I followed the bartender. He continued south. I slipped along in the dark. Soon, two odd-looking fellows appeared out of nowhere and joined him. The bartender decided they'd go to the mountain in the morning. I heard him say, 'we leave the highway on the other side of the bridge and follow the path up the river.' So I crossed the bridge and slept in the trees that night," Arnold said.

Bonnie heard the big clock strike 12 times. Arnold stuck his nose in the air. In a bizarre way, he moved his head from side to side as he sniffed. Then he slapped the table. As he bounced up and down on the chair, he yelled, "It's time to eat."

"Ronald, shall we serve your lunch in here, so you can keep on talking?" the aide asked.

"Yes, I want to help these people." Arnold glared at the aide and wrinkled his forehead. "I can eat and talk. Don't you think I can do two things at once?"

"I know you can. We have chicken salad or tuna fish sandwiches, which would you like?" the aide asked.

"I hate fish. We will have chicken salad." Arnold's eyes surveyed the room. He wrinkled up his nose and said, "If any of you order fish, I'll know it, cause I can smell the stuff."

We better eat chicken salad, Bonnie thought. She noticed everyone ordered chicken salad and coffee.

"The coffee is lukewarm," the aide said.

The waiters were on their way out when Arnold yelled, "I want soda pop." Arnold paused. "Where did I stop?"

Bonnie noticed Arnold rubbed his hands together, looked at the lights in the ceiling, then he stared at the aide on his left.

He acts like his mind has failed him, she thought.

"Where in the name of hell did I leave off," he asked the aide.

"You had spent the night in the trees," the aide said softly.

"Oh yes! Oh yes! That was a rough night, the ground was cold and the pine needles stuck worse than if I had tried to sleep with a porcupine," Arnold said.

The aide on Arnold's right peered at Arnold in a peculiar way and laughed.

Arnold, don't stop now. You must keep talking. Bonnie saw the big door open. Two men entered. One was pushing a serving cart with sandwiches and drinks.

The waiter served Arnold's sandwich. Arnold lifted the top piece of bread from one half of his sandwich, stuck his finger in the filling, licked it and smiled. "This chicken salad is okay." He picked up the other and inspected it, then laid it on his plate. He stood, leaned on the table, and sized up everybody's lunch. "Mine is just as big as any of yours," he said and stuffed half his sandwich along with a big gulp of soda pop in his mouth. "Hey you." He pointed at Art. "What year is it?"

"Nineteen-eighty-seven," Art said.

Bonnie saw Arnold's lower jaw drop, and some of his sandwich and pop oozed out of the corners of his mouth and down his chin. He wiped his chin on his blue denim shirt sleeve and asked again. "What year is it?"

"It's 1987," Mike said.

"Mister, it can't be. I just read in the morning paper that President Roosevelt thinks Hitler will invade Poland," Arnold said.

"Remember Ronald," the aide on Arnold's right said, "you had just spent the night in the woods."

Arnold ran his fingers through his wavy white hair. Before he said another word, he scratched his head and crunched in another huge mouthful of his sandwich. Then he stood and leaned forward. With his mouth open, he chewed on the last bite of sandwich while his eyes scanned the table.

Bonnie wondered what Arnold found so interesting. She had only eaten a small piece of her sandwich, which tasted delicious. Arnold reached across the table, and with both hands, he grabbed the balance of her sandwich. Before Bonnie had time to recover from that shock, Arnold stooped over, jerked off his slipper, and put it on the table. As Arnold raised his leg, he pulled up his pant leg to the knee then tried twice before he got his foot on the edge of the table. He scratched the bottom of his foot and between his toes. "Damn," he said, "how my foot itches." He put his slipper on, removed his foot from the table, and stood shaking and wiggling.

I hope Arnold gets that pant-leg straightened out soon. I didn't see any scars on his leg, so Snapper didn't bite him, she thought. Bonnie watched him snatch the balance of Art's sandwich and his cup. Before Arnold sat, he drank the rest of Art's coffee, set the cup on the table, and stuffed the balance of Art's sandwich in his mouth. With a big grin on his face, he patted his stomach and said, "Ah, good lunch."

Arnold rolled his eyes toward the ceiling. "Where was I?" He paused. "Oh yes. I saw the three men riding across the bridge on their motorcycles. They turned up the path along the river. I was running as fast as I could to try and keep close enough to hear their conversation. Besides, I didn't dare let the three see me."

Bonnie kept listening to Arnold's story. *This is the biggest line of bull I've ever heard, she thought. On the other hand, he keeps the story moving and not repeating himself. Is this the closest thing to the truth that I've heard yet?* Arnold's voice got her attention.

"The three stopped to rest. One man found an old can in the bushes. He brought some fresh water from the river. I heard another man mention the Pennsylvania prison. Then the other one laughed about how they escaped. The two smaller men called the big fellow Dizzy. One of the smaller men asked Dizzy what he was in for."

Arnold giggled then he said, "Any idiot should know when you're in prison you've committed a crime. Dizzy told them he stole an old man's car and dumped him beside the road with a bullet in his head. Dizzy said if he were ever in Pennsylvania again, he was gonna beat the hell out of the crooked-assed fellow that was on the jury." Arnold laughed even louder than before. He stood and waved his arms again. "I've never heard of one of those fellows. What do you suppose a fellow like that would look like?" Arnold glanced around the room.

Bonnie wondered why Arnold rolled his eyes so much, at times, only the white eye ball showed. *Is he having some kind of a fit?* He paused for what seemed like forever to Bonnie.

Then Arnold began again. "Dizzy said he knew that queer swayed the jury and that's the reason they found him guilty."

Bonnie wanted to tell Arnold to keep on with the story but thought it best to keep quiet.

"The three climbed on their motorcycles and continued up the narrow path along the river. When the path made a turn up the mountain, Dizzy wanted to follow the river until they came to the creek. This way, they could approach the house without being noticed. They traveled much slower from there on, because the path ended and the brush was thick. Each time they stopped, I'd have time to catch up. All they talked about was prison life and how good it felt to be free," Arnold said.

Dizzy admits he was in prison. As far as I can tell, Arnold stays on the same track. One sure thing, Mike can follow through on the prison. If this is true, Arnold could be giving us some facts, Bonnie thought.

"When they got to the creek, they rested for sometime. Again, I was able to overtake them. From here on, the two smaller fellows struggled to get their motorcycles along the stream to where a path came from another direction. They lit a small fire, boiled a pot of coffee, then ate some cold pork and beans with bread. I was so hungry, I never knew coffee could smell so good." Arnold sniffed again, as if he could still smell the coffee.

"I spent the night in the brush and trees." After another gulp of soda pop, Arnold continued. "It was raining. I should have said pouring. I was soaked. In the morning, they made another pot of coffee, ate some bread, poured some water on the fire, and started up the steep path. I found four slices of bread in the wrapper that they left. That was my breakfast.

"The two men were ahead of Dizzy. About half way up the path, the two got in an argument. They were having trouble pushing their bikes up the hill. I could hear them arguing. Dizzy kept telling them to shut up, and each time I could tell he was more upset. Then without saying a word, he pulled a gun out of his coat pocket and shot each of the men in the back of the head."

Arnold glared at Art and shouted, "Bang, bang." Art jumped. Then Arnold laughed even louder. "Does bang, bang scare you?" Arnold roared.

After a minute, the aide next to Arnold said, "Ronald, you said Dizzy shot the two men."

"Oh yes! Oh yes! Dizzy dragged them over the bank and hid them in the brush. He threw their motorcycles over the hill side. I could hear the noise when they landed. Then I saw Dizzy turn the other direction and hide the gun in a dead tree trunk. He hurried to his motorcycle, got another gun out of the bag and put it in his pocket. He's a big man and strong as an elephant. He pushed that cycle up that steep path easier than I could a baby's tricycle," Arnold said.

I'll be, Bonnie thought. *The guards found two men shot in the head and their motorcycles dumped over the bank. Has this nut told us what really happened?*

"When Dizzy saw the big white house, he got so excited he started talking to himself. He kicked open the door. A dog started barking, and Dizzy screamed. I think that's when the dog bit him, because he had blood on his pant leg. Then I heard a shot. I guess that was when Dizzy killed the dog that was on the floor inside the kitchen. Dizzy yelled again, 'Don't move old man, or I'll blow your brains out,'" Arnold said.

By now, Bonnie thought she would faint, but knew she must stay calm, or she would never get through this. *I wonder if Art can control his emotions long enough for us to hear the rest of his story? I must remember this is Arnold but he wants us to call him Ronald*, Bonnie thought.

Arnold continued. "I slipped up to the door so I could watch Dizzy. He grabbed Donald's arm and broke it over the top of the kitchen chair. I heard Donald scream. All this time, Dizzy was yelling at him and asking where he hid the boxes of money. Donald kept telling him that all the money he had in the place was in his bill fold. If Dizzy wanted more Donald would go with him to town and get some but if he killed Donald, he'd never get a cent.

"Dizzy asked, where are the boxes of money. That time he must have knocked Donald to the floor, because I heard Dizzy tell him to get up or he'd kick the living life out of him." Arnold giggled and waved his arms in the air. Then he said, "I felt good. Dizzy was beating the devil out of Donald because Donald took Marie away from me."

Bonnie wondered if she could keep down what little sandwich she had eaten. She took a handkerchief out of her pocket just in case. She heard Arnold when he said, "Dizzy's voice kinda drifted away, and I got closer to the kitchen door. Dizzy had taken Donald into the living room. I slipped inside so I could see better. Dizzy had Donald tied in a rocking chair slapping him around the head. Again Dizzy yelled, 'Where's the money? You better talk, or you'll never speak again.'"

This lunatic is telling us what I saw on the mountain Sunday, the day Donald died, Bonnie thought.

"When Dizzy said that, he hit Donald in the right jaw with his big strong left fist. Dizzy hit Donald so hard that I hoped it broke his jaw. Donald coughed, and some of his teeth fell into his lap. That tickled me more than ever, because Donald was getting just what he deserved. Arnold kept slapping his hands together as he said, "Why I mean Dizzy must have hit Donald a 100 times."

I know that's a lie, because from the looks of Donald's face, Dizzy couldn't have hit him more than once or twice in the jaw.

Arnold doubled up his right fist, hit the palm of his other hand, and shouted, "Hit Donald again, Dizzy. Give it to him. He has it coming."

Bonnie peeked at Art. His face was drawn and his eyes were red.

She wondered if he could endure any more. She reached over and squeezed Art's arm.

Arnold sprang to his feet and lunged across the table. He grabbed Bonnie's arms above the elbow and began shaking her. "Marie, why are you making over him? Do you have to put your hand on every man that comes along?" Arnold bellowed.

Art and Mike jumped up and tried to release Arnold's hands. Art screamed, "Ronald, this is Bonnie, not Marie. She's my girl."

Arnold stopped. Green eyed, he stared at Art. "She's your girl?" Then Arnold shifted his eyes to Bonnie and the most weird look crossed his face.

"Yes, she is. I can understand how you made a mistake," Art said.

Arnold slid off the table and fell on the chair. He fixed his eyes on Bonnie again. In a hateful way, he said, "You're right, she ain't Marie." His face glowed with excitement when he whistled. "The more Dizzy worked Donald over, the better I felt."

Arnold got so excited that his body shook. "Then Dizzy grabbed the flower vase off the table, dumped the flowers and water on the floor and swung it so close to Donald's head. I'm not sure if Dizzy meant to hit Donald on the head or not, but he did. Donald's head fell forward. I hoped Dizzy had killed him." Arnold's clenched his fists and whammed the table.

"What did Dizzy look like?" Mike asked.

It surprised Bonnie when Mike spoke.

"I hurried out of the kitchen, but before I left, I made sure to get a good look at Dizzy," Arnold said in a happy manner. "I hope some day I can do something for him. He's a good-looking fellow, clean shaven, light skin, and small blue eyes. He has a large round face with big ears, and his hair is short. He's lost it in front. I'd say he's about six feet tall and would push the scales up to 250 pounds." Arnold pounded the table with his fists so hard that his hands warped out of shape. They reminded Bonnie of bent strips of metal rolled into a ball. He began to scream at the top of his voice. "I'll kill him."

Bonnie noticed a change in Arnold. At times his eyes were wide open, but he rolled the pupils so far back in his head only the whites showed.

The aide on Art's right slid his chair under the table and yelled, "You folks better get out of here fast."

Bonnie noticed Arnold's face was a fire-wagon red. He leaped to his feet, grabbed the back of his chair, and slammed it on the table so hard it broke the chair in pieces. He was bellowing like a mad Brahma bull.

Bonnie froze too scared to move. She sat there and stared at Arnold.

She heard Art when he yelled, "COME ON BONNIE," but she couldn't move. Mike grabbed her left arm above the elbow and Art the right. They pulled her backwards and finally, her chair tipped over onto the floor. The two men dragged her over her chair and into the hall. All this time, her eyes were on Arnold. She saw him pick up one of the aides and throw him across the floor.

A nurse ran in and gave Arnold a shot in the arm. Art slammed the door behind them and lifted Bonnie onto her feet. With Art holding one arm and Mike the other, she never ran so fast in her life. When she couldn't keep up, they swung her between them.

"Hurry Bonnie, please hurry, let's get out of here," Art yelled.

By the time they got to the car, she began to realize what a terrible sight she had seen, and now she wondered if Arnold had the strength of a Brahma bull. *Without that shot to force Arnold to calm down, I don't think the four aides could have managed him.* She noticed Art's hands trembled so much he couldn't get the car door unlocked.

"Give me the keys," Mike said and held out his hand.

Art handed Mike the keys and said, "I think you better drive."

Mike opened the car door and hurried around the other side. Art pushed Bonnie into the car and leaped in beside her. Art had shoved her so hard, she was still picking herself up from under the steering wheel when Mike tried to get in.

As soon as Mike got in, he turned to Bonnie. "Did we hurt you? I never dreamed you'd just sit there."

"To answer your questions, you didn't hurt me. With all that shouting and the crash when he broke that chair, I just couldn't move," she said.

"Let's get as far away from this place as possible," Art said.

Mike thanked the guard at the gate and drove onto the street. "Let's get a hot cup of coffee. I think it will be good for all of us," Mike said.

"I agree," Art said. He laid his arm around her neck and gently pulled her toward him. "Sorry I handled you so rough. You and Mike will never know how I felt when I saw what looked like my dad turn into a wild, raving maniac. I'll see those crazy eyes as long as I live."

Mike turned into a hamburger stand and stopped at the window. Mike handed Art and Bonnie each a cup of steaming coffee.

"Doesn't this smell good? I never wanted a hot cup of coffee so much in my life as I did at lunch. I did learn one thing in this place," Bonnie said. "When they serve your lunch, you better eat fast or you'll starve."

"Arnold can really poke it in," Art said.

"What did you think was going to happen when he took his shoe off?" Mike asked,

"I had no idea, but at least his feet didn't smell," she said.

Art and Mike seemed to relax, and Bonnie knew she had.

"We better go to the Pennsylvania prison and find out if Dizzy, the bartender, is an escapee," Mike said.

"If we keep on bringing these stories to Windcove, we'll put your little town in the headline's nationwide," Bonnie said.

"If Dizzy was a prisoner there, they'll have pictures and information that could help us," Mike said.

"I must go to the cemetery and see if Ronald's name is on his stone. Would you folks like to ride along?" Art asked.

"By all means, I'd like to," Bonnie said.

"I'm with her," Mike said.

They got out at the cemetery. Bonnie felt the cool breeze. As she walked up the slope to Mrs. Rigby's and Ronald's graves, she pulled the light jacket close around her waist then folded her arms across her chest. "Ronald's stone is a perfect match. It's very sad when one brother takes another brother's life," she said.

"The Snow Funeral Home did a good job," Art said and heaved a big sigh. "Let's go to the hotel and call it a day, such as it is."

"Any place or anybody you want to talk with or ask about while we're still in Augusta?" Mike asked.

"No! I think this will do it. How about changing for dinner, and let's have a drink in my room before we go to the dining room?" Art asked.

"Thanks Art. After what I've gone through today, I'd like to try and relax before dinner," Bonnie said.

Mike drove back to the hotel. They rode the elevator to their floor, and Art escorted Bonnie to her room first. "See you later," Bonnie said as she unlocked the door.

Bonnie slipped into a pink dinner dress. When she got to Art's door, she saw the waiter leaving. They talked for nearly an hour before deciding to have dinner.

The following morning, the three boarded a plane for Harrisburg. After they landed, Art rented a Ford and drove to Camphill. When they met Warden Cy Jones, Bonnie thought he seemed friendly. After Mike explained why they were there, Cy said, "I'll help anyway that I can."

Mike showed Cy two pictures. "The sheriff's deputies found these men shot in the head and dragged off a path on Wilms Mountain. They were traveling with a large, heavy set fellow called Dizzy," Mike said.

"I think you're talking about Dizzy Welch. He and the Ryan

brothers escaped about six months ago," Cy said.

"I'm working from a madman's description. Dizzy is heavy set, blond hair, receding in front, blue eyes, and a round face. Does that sound familiar?" Mike asked.

Cy rubbed his hand over his black hair and asked, "A mentally ill man gave you that description?"

"Oh, he's crazy, but on good days he talks like a normal person," Mike said.

"Your description makes me believe it's Dizzy, and the two men were the Ryan brothers. They were here on robbery and rape charges. Dizzy was serving a life sentence for murder."

Maybe we can solve Donald's case, Bonnie thought.

"He brutally killed Art's father. We're hoping to get a picture of Dizzy. It will help us in our search," Mike said.

"I'm sorry to hear that," Cy said, and he handed Mike a piece of paper. "The local newspaper printed this picture along with the story of the escape. It should help. Looks like your madman gave a good description of Dizzy."

"Yes it does, but I can't put him on the stand," Bonnie said.

Art and Mike got into man's talk with Cy. Bonnie excused herself and left the room.

Soon Art, Cy and Mike joined her in the hall. Art held his business card out to Cy and said, "Please let me know if you learn of Dizzy's whereabouts, and I'll do the same."

"Be glad to," Cy said.

"Thank you," Art said, as he shook hands with Cy, and they got in the car.

The three drove to the airport. While they were on the plane to Boise, Bonnie relaxed. She heard Art talking on the phone. "We're on flight 620 meet us in Boise."

I'll soon be in Windcove, and here's hoping I never go to Maine again in search of the Rigby's. I'm so tired. I'll sleep tonight, she thought.

CHAPTER 13

They arrived in Windcove around 2:00 p.m. Bonnie did little for the rest of the day, and awoke early after a restful night. She could hear Art making calls on the phone in the office.

She walked in with a friendly "Good morning." Art motioned for her to sit in the chair on the other side of the desk. He finished his call with a pensive look on his face and turned to face her. "We have to talk." He shoved the papers aside and dropped his glasses on the desk. "How much of my family's past will you have to make public?"

"I've no idea at this time. Should I find out there's anything I have to expose, I'll tell you ahead of time."

Art pushed the Boise paper over to Bonnie. "Read this. It scares me to think what the Windcove paper has in it."

Bonnie held up the morning paper. The first thing she saw was a large picture of Arnold Rigby on the front page. Below the picture in headline size letters: "THIS MAN IS DANGEROUS. He escaped recently from the Augusta sanitarium in Maine." The lead story continued warning residents to be cautious and to call authorities if they saw the fugitive or had any information. Bonnie paused for a second and said, "I guess it won't matter what I say now."

Art slowly opened the middle desk drawer and locked the papers he had been reading in it.

From the open door, Mike's voice was suddenly excited. "Have you had the television on?"

"Not this morning. Why?" she asked dreading, to hear Mike's answer.

"Donald's picture is on the screen. They're comparing Donald with Arnold Rigby. They've already repeated everything that's in the morning paper."

Art turned the television on in time to hear the announcer. "This appears to be the man who was reportedly seen several weeks ago in Windcove." The announcer continued carefully to report that numerous calls had been received by the station asking if Donald Wilms was still alive and if perhaps another body had been placed in the local cemetery. With concern for the legalities of suggesting something that had not been proven, but fully aware of the news value of this breaking story, the announcer fairly sparkled with controlled excitement.

For the first time since they left the sanitarium, Bonnie had a good chance to watch Art. His shoulders were bent, and he walked with the defeated attitude of a nursing home patient who had totally given up on life.

Art tossed the picture of Dizzy Welch to Mike and said, "I think we better talk to the sheriff about this fellow."

"After listening to Arnold Rigby, I think it's time we hear Bob's side of this story," Bonnie said as she got to her feet. "He's going to ask a lot of questions and want some answers."

"Well, he can keep on wondering," replied Art. "I have no intentions of satisfying his curiosity this morning."

Fifteen minutes later, Art pushed the door open into the sheriff's office, and it somewhat surprised Bonnie to see Bob in his favorite position—half asleep and feet on the corner of his desk. *Seems like a strange time to be dozing. There can't be that many "breaking stories" in this town. All I've heard is how hard he works.*

Art chuckled and asked, "Is this what our sheriff does all day?"

Bob half opened his eyes, removed his feet from the corner of the desk, and said, "Hello, I worked until 3:00 a.m. Some punk held up the Chicken Inn."

"Anyone hurt?" Mike asked.

Again Bob yawned, rubbed his face and said, "The punk was holding the employees at gunpoint, and our man had to shoot him. He's in the hospital."

Bonnie noticed the morning paper spread out on Bob's desk with Donald and Arnold's pictures side by side. *Art will have to tell Bob the whole story.*

"Can you explain this?" Bob asked.

"It's a long story. I'm not here to talk about my dad," Art said. He pulled the picture of Dizzy Welch out of his pocket and put it on the sheriff's desk.

"Is this character supposed to mean something to me?" Bob asked.

"That's the fellow who beat Donald to death. He used to work at the Cross Roads Bar."

"Charles Robbins killed Donald. His fingerprints were on the murder weapon," Bob said.

The sheriff is certain that he has the killer. Art will never convince Bob otherwise, Bonnie thought. *It's almost as if he doesn't even want to consider anyone or anything else.*

Art gave Bob a copy of the newspaper article on how Dizzy escaped from the prison in Pennsylvania. "Read this, then see how you feel." Art picked up the picture of Dizzy that he had put on Bob's desk. "I'm taking this to the local paper," Art said. "I know the so-called media reports a lot of really bad news. Our paper is professional and will run this article, and they can be a lot of help to your office."

"What's your hurry? I have a lot more questions," Bob said.

"Maybe later, but right now I don't want to talk to anybody," Art said and turned to leave.

Bonnie and Mike followed Art out. In the car, Art said, "I'll bet Bob will be over to see us. He'll probably be waiting at the house."

She waited in the truck as Art and Mike took the articles into a city editor. *Art resents Bob Ingram, but I can't figure out why? What is his background?*

When they returned, Mike was talking. "I don't think the editor believed you when you told him that this is a picture of the man who we believe killed Donald."

"It's scary," Art said. "You'd think we were telling them Donald beat himself to death. But remember, lots of false leads come in every time there's a story like this, and they have to be very cautious."

They all chuckled as they turned into Art's driveway. "He's here, just like you knew he would be," Mike said.

"I knew it. He's so inquisitive, but let's face it. He does have a job to do."

"Hello Bob, haven't we seen you some place else today?" Bonnie asked.

Bob gave Bonnie a dirty look, then a sarcastic reply. "You're getting as secretive as Art. He's such a tight mouth. I can't get any information out of him."

They left the car and Bonnie followed the three men into the house where they all found chairs in the office. Art turned his back on the group and looked out the window.

"Damn it Bob, you blab everything all over town. I used to tell you a lot of things. One day I heard my customers repeating what I had told you. Then I knew it was time to keep my mouth shut," Art said.

OK. So that's one reason Art has it in for Bob.

Bob got out of his chair and paced around the office. Bonnie saw the strange way Bob looked at Art with an obvious question on his mind.

"You'll never convince me that identical triplets were born to different parents. Sorry, buddy, but it just isn't done that way! So what's the scoop?" Bob asked.

Bonnie watched Art as he slowly sat in the chair at his desk. He sighed deeply and began slowly. "Perce and Irene Rigby had triplets. The three were so much alike they wore wrist bands with their names on them." Art gestured for Bob to sit again. "My grandparents named them Arnold, Ronald and Donald. Donald graduated from college and relocated in Florida. While he was there, he changed his name to

Wilms and married my mother, Marie Wells, in 1937 in Phoenix, Arizona. That's the story," Art said.

"Donald disowned his family?" Bob asked.

Art slapped the desk in an angry and disrespectful voice. "That's what I hate about you. I didn't say that he disowned his family. Those are your words. That's the trouble, Bob, you always change the story."

From the sound of Art's voice, Bonnie knew he was upset.

"What about the picture of Dizzy Welch that you showed me?" Bob asked.

"He's the man who killed my dad, and I think Robbins can help us prove it. Before we're through, I think we'll find out that Dizzy killed the Ryan brothers, too."

"The way you talk makes me believe Arnold Rigby is one of your relatives." With that, Bob charged out and slammed the door.

Art had a big grin on his face when he said, "Bob believes I'm as crazy as Arnold."

"Bob will insist on hearing the whole story," Mike said.

"I know, but let him keep his water warm a little longer!"

"We should listen to Arnold's story again," Mike injected. "I'll admit he's as nutty as a sack of walnuts and as clever as a wild fox."

"What part of your brain figured that out?" Art asked.

"Oh, the section that's as good as new, because I've never used it." It was good to have a bit of revelry; the tension was beginning to take its toll on all of them.

Art was smiling. Bonnie watched him as she made notes on the columnar pad open on the desk.

"I just had a thought," Mike mused. "Call Bob back. Let him hear this too. You know, I think Dizzy just might be dumb enough to break into Donald's place hunting for the money that he thinks is hidden in that house on the mountain."

Art ran out and motioned Bob to come back. With a frown on his face, he backed up and parked again in the driveway.

Inside, Art said, "Have a chair Bob. Mike has an idea that you better hear too."

Mike repeated what he had been thinking and the expression on Bob's face softened. It presented an entirely different person, and Bonnie watched him lock his fingers behind his head. He answered thoughtfully. "If Dizzy is the murderer, running from the law, desperately in need of money, he might be fool enough to break into Donald's house." Art spoke again, with difficulty. Obviously, he had come to a decision. "Take your coat off, Bob, and make yourself comfortable, because I've quite a story to tell."

Art threw the pen that he was holding on the desk so hard it bounced off on the floor. He whirled around in his chair. Slowly he walked to the north window and crammed his hands in his pant pockets. Beads of perspiration covered his forehead. He jerked a handkerchief out of his pocket and wiped his face and hands.

As he nervously sank into the chair facing his three visitors, he continued as if they were not even there. "When my dad graduated from college, he wanted to see his mother. He didn't expect to fall in love with Arnold's girlfriend."

"Arnold is the triplet in the asylum?" Bob asked.

"Yes," Art said, as he looked at his dad's picture on the corner of his desk. "It isn't easy to admit that your brother and my uncle is nuts!"

He shifted his attention to Bob and wearily continued. "Arnold swore he would kill Dad. So Dad and Marie ran away. Dad settled in Florida and Marie in New Orleans. The triplet we saw walking the streets of Windcove called on me at the garage. He said his name was Ronald, but that was Arnold. He escaped from the sanitarium and stole Ronald's identification."

"You talked to him?"

"Yes! Arnold told us many things. Most of the time he was as normal as anyone. The police picked him up in Minneapolis and returned him to the nuthouse."

As Art told Bob where we had gone and who we had talked with, Bob stared at Bonnie. "I can't believe you were stupid enough to follow these fellows into a nuthouse for information," Bob said. "Did you see Arnold?"

"Yes. Mike, Bonnie and I waited around for a week before Arnold decided to talk. It took that long for him to get into the mood, but when he did, he talked for most of a day. He told us how Dizzy shot the Ryan brothers, and he also told us how Dizzy abused Dad. It's really sad, you know, but Arnold was still so angry at Donald that every time Dizzy would hit or hurt Donald, Arnold would really take off with joy. He kept saying it served Donald right for taking Marie away."

Bonnie held out a piece of paper to Bob and said, "I think you should see this. It's a sketch of the fellow an artist drew from the description Arnold gave us." She showed Bob the front page of the Harrisburg Times. "You'll be interested in this. Now compare that drawing with this picture of Dizzy."

"I'll admit they do look alike," Bob said, "but you can't convict on that."

"We can't question the fact that Arnold saw Dizzy, because this proves he remembered him. So why should we doubt Arnold's story?" Bonnie asked.

"It does make you think, but remember this is a madman. He's crazy! And to believe such a person is ridiculous," Bob said. He paused for a moment. "Besides, the only fingerprints on the vase were Charles and Tom Finch's. Tom has an alibi."

"The only thing Arnold seemed confused about was the date. He's living in 1937, only 50 years behind the times," Mike said.

"Did you ask Arnold how and when he left the mountain?" Bob asked.

"No, he pretty much lost it and couldn't concentrate on anything."

"Mike and I feel like Dizzy will go back to the house hoping he can find the money he thinks is in Dad's house. As you know, I had an alarm system installed that will ring in your office, in the garage and here if anyone breaks in," Art said.

"We have the helicopter ready if we need it. We're planning on policing the paths, whichever way anyone goes in, if he does, we're ready," Mike said.

"Does your helicopter have a spot light?" Bob asked.

"Of course."

"I'll keep a man stationed at the railroad tracks across the river. We can always get someone at the bridge if that's the way he goes," Bob said.

"If you get any static at having an officer on the tracks, put him on my payroll," Art said.

"I'll remember that. I've got to get to work." Bob stood and, hesitating as if it hurt to say it, he left with a quiet, "Thanks for the information."

After Bob had gone, Mike said, "Well, Bonnie, plan on my being on your side as long as you feel like representing Charles. I'll do anything I can."

"Thanks Mike, no doubt I'll need your help, since the district attorney is charging Charles with three counts of murder. I must go over everything with Charles again," Bonnie said. She put some papers in her briefcase and picked up her coat. "Is that Thunderbird still at my disposal?"

"Anytime, just keep the keys. Goodness knows I have plenty of rigs," Art said.

"Thanks, maybe I can do you a kindness sometime," Bonnie said.

"You already have. I'm trying to catchup," Art called out, as Bonnie and Mike waved goodbye.

After they talked to Charles at the jail for an hour, they returned to

Art's place. Bonnie and Mike sat across from each other and Art stood lounging against the cookstove. He lowered his head and peered over his glasses. "This must have been an interesting interview. Is Charles as independent as he was before?"

"That man simply hasn't accepted the seriousness of his situation. At least, he hadn't until Mike told him in no uncertain terms that he might go to prison for the rest of his life. That got his attention. It didn't hurt, either, when Mike told him it was possible he could get the death penalty."

"Someone better buy him some descent clothes, and he needs a hair cut. Put it on my account at Barney's Men Shop," Art said.

"Why are you buying him clothes?" Bonnie asked.

"So I'm an easy touch. Sue me," Art said. "Besides, Charles can't go to court without some decent clothes. The rags he's wearing are disgraceful."

"Charles has an idea that people don't go up for crimes they haven't committed," Mike said.

"When the judge holds him over for trial, he'll get an education in a hurry," Art said.

"The preliminary hearing is Monday, July 13th," Bonnie said.

CHAPTER 14

Monday found Bonnie ready to go to court looking very much big city in sensible low-heeled pumps and her trusted blue suit.

"Mike and I guessed at the size of a suit for Charles," Art said.

"I held it against him," Bonnie hesitated, "it looked okay."

"You folks go on ahead. I'll be at the courthouse in a little while," Art said.

Bonnie reached her seat next to Charles, just seconds before the bailiff called out, "All rise." Judge Rowland took the bench, and the bailiff intoned, "You may be seated."

"Is the prosecution ready to proceed?" the judge asked.

"We are, your honor," Frulik said.

"Is the defense ready?"

"Yes, we are, your honor," Bonnie said.

Frulik called Dr. Phillips, the county coroner who explained how Donald died. Then Frulik called Sheriff Ingram. He testified that Donald's blood was on Charles' shirt, Charles' fingerprints were on the murder weapon, and that Charles stole Donald's jewelry and motorcycle.

Billy Pile rattled on about the Friday night at the Cross Roads Bar. He told how interested Charles was when he heard the men talking about the old man on the mountain. The story was that Donald Wilms lived alone, with his money hidden in the house.

He also testified about other rumors he had heard at the Cross Roads Bar the Friday night before, Donald was killed.

Bonnie tried to persuade the judge that Frulik had based the charges against Charles on circumstantial evidence only. She noticed Judge Rowland sat quietly for a few moments, but then announced that he felt there was sufficient evidence to bind the defendant over for trial. He picked up a small calender. "Will September 9th be satisfactory?"

"Fine with me, your honor," Frulik said, and Bonnie added that it was satisfactory with her as well.

"Court is adjourned," Judge Rowland said, and he hurried from the courtroom.

Bonnie noticed the officer was moving toward her table. "Let's go young fellow," he called out.

Charles looked at Bonnie. "Why is he taking me back to jail?"

"The judge held you over for trial on three counts of murder." It almost seemed like, until that moment, Charles had not fully understood what was happening or what might happen in the future.

During the week following the preliminary hearing, Bonnie, Mike and Art stayed close to the security system, and even took turns monitoring it closely. Nothing happened at the house on the mountain, and Art didn't hear anything from Bob about Dizzy.

On the morning of July 26th, they sat in the office, and Bonnie could see that the waiting and the total lack of information or action was taking its toll on Art.

"Mike, I guess that hunch you had about Dizzy returning to the mountain was wrong," Art said.

"If he doesn't, he'll be the first fellow that I've ever heard of who needed money and didn't go where he thought he could get it," Mike said.

"Staying near these alarms night and day is getting monotonous," Art said.

For lack of anything else to do, Art suggested the garage. Bonnie and Mike went with him, and for the next several hours, they filled in time with routine auto duties. But all of them were feeling the pressure. Bonnie, especially, found herself restless and worried.

Art would sit for a few minutes then walk the floor. This made Bonnie feel worse. She kept thinking about what the guard told her about Dizzy. After two hours of this, Art decided to go home.

On their way, Bonnie asked, "Mike, if that alarm goes off, are you and Art going to the mountain?"

"On the double," Art said.

"You better hear a tape I made at the Harrisburg Prison while the two of you and Cy were chatting." At the house, she excused herself and hurried to her room. When she returned with two tapes and her recorder, she noticed Art and Mike were so quiet her soft soled sandals sounded on the carpet.

Mike spoke first. "Very seldom do I see you in this mood. What's wrong?"

She took a small drink of coffee. As she opened her recorder and placed it on the desk, she said, "When Cy, you and Art got started on man's talk, I wandered into the hall. A guard introduced himself, invited me into his office, closed the door, and played some tapes for me.

"Then he said, 'I understand you're a defense attorney. Are you going to be cross-examining Dizzy Welch?' I told him probably. He gave me six pictures and said, 'I think you should see these. I snapped them of Dizzy in his cell one night. So help me God that man acts like a wolf.'"

"What in the hell are you saying?" Mike asked, "And why haven't you shared this with us before now?"

She opened her purse, handed Mike a few more pictures and her magnifying glass. She leaned back in the chair with her coffee cup in her hand and watched their expressions as Mike and Art studied the snapshots. She noticed that the more they looked at them, the more curious and interested they seemed.

"Did he tell you how and where he took these?" Art asked.

"Yes, late one night he heard what he thought was a wild animal howling. He ran into the hall. There was a dim light on in Dizzy's cell. Dizzy was on all fours with his nose in the air giving the wolf's mating call, and over a couple of weeks he got these pictures. I asked if that were general knowledge around the prison.

"He said it was not, but said he had told Cy, who told him to keep his mouth shut for the time being. I guess that's why I haven't shared this until now. I've just been waiting, but I'm not sure for what.

"The guard went on to say 10 years ago he heard some queer stories, which fascinated him. He said he took a month off and traveled over a 1000 miles through the north country. He drove for miles where the only signs of life were wild birds and wild animals that darted across the narrow dirt road.

"He just kept on talking and staring at the wall. In an odd sort of way, I think he was so glad to be able to tell someone, that when he started talking he almost forgot I was there.

"He told me that he would never forget an old shack that he came across. He described straight up and down footboards, no paint and dirty, dirty windows, one on each side of an old broken down door.

"He said he couldn't see in, so he knocked on the door. Said it was so shaky and broken and the hinges were so loose that he thought it might fall off. But it didn't, and he heard a weak voice telling him to come in. He told me he opened the door, came face to face with a small gray-haired man sitting in an old homemade rocker."

Mike and Art were fascinated with this new information that they had not before been made a part of.

Bonnie went on with her story as she repeated what the prison guard had told her. "There were a few dusty cans of stuff on the shelves and the place had dust on everything.

"But he said the old man was conscious and lucid and said he had been there for almost two months because he had no way of getting out. His horse, he called him his nag, had fallen and the old man had to shoot him. He had apparently survived on what canned beans there were in the cabin."

Bonnie sipped her coffee and continued relating her story. "The guard said the old man said to take anything he wanted. Said he had rationed his food, but it finally had run out. What little he had in the way of clothes he had packed in a ragged old suit case, and the guard said he put it and the old man in his car, and gave the man some cold coffee and a sandwich he had in the back seat.

"I guess the guard finally realized I was there and he was a little embarrassed at having talked so long. But he laughed and asked if I would believe the old man drank that coffee as if it was the best he had ever tasted.

"The guard told the old man about the rumor." Bonnie continued. "The old man recalled that he had lived in this area for over 65 years. One day, a well-dressed young couple came in the store. They were riding a matched pair of Arabian ponies and leading two overloaded mules. The stranger said he always wanted to be a trapper, and at last he was going to do it.

"According to the guard, the old man said that he then saw them about three months later, bought their hides, and they stocked up for the winter. He said that went on for more than 20 years, but that after about three years they came in one day with a baby boy. He was about six months old, and they called him Dizzy.

"The boy, according to the guard, who continued to tell what had been told to him, was unusual. His right hand had a bandage on it, and his eyes were different. But then, he said, it was as if the couple disappeared. I never saw any of them for about 15 years. One day, the woman and her son came in the store. The old man said he asked about her husband, and she said he went out to check his traps, and neither him nor the pony returned.

"The old man said the woman wanted to sell a small box of jewelry, and he paid her $35 for it. He never saw them again, but a few years later Dizzy came in and wanted a job. There was nothing I could give him," the man's story continued, "and that's the last I ever heard of any of them."

Bonnie ended her story by saying that the guard told her he had put the old man on a bus to his daughter's.

"Did he ever say what Dizzy was like and how he got along with the men in the prison?" Mike asked.

"No. He did say I should watch him, as you can't tell from one minute to the next what he'll do. Also, when he's angry or not sure of himself, he pulls his upper lip back over his teeth. You may get a surprise. Now that you two have heard this story, are you still going to the mountain alone?" she asked.

"If that alarm sounds, we must get the killer," Mike said.

Bonnie didn't like Mike's answer, but tried not to show it. She put all her records in her case, bid Art and Mike good night and left the office. In her room, she changed and laid her head on the cool pillow and in no time was sound asleep.

The loud clanging of the bell woke her with a start, and she heard Art yell from upstairs. "I ordered a medium bell, not one that would scare the devil himself off the mountain."

Bonnie dressed and rushed to the kitchen. She saw Art and Mike wearing their guns. That wasn't so bad, but when she realized Mike had on his bulletproof vest, she knew they were preparing for the worst.

"Are you getting ready for war?" she asked.

"It always pays to go well, prepared," Mike said.

"I'll be here by the phone if you need anything," she said and followed them out.

"Good," Mike answered.

"Be careful," she called to them as they backed out of the driveway.

Three hours later, Art and Mike returned. "Did you get him?" Bonnie asked.

"Yep, Dizzy was stupid enough to break into Donald's house," Mike said.

Art smiled and asked, "Will I have time to make a short phone call and wash up?"

"Yes, I can't cook that fast," Bonnie said. She stood by the range turning the ham in the skillet. As Art went by, he gave the tie on her pink and white ruffled apron a jerk.

Mike laughed. "When Bob and I walked in on Dizzy, he fired at us. You should have heard him complain when Bob fired back nicking him in the arm."

After breakfast, she remembered Mike's description of how Dizzy complained when they arrested him. *I'll bet he howled like a dog,* she thought.

Mike and Art walked outside. The big Doberman followed Bonnie into the office. Bonnie sat at the desk, and Millie dropped on the floor next to her chair.

I've a start on Charles' case. September 9th will be here before I know it, she thought.

"Well, Millie, would you like to hear what I think about Dizzy?" She peeked at Millie. The dog raised her head and wagged her tail. "I thought so," she said.

Bonnie spread all of Dizzy's pictures and newspaper articles on her desk. *He's a cold, heartless looking man. I imagine he will be difficult to question on the witness stand.*

She remembered Arnold Rigby telling how Dizzy abused Donald Wilms, also Cy Jones and the guards' description of him. *I may have to use a different approach,* she thought, as she took a second look at Dizzy's picture.

Bonnie heard the kitchen door open, and since Mike was away, she assumed Art had come in from his self-appointed job as chairman in charge of trimming roses.

A high-pitched screeching voice yelled at her. "You're the witch that's trying to come between Art and me."

Bonnie swivelled her chair and stared at a woman that she had never seen. "You must be Zeeta?"

"Yes I am, old girl. If you think you can come into this town pretending to be a big city lawyer and win Art away from me, you're nuts!" she screamed and stomped her right foot.

I've no place to run! There's no way out of here! Bonnie watched the strange woman inch herself closer and closer. Trying to appear calm and composed, she said, "Wait a minute, let's talk about this."

Zeeta's upper lip snarled. With a nasal twang, she angrily roared, "Old girl, you're getting out of here TODAY."

Bonnie kept talking as she noticed Art slipping up behind Zeeta. "I'm going to court in a few days. As soon as this trial is over, I'm going home."

"I've decided you're leaving RIGHT NOW," Zeeta yelled and pulled a gun out of her jacket pocket.

At almost the same moment, Art grabbed her right arm forcing her hand upward. While he choked her with his left arm, he pulled her backwards into the kitchen. During their scuffle, Bonnie heard the gun fire. The bullet hit the oil-painting of Donald, sending it crashing to the floor.

Bonnie grabbed the phone and thanked heaven for programmed dialing as she pushed the button for the sheriff's office. A second shot sounded from the kitchen.

As soon as Bob's phone clicked, Bonnie said, "Hurry, Zeeta's here with a gun." She laid the receiver on the desk and hurried to the kitchen. As Bonnie entered, she saw Art holding the gun in his right hand. His left shoulder was bleeding, and he was still scuffling with Zeeta.

Bonnie took the gun from Art and opened a kitchen drawer. She laid the gun in the drawer and grabbed a large ball of heavy twine, which she put into her pocket. Art shoved Zeeta into the corner and held her so tightly against the wall that she couldn't move.

While trying her best to kick him, Zeeta kept calling Art every name imaginable. Some were so filthy Bonnie wondered where they came from.

Bonnie took the large ball of twine from her pocket, took a paring knife from the dishwasher, and cut off a long piece. She got on her hands and knees and crawled between Art's legs, twisting the twine around Zeeta's ankles as she dodged the frantic kicking. Holding onto the twine, Bonnie backed from between Art's legs and gave the cord a hard jerk. Zeeta landed on her butt still kicking and screaming. Art immediately pulled Zeeta's arms around her back and Bonnie tied her wrists together.

Bonnie called Dr. Crugar. "Art's been shot. We need you right away."

"I'll be right there," was his immediate response.

Zeeta continued to swear at Art and Bonnie.

"I think she needs a cooling off." Bonnie said. She got the pitcher of ice water and slowly poured it over Zeeta's head. "Maybe that will close that big mouth." It amused Bonnie at the expression that crossed Dr. Crugar's face when he saw Zeeta on the floor with her legs and hands tied. Her hair was so wet that water was steadily dripping onto her dress. The doctor packed Art's shoulder, but from time to time he glanced at Zeeta and smiled. "Art, you've bled so much I suggest a short stay in the hospital," Dr. Crugar said.

At that moment, Bob Ingram and two deputies rushed in. When Bob saw Zeeta on the floor in a puddle of water, he glanced at Bonnie and started laughing.

"Zeeta got so mad Bonnie thought she needed cooling off," Art said.

Bonnie explained what happened.

"Art, when you got shot, did Zeeta have the gun?" Bob asked.

"Yes, neither of us could get her to listen. She came here to kill Bonnie," Art said.

"Mrs. Cockran, do you have a permit to pack this gun?" Bob asked.

"I don't need a permit. I'm here to scare that would be lawyer out of town," Zeeta snapped.

"Is the gun registered?" Bob asked.

"Of course not. I didn't pay for it," Zeeta roared.

Bob advised Zeeta of her rights. "Take her in," he said and motioned to the other officers.

Art twisted around on his chair. "You better keep her tied. She kicks like a mule and watch that mouth of hers. You could put a teacup in it and still eat a sandwich," he said.

Zeeta spit at Art. "Before I get through with you, you'll wish I'd never been born," she screeched as the officers escorted her away.

"I insist you go to the hospital," Dr. Crugar said.

Mike walked in and asked, "What happened?"

"Oh, Zeeta showed, we had a scuffle, and I got shot," Art said.

Mike held onto Art's right arm. "Come on, let's go," Mike said and glanced at Bonnie. "I'll be back as soon as I know our patient is okay."

"I'll be by later," Bonnie said and closed the door.

CHAPTER 15

Two hours later, Mike returned from the hospital. "The bullet damaged an artery. He bled so much that Dr. Crugar gave him a transfusion," Mike said.

"I'll stop by later." Bonnie thought for a second. "Bob and Frulik are going to meet with Dizzy today. I'd like to hear what he has to say." She slowly put her hands on the arms of the chair and pushed upward. She picked up her briefcase and the car keys and held out her hand to Mike. "Let's go."

Mike picked up his briefcase that was by Art's desk and examined the handle. Bonnie had seen Mike replace the batteries in his recorder many times before.

Ten minutes later when they arrived at the jail, Bonnie said, "I feel like the bottom is dropping out of everything—like we're in for a big surprise, but I don't know what it is."

"Do you mean Dizzy or the district attorney?" Mike asked.

"Probably both."

Mike opened the door to the room next to the interrogation room. As Bonnie entered, she could see Bob and Lyle Frulik.

Mike pushed a button by the window casing, and immediately Bonnie could hear everything from within the room. Frulik's voice was clear and concise as he said, "Dizzy swears he can tell us who killed Donald Wilms."

Bonnie stared at Mike. "Could it be that we're all wrong?"

Mike spoke slow and in doubt. "I don't know. I've noticed that every time we think this case is under lock and key, someone throws a monkey wrench in the works."

The door to the adjacent room opened and Dizzy Welch entered with the chain on his ankles scraping on the floor.

"He's a meaner looking brute than his pictures make him out to be. I can see why Donald Wilms never had a chance," Bonnie said.

Dizzy sat on the other side of the table from Bob and Frulik. In this position, Bonnie could see Dizzy's face.

"You wanted to talk, so let's hear what you have to say," Bob said.

"I know who killed that old man on the mountain, but before I tell you a thing, I want to make a deal," Dizzy said.

"Mike, I told you I felt something was coming!" Bonnie's voice trembled slightly.

"You have every right to a lawyer, you know," Frulik said, "and perhaps you should think about that."

"I don't need one of those smart-guys for this. Here's the deal I want. If you don't charge me with breaking into the house the other evening, I'll tell you who killed the old man."

Bonnie glanced at Mike. "You thought somebody threw a monkey wrench in the works. I just saw a box car roll in," she said and turned her attention back to Dizzy.

Frulik walked slowly and cautiously around the table. "How do you know who killed Mr. Wilms?" he asked.

"I was watching."

Both Bonnie and Mike sat back in shock. This was not what they had expected to hear.

"Dizzy, you fired a shot at the sheriff," Frulik said and swiftly returned to his seat.

"Yeah, but I didn't hit him." Dizzy's attitude was smart and know-it-all. His whole bearing suggested that he felt he was in control of the conversation.

Frulik made no secret of the fact that he didn't like Dizzy, but Bonnie's feeling, nevertheless, was that they were headed toward a deal.

"I realize you didn't shoot anyone, but we know you tried. If you're willing to testify in court about who killed Donald Wilms, and we can prove it, I'll grant you immunity," Frulik said.

"Put it in writing," Dizzy said, and crossed his arms on top of his fat belly. "After you assure me immunity, I'll tell you who killed Donald Wilms, because like I said, I saw him do it."

"Dizzy is a lot smarter than he appears. Most people would never think of getting it in writing," Bonnie said.

"Before I make a move, I want to know who killed Donald Wilms," Frulik said, "and I repeat, we've got a deal only if we can prove it court."

"You have the moron in jail right now. It was Charles Robbins," Dizzy said maliciously gloating.

Bonnie listened for over an hour to Dizzy tell Frulik and Bob how Charles killed Donald as well as the Ryan brothers.

"He's repeating the same thing Arnold said. Of the two, I'd believe Arnold Rigby first and I think Dizzy is lying," she said.

"What will you do if you find out that Arnold lied to us, and Dizzy is telling the truth?" Mike asked.

"I'll feel like the idiot of the 20th century."

Mike laughed and said, "You're not the only one, everybody else will think so."

Bonnie and Mike hurried from the jail. Outside on the steps, Mike said, "You can't put Arnold Rigby on the stand. Billy Pile hasn't said a thing that will help Robbins. Who can you find that will testify in Charles' favor?"

"I don't know." Bonnie got in the thunderbird, on the passenger side, and Mike climbed in under the wheel. He stopped at a drive-in and ordered two colas. He pulled in under a large tree in the park, shut off the motor and swivelled in the seat. "You've taken some of the damndest cases, but Robbins beats them all." He lifted the top off one drink and gave it to Bonnie.

Mike is right. I do have myself in a corner, Bonnie thought. She changed her position so she was facing Mike. She tasted her cola and eyed Mike. "I don't have an answer to your question, or a witness who I can put on the stand. I wish I knew somebody who could testify to Charles' character. All I know about Charles is that he gambles, uses dope, is a thief, has a head full of lice and never takes a bath," she said.

Bonnie saw half a grin on Mike's face. In a slow Mike Dailey drawl, he said, "That's go-o-o-o-d. With a character reference like that, you'll win hands down!"

"Oh, go ahead, laugh at me. I'll still try to get Charles out of this."

Mike drove to Art's place. As Bonnie tried to open the kitchen door, she found that the knob wouldn't turn. "I forgot Art's in the hospital." She waited for Mike to unlock the door. After Bonnie had taken a few steps inside, she said, "Please come to the office. I want us to listen to all the tapes again. We must have missed something!"

Bonnie walked ahead of Mike. He slipped into the big chair and put his right ankle on his left knee. He rested his head on the soft pillow and shut his eyes.

Bonnie watched with affection for this man with whom she had worked so closely. *I've seen him sit like this so often and search for a clue.* She put in the tape of the first interview Mike had with Charles. Next, she chose the tape of Arnold Rigby's report of how Dizzy killed Donald.

After the tape ended, Mike asked, "What's your point?"

"I got the idea from Arnold's description of what happened that Sunday that he didn't see anyone but Donald and Dizzy. Bear in mind that Arnold had followed Dizzy and the Ryan brothers since Saturday morning. No place does Arnold mention he saw or heard anybody or anything like a wild animal except Donald's big Collie that Dizzy shot. Here's what Billy Pile told us," Bonnie said, as she got another tape. When Billy finished, she shut off the recorder. "I didn't hear anything new or anything we had missed. Did you?"

"Not really! But then I haven't heard or seen anything, up too now, that Billy Pile has said to be of any significance." Mike paused. With his brown eyes staring at her, he asked, "Who will reimburse you for all this expense?"

"Ah. Money raises its ugly head. Who's not getting paid?" Art asked as he pulled a chair alongside Mike's.

"How did you get out of the hospital?" Mike asked.

"Dr. Crugar wanted me to stay the night. I had to promise to take it easy and keep my arm in this sling," Art said. "What were the two of you talking about when I came in?"

"I asked Bonnie who will pay her for all her expenses," Mike said.

"I've taken other cases, pro bono," Bonnie said.

"Bonnie, if you can prove who killed my dad, I'll see that you're well-paid," Art said.

She felt sorry Art heard Mike's question, but she never let on. "Today is September 8th. We go to court tomorrow. Will you be there?" Bonnie asked and glanced at Art.

"Everyday."

CHAPTER 16

The following day, as Bonnie got ready for court, she put on a black tailored suit and tiny pearl earrings. Art watched her carefully, and she wondered what he was thinking.

"Is that your fighting outfit?" Art asked.

Bonnie laughed. "Not really, but the first impression is very important. It's good common sense to let the court know you're there and ready to present your case." She opened her briefcase, added two pads and a couple of pencils as well as her notes. She glanced around and noticed Mike. "I see you, too, have on your Sunday go-to-court wear."

"I saw the way you were packing your case. Why are you so nervous?" he asked.

"I didn't know it showed, but I guess you know me too well." She slowly closed her case, rested her hips against the desk, and faced Mike. "I have so little to go on, a weak client, and a hard-nosed district attorney who I understand is a very poor loser."

"I know. You've done it before, and you'll do it again," he said and picked up her briefcase.

As Bonnie and Mike started for the door, Bonnie glanced at Art. "Are you going with us?" she asked.

"I'll join you later," he said and followed them outside into the sunshine. Mike put their briefcases in the thunderbird and stood with the car door open for Bonnie.

Mike parked in front of the courthouse, and for the first time, she really observed the building. "I never noticed how old and weather-beaten this courthouse is," she said.

Mike grinned at her. "That's because the first day you were here, it was a cloudy day, and we came in the back way."

She started up the front steps. This was the first time she saw how chipped and cracked the old gray pillars were. The four wide steps looked as if someone had used a sledgehammer on them. As she reached the top step, it seemed like reporters came from all directions and began calling out questions fast and furiously. She had no intention of answering any.

"She has nothing to say," Mike said as he pushed and shoved their way through.

Inside the courtroom, it surprised Bonnie to see so few spectators and so many eager reporters. *In this small town, I never expected reporters to flock in like this.*

Art chose a seat in the third row from the front and Mike sat directly behind Bonnie.

Lyle Frulik and his assistant sat on Bonnie's right. Sheriff Ingram was next to the aisle near Frulik.

The deputy sheriff escorted Charles to a chair beside Bonnie. She could see a change in Charles' appearance. *At least I'm defending a fact-simile of a man,* she thought, and smiled at Charles. She leaned toward him and whispered, "You're handsome."

"All rise. The Honorable Judge Rowland presiding," the bailiff said.

Judge Rowland entered and looked over the court. "Good morning. The case of the state versus Charles Robbins. The jury has been selected and sworn in. Is the prosecution ready?"

"Yes, your honor," Frulik said.

"Is the defense ready?"

"We are, your honor."

"Very well. The prosecution may proceed with your opening statement."

Bonnie wondered what Frulik would be like in court. She didn't have a license to practice law in the state of Idaho. Her assistant recently passed the bar and knew nothing about him.

Slowly, Frulik walked over, stood in front of the jury, and said, "Your honor, ladies and gentlemen. Before this trial is through, I will prove the defendant, Mr. Charles Robbins, committed the most brutal crime. He murdered Mr. Donald Wilms, an old man who was almost helpless." Bonnie's trained ears picked up the train of his comments.

He makes it sound like Donald Wilms was an invalid. From what I've heard, he was a very active man for his age.

Frulik continued. "I can't think of one thing that would be worth a human being abusing another in the manner that we are prepared to prove that Mr. Robbins tortured Donald Wilms, who was one of the most kind and respected citizens in our community. The state will prove that Charles Robbins murdered Mr. Donald Wilms for a few pieces of silver, some jewelry and his motorcycle. We'll prove also that he shot his two partners, Harry and Paul Ryan, brutally, in the back of the head. And we'll prove that all this brutality was simply because he didn't want to share all the money he planned to steal from Mr. Wilms. You will have no alternative but to find Mr. Robbins guilty on three counts of first degree murder. I thank you."

"Miss Cole, do you intend to make an opening statement?" Judge Rowland asked.

"I do, your honor." Bonnie rose and moved to the middle of the courtroom floor. She nodded at Frulik, faced Judge Rowland, smiled, and said, "Your honor." Slowly, she turned to the jury. In a friendly but businesslike manner, she smiled. "Members of the jury. We're here today to prove Mr. Charles Robbins, a young man born to a widowed mother, did not kill Mr. Donald Wilms, nor did he kill Harry and Paul Ryan. Mr. Robbins did steal Mr. Wilms' rings, wristwatch, some change and his motorcycle. But murder three men, never!"

Bonnie shook her head at the jury in a decisive way. It was a trick her years of experience had taught her—shaking her head in this manner conveyed the feeling to the jury that she truly knew her case and was confident in the truth of what she was saying. It was important to get the jury on her side early in this case. "I thank you." Bonnie turned to the judge, nodded, smiled, and walked slowly back to her seat.

"All of the witnesses have been sworn in. Mr. Frulik, you may call your first witness," Judge Rowland said.

Bonnie watched her client as best she could from where she sat. *He's a weak, pitiful specimen of a man who will lie and steal, but I don't believe he's capable of killing.*

Frulik rose and spoke in a commanding voice, "I call Mr. Art Wilms."

Bonnie didn't think the district attorney had to put Art Wilms on the stand. *We all know every witness will go over the case.* Art came forward. *His face was pale, and he seemed so tired.*

"I'm sorry to have to ask you these question," Frulik spoke softly. "You went to Mr. Donald Wilms' house on the mountain Sunday afternoon, May 3rd."

"Yes, that Sunday was my dad's birthday. I intended to spend the afternoon and evening with him," Art said.

"What did you find?"

Art laid his arm on the railing and in a sad low voice, he said, "I found my dad murdered."

"I understand you received a call from your father?"

"Yes, at 12:30 p.m."

"What did he tell you?"

Art rubbed his forehead. "In a really scared voice, Dad said, 'Hurry Son, please hurry, I'm hurting.' And then the receiver slammed so hard it hurt my ears."

"What did you do then?" Frulik asked.

"We left immediately for Dad's house on the mountain. When we arrived, you know what we found, and I was in such a state of shock that it was Miss Cole who called the sheriff." Art's voice faltered as he tried hard to compose himself.

"Thank you, no more questions." The judge looked toward Bonnie with a questioning expression and she shook her head. "No questions."

"You may step down. Mr. Frulik, call your next witness," Judge Rowland said.

"The county coroner, Dr. John Phillips."

Bonnie noticed Dr. Phillips seemed much older than he had appeared the day he was at Donald's house. She remembered his white hair, but she never realized how bent his shoulders were and how short and awkward his steps appeared.

"What time did you arrive at Mr. Wilms' house?" Frulik asked.

"It was 2:00 p.m. Sunday, May 3rd. One of the first things I saw was a large collie on the floor just inside the kitchen door. She had been shot in the head."

"What were your findings?"

"The forensic team found blood and human flesh on the dog's teeth. I could hardly look at that corpse. We know Mr. Donald Wilms was alive at 12:30 p.m. He died between 12:30 and 1:00 p.m., Sunday, May 3rd," Dr. Phillips said.

Bonnie had always assumed that coroners saw so many dead bodies, one was the same as another. When Dr. Phillips mentioned Donald and the condition in which he found Donald's house, Dr. Phillips also found his voice faltering and he fought hard for composure.

"Doctor, please explain to the court in what condition you found Mr. Wilms," Frulik said.

"He had received a severe beating to his head and shoulders. He had a compound fracture of the right arm." Dr. Phillips' head moved back and forth rapidly as if he had palsy. The doctor raised his head and stared at the judge. "Your honor, the killer cut off the little finger and part of Mr. Wilms' left hand apparently to get the valuable ring he had worn for over 40 years. Also, the killer knocked out many of his teeth," Dr. Phillips said.

"What was the cause of death?"

"Mr. Wilms had a bruise on the right side of his head which rendered him temporarily unconscious. The blow that killed him crushed his skull on the left-side." Dr. Phillips paused and continued. "The longer I think about Donald Wilms' condition, the more convinced I am that his attacker was a lunatic," he said and laid his arms over the railing.

Bonnie objected quickly. "I request your honor order the jury to disregard the witness last comment."

"Sustained." Then the judge said to the jury. "You'll disregard the witness' last remark."

Frulik picked up a glass vase off his table. In front of the witness stand, he asked, "Is this the murder weapon?"

"Yes, I found Mr. Wilms' blood and hair on it. The design on it matches the indentation on the left side of Donald Wilms' skull," Dr. Phillips said.

"Your honor, I'd like this vase entered as prosecution's exhibit number one," Frulik said.

"No objection," Bonnie said.

"So ordered," Judge Rowland said.

"Had Mr. Wilms been drinking?" Frulik asked.

Bonnie dreaded to hear the doctor's report, and sighed with relief when she heard Dr. Phillips say, "No."

"You also did an autopsy on Harry and Paul Ryan, is that correct?"

"That's correct. The Ryan brothers had been shot in the back of the head. This happened sometime between 9:00 and 11:00 a.m., Sunday, May 3rd."

Frulik looked at Bonnie. "Your witness."

"Does the defense wish to cross-examine?" Judge Rowland asked.

"Yes, your honor," Bonnie said and turned to Dr. Phillips. "Doctor, in as much as Mr. Tom Finch heard two shots at 9:30 a.m., Sunday, May 3rd, could the Ryan Brothers have died about that time?" she asked.

"Objection," Frulik called out.

"I wanted to save the court some time. However, Mr. Finch will gladly testify to that fact," Bonnie said.

"Overruled," Judge Rowland said.

"If Mr. Finch heard two shots, it's entirely possible the two men died at that hour," Dr. Phillips said.

"The blood you found on the dog's teeth, what was the type?" Bonnie asked.

"It was type 'A'," Dr. Phillips said.

"Thank you," Bonnie replied. "It has already been established that Mr. Robbins' blood is type O. I have nothing further."

"That will be all," the judge said.

"It's now 11:30 a.m. Court will recess until 2:00 p.m.," Judge Rowland said.

Bonnie noticed Charles' head bent forward. "I gotta talk to you," he whispered.

"May I have a few minutes with my client?" she asked.

The officer nodded and stepped away. Bonnie motioned for Mike to wait. Instead, he rushed over. "What do you want to tell us?" she asked and wondered why Charles seemed so worried. His eyes moved around the empty room, then at her.

"Guess I ain't told you yet, but after watchin' the fellow on the old motorcycle go over the railroad bridge, I rode up the path and went in the house. That old man was still alive, because he made a funny noise and tried to tell me somethin," Charles said.

"What did you think Donald tried to say?"

"I coulden figure that out. Besides, I had to get somethin to peddle or find some dough and get out of there," Charles said.

Bonnie saw Mike's eyes flash and his jaws tighten. It was all he could do to keep his hands off Charles. "Are you telling us you didn't even try to help him?"

From the way Charles was acting, Bonnie felt like he couldn't decide what to say or do, but she made it clear that she wanted absolutely nothing at this point except the truth. "Charles Robbins, you better tell us what happened."

"I didn't have no time. Suppose someone got in there. They'da blamed me for beatin the old guy up," Charles said.

"Charles Robbins, you knew Donald needed help at once. How could you have been so heartless?"

Again, he paused and looked off in the other direction. "Like I toll ya, I had to get outta there. I couldn't know what he was tryin to say." Charles said.

He's lying, but why? At that moment, she could have knocked him across the room. "You haven't told me the truth about how your fingerprints got on the vase."

Charles rolled his eyes at the bench then he peered at Bonnie. "Yea, I huffed it around the chair. On the way, I kicked the vase. I grabbed the darn thing and set it on the table. I swear that's what happened."

Bonnie stared at Charles, then at Mike. *Had Charles told another lie? Pictures of the crime scene show the vase on the floor.*

"Why didn't you tell me this weeks ago?" she asked.

"I didn't think it mattered none. He was still a mumbling and a groanin when I got outta there."

"Hell! You need to go up for about 20 years. Maybe you could learn something," Mike said in a loud voice.

Bonnie watched the deputy take the man away and wondered why she felt she must help Charles. *He doesn't deserve it, but for some reason, I've got to help.*

Bonnie, Art and Mike cut their lunch short so they could be in court at 2:00 p.m. She stepped up to her table as the bailiff called out. "All rise."

It was 2:00 p.m. when Judge Rowland resumed.

"Mr. Frulik, call your next witness."

"Sheriff Ingram," he said.

Bob glanced her way as he went by, and she wondered how much of Donald's life Bob would describe and how many snide remarks he would attempt to drop into the testimony.

Frulik leaned on the witness stand by Bob for a second, and his eyes wandered over the court room. Bonnie wished he'd get on with it. She was most anxious to hear what the district attorney would ask, and how far he intended to explore Art's family history.

Frulik straightened up as fast as he had leaned on the witness stand. He whirled around and faced Bob. With a snap in his voice, Frulik said, "Sheriff Ingram, did you go to Mr. Wilms' home on the mountain May 3rd?"

"I did."

Again in a cold hateful voice, Frulik asked, "What did you see or hear while you were there?"

"What I assumed was Mr. Wilms' breakfast was still in the skillet on the floor. In the large front room, I saw the worst sight I've ever seen in my life," Bob said.

"Objection, your honor. The witness is stating an opinion. Move to strike his last comment," Bonnie said.

"Sustained. Strike the last statement from the record," Judge Rowland said.

"In what condition did you find the deceased?" Frulik asked.

"Mr. Donald Wilms was in a rocker, his hands tied behind it, and his feet fastened to the front. Mr. Wilms' head had fallen forward with the left side of his scull caved in," Bob said.

"Did you find any sign of forced entry?"

"Yes, someone had kicked in the kitchen door."

"Do you know of anyone who hated Mr. Donald Wilms enough to kill him?"

"No one despised him that I know of, and I've lived and worked around here for 45 years. Mr. Donald Wilms had befriended almost everybody in this area at one time or another," Bob said.

"Then the defendant is not from this area?" Frulik asked.

"No, he was just passing through."

"Have you located Mr. Robbins' permanent address?"

"No, he seems to move around so much that home is wherever he happens to be at the moment."

"What condition did you find Mr. Donald Wilms' house?"

"The bedroom showed someone was looking for something, I

suppose money, because I found clothes, papers, even his dresser drawers were emptied on the floor," Bob said.

Frulik picked up a stack of pictures off his table. He showed them to Bonnie and the judge. Then Frulik said, "I'd like to enter these photos as prosecution exhibits two through 11."

Bonnie didn't object so Judge Rowland ordered the exhibits into evidence.

After the bailiff marked the pictures, Frulik passed them to Bob. "Do these accurately represent what you saw in Mr. Donald Wilms' home the morning of May 3rd?" Frulik asked.

The sheriff studied the pictures carefully and then looked at the jury. "I believe you can get as good an idea of the conditions that house was in as pictures can produce," Bob said.

Frulik quietly walked across the courtroom. He handed copies of the pictures to the judge and the foreman of the jury. Frulik waited while the jury studied them.

As soon as the foreman gave the pictures to Frulik, he laid them on the evidence table and walked to his chair. He picked up a shirt, held it up so the judge could see it, then said, "I'd like to introduce this as prosecution exhibit number 12."

"No objections," Bonnie said.

"Bailiff, mark the exhibit," Judge Rowland said.

Frulik presented the dirty shirt to Bob. In a disgusted tone, he asked, "Where did you find this?"

"It was in Mr. Robbins' room in Denver," Bob said.

"What's on the sleeve?"

"Tests prove it's Donald Wilms' blood."

"Mr. Robbins got in town a day or two before the murder. The only time that blood could have gotten on Mr. Robbins' shirt was Sunday, May 3rd, when he killed Mr. Wilms," Frulik said.

Bonnie jumped to her feet. "Your honor, our district attorney states what he assumes are facts. How does he know what Charles Robbins could have seen at Donald Wilms' home? It's possible Charles Robbins could have seen Mr. Wilms on Saturday. I object to this," Bonnie said.

"Mr. Frulik, I agree with Miss Cole. You're assuming a lot and proving nothing. Rephrase in the form of questions," the judge said.

Frulik picked up a sheet of paper. "Sheriff Ingram, whose fingerprints were on the glass vase?"

Bob slid forward in the witness chair, laid his hands on the railing, and in a clear decisive voice, he said, "We found Mr. Tom Finch's and the accused, Mr. Charles Robbin's, prints on the vase."

"Your witness," Frulik said.

Six feet from the witness stand, Bonnie said, "Mr. Robbins has already admitted he took Mr. Wilms' watch." She stepped to the exhibit table, got Donald's watch and slipped it on her wrist and returned to face the jury. She held her arm up so the jury could all see the band. "Since someone had tied Wilms' wrists together, Charles Robbins had to cut the cords around Mr. Wilms' wrists before he could take off this watch." She turned to Bob Ingram. "Could the blood have gotten on his sleeve when he removed the watch?"

Bob hesitated, looked at Bonnie, and said, "Yes, I suppose it could have."

"Did you find Mr. Finch's prints any place else in Mr. Wilms' house other than on the murder weapon?"

"Yes, several places."

Bonnie moved across the court room floor. She laid Donald Wilms' watch back on the exhibit table. Then she faced Bob Ingram. "You only found the defendant's prints on the vase and no place else?"

"That's correct."

"Don't you find that strange?"

"Maybe Mr. Robbins wore gloves."

"You mean he put on gloves to search the house?" Bonnie said.

"He must have," Bob said.

Bonnie gracefully walked across the floor and faced the jury for a second time. With a puzzled expression on her face, she said, "If I understand your report of the events." Bonnie paused, thought for a second, then said, "Mr. Robbins came in the kitchen with his gloves on. Then he removed his gloves, picked up the vase and hit Mr. Wilms. Now sir, according to your testimony, he put his gloves on again and searched the house?"

She glimpsed at each member of the jury. She put her hands in the air and shook her head.

Bob hesitated and said, "Well…"

Bonnie pivoted and stared at Bob. She interrupted. "How else do you account for the fact that Mr. Robbins' prints were on the vase and no where else in the house?"

"Objection," Frulik said. "Miss Cole is trying to get the witness to speculate."

I could withdraw the question, but I'll be darned if I'm going to. She turned and faced the judge. "Your honor, I feel my last question was a legitimate one, and the sheriff should answer it," Bonnie said. With those big brown eyes of hers, she stared the judge in the face.

The judge looked at Bob Ingram, then the district attorney, and finally at Charles Robbins. The judge's voice was sympathetic, more like a father might reprimand an older brother for teasing a younger one, when he said, "Mr. Frulik and Sheriff Ingram, between the two of you, you have pounded away at Mr. Robbins. Each time Miss Cole has proven you wrong. I agree with her. Mr. Ingram should answer the question. Do you feel the court is being partial to the defense?"

"No, but she does pick everything I say to pieces and in a know-it-all manner," Frulik whispered.

"Ye gads, she's a defense attorney, and a good one, I might say. That's the reason she's here," the judge said.

"I didn't think about what I said, and I'll admit it was rude," Frulik said.

"Very well and no more remarks," Judge Rowland said.

"I agree," Frulik said in a softer voice.

"Sheriff Ingram, answer the question," the judge said.

After Bonnie repeated her question, Ingram said, "We only found Charles Robbins' fingerprints on the top of the vase."

"Then you would say there was no way anyone could have held that vase like Charles Robbins did and hit Donald Wilms hard enough to kill him?" Bonnie asked.

"I don't think it would be possible."

"Thank you. I have no more questions for this witness," Bonnie said.

Bonnie looked at Frulik. His face was red from anger. Out of the reach of the judges' ears, he muttered, "For the second time today, a petticoat won."

Bonnie felt Frulik didn't intend to utter those words out loud, but she resented it. "Will the district attorney please repeat his last remark loud enough so the judge can hear him?" Bonnie said and looked at the judge.

"Please do! I'd like to be aware of everything said in my courtroom," the judge said.

"It was a silly thought that I never intended to leave my lips," he said.

"Since you put your thoughts into words, I suggest counsel come to the bench."

At that moment, Bonnie wished she had kept her big mouth shut, because, from Frulik's expression, she was confident he would be hard to get along with from now on. Her steps were short and soft as she approached.

In a low voice, the judge said, "Repeat your remark."

After Frulik answered, Judge Rowland said, "I think your remark was uncalled for. It's now 3:30 p.m. Court will adjourn until tomorrow at 10:30 a.m." Then the judge left the room.

She stood at the end of her table and pretended to pick up her papers, but all the time she kept her head turned so she could watch Frulik. He threw his notepad and pen in his case and slammed the cover, then departed on the run.

Bonnie turned to Charles. "How did you get blood on your shirt?" she asked.

"When I reached over to cut the strings on Donald Wilms' arms, my shirt touched against the wet sleeve on his broken arm," Charles said.

Bonnie nodded and picked up her case. She and Mike left the courthouse, got into the thunderbird and waved to Art as they drove away. She noticed Mike had a grin on his face and seemed mused about something. "Where do you get the plain old guts to take on these fellows?" he asked.

Bonnie laughed. "I'm a daughter of Fred Cole. If you'd meet him, you'd have your answer."

"I'm going to meet that man, if it's the last thing I ever do," he said and smiled at her.

CHAPTER 17

The next morning as Bonnie entered the courtroom, she wrinkled up her nose and whispered to Mike. "This room smells terrible."

As the bailiff walked by, Mike asked, "Will any of these windows open?"

"Yes, we do need some fresh air," the bailiff said. While Mike and the bailiff opened the windows, Bonnie moved to her table.

Frulik came to her table with his hand outstretched. She stood and met him with a smile. "I tried to get a continuance for a couple of days, as I was in bed last weekend with an attack of kidney stones and needed a couple of days to recuperate."

"I'm sorry. I haven't made things any easier for you."

"You're good and I admire your spunk. Oh, I'll fight you all the way, but I guess that's what we are here for," Frulik said and returned to his table.

At 10:30 a.m. the bailiff called out, "All rise."

Judge Rowland took the bench. "Good morning counsel. Mr. Frulik, call your next witness."

Frulik wearily got up and said, "I call Billy Pile."

As Billy passed Bonnie, his face was pale and drawn. He was obviously scared out of his wits. She remembered the last time she had seen him and remembered his fast gait and his cock sure appearance. When his 300 pounds settled in the witness chair, she heard the chair squeak and his head and shoulders were way above the railing. Surprisingly, he seemed either unaware or simply ignored the judge and jury.

"Mr. Pile, you were in the Cross Roads Bar Friday night on May 1st?" Frulik asked.

"Yes, when I got to the Cross Roads, the place was full. The bouncer had to bring in a small table and two chairs for us. We sat not six feet away from the bar."

"I see! Do you recognize anyone in court today who was at the bar?" Frulik asked.

Billy looked at the defendant and said, "Charles Robbins." He glanced around the room. "My friend that was with me that night is here; that's all I remember."

As often as he frequents that bar, it seems to me that he should be able to recognize others in this crowd, Bonnie thought.

"What else happened that night?" Frulik asked.

"The heavy set fellow who sat on the stool beside Mr. Robbins talked so loud that everybody in the room could hear him. He told how some old man on some mountain had lots of money and kept it packed in shoe boxes in his closet."

"Do you mean the heavy set fellow was referring to Mr. Donald Wilms as the old man on the mountain?" Frulik asked.

"He must have because Donald Wilms is the only man living on a mountain around here that I know of, and I've lived here all my life."

"Did Mr. Robbins ask any questions?"

"Yes, he asked how far it was to Mr. Wilms' house," Billy said.

Bonnie peeked at Charles. He leaned over and whispered, "I never done that." She wondered whether Billy had lied or just made a mistake.

"Your witness," Frulik said.

Bonnie moved forward so she stood in front of the jury. "Mr. Pile, was anyone else interested in the story about the old man?"

"The bartender listened to the conversation. He was so interested that the cocktail waitress had to wait for him to fill her orders. We waited 20 minutes to get our drinks. When we did, he gave me all mixer instead of half whiskey," Billy said.

Bonnie's next question brought hesitation from Billy, and Bonnie noted the pause with interest. "Did you notice anything else that evening?"

"Well," Billy said.

Bonnie was certain he dragged the word out long enough to have answered four questions. "Please answer."

"About this time, the fellow at the end of the bar called it an evening, and Tom Finch sat on his stool," Billy said.

"Was Mr. Welch still interested in the story about Mr. Donald Wilms?" Bonnie asked.

"Who?" Billy asked.

"Mr. Dizzy Welch, the bartender."

"I never knew his last name. Yes, he urged the fat man to keep on talking. Finally, Mr. Welch asked him how to go up the mountain to the old man's place. The fat man told Mr. Welch that you have to follow the crooked path up the Snake River."

"Mr. Pile, you said Mr. Robbins asked how to get to Wilms' place. Apparently you must have been mistaken before."

"Oh, yeah. I was mixed up. The bartender asked the fat man that question, not Mr. Robbins," Billy said.

Bonnie glanced at Frulik. He shook his head. "You've done it again," he said.

"Then you noticed that Mr. Welch also had a fascination for the story about the old man. Could there have been others?" Bonnie asked.

"Objection. Miss Cole is trying to get the witness to speculate," Frulik said.

"Sustained," Judge Rowland said.

"Nothing further," Bonnie said.

"You may step down. Mr. Frulik, call your next witness," the judge said.

"I call Dizzy Welch."

"Bailiff, bring Mr. Welch into the courtroom," Judge Rowland said.

In a few minutes, the door to the hall swung open. As Dizzy appeared in the doorway, Bonnie thought, *this fellow is good. I bet he's been in court many times.*

Dizzy sat in the witness chair and smirked at the jury. She quickly eyed each member. From the expression on their faces, she figured many members didn't like Dizzy and others appeared to be actually afraid of him.

"Mr. Welch, did you go to Wilms Mountain on May 3rd?" Frulik asked.

"Yes I did. I was curious about the conversation I heard at the Cross Roads Bar on Friday night."

"How did you go up the mountain?"

"Early Saturday morning I got on my motorcycle and rode up the path along the Snake River. I saw a steep path up the mountain, but I followed the river to the creek, then up along the creek for several miles, where I spent the night."

"What did you do Sunday morning?"

"It rained Saturday night. I was wet and cold. I built a small fire and made a cup of coffee. As I climbed up the path, I heard voices ahead of me. I hid behind a big bush that had branches and leaves on the ground. Two men climbed up the bank and tried to push their cycles up the path. I saw a third man come out from the trees and follow them," Dizzy said.

"What happened then?" Frulik asked.

Before Dizzy answered, he wiped his nose on the left sleeve of his shirt. "The two men in front would not shut up. The third fellow told them to be quiet, but they were mad and paid no attention. The third guy pulled his gun and shot each in the back of the head. As he dragged the first body over the bank, I saw his face."

"Do you see the third man in the courtroom?" Frulik asked.

"Yeah, that's the guy next to that good looking broad," Dizzy said. He raised his left hand and gestured toward Bonnie.

"Mr. Welch, you will not refer to any lady in this court in that manner," Judge Rowland said.

"Did you point to the defendant, Mr. Charles Robbins?" Frulik asked.

"Yeah, if he's the little tramp next to her," Dizzy said.

"What did Mr. Robbins do then?" Frulik asked.

"He dragged the second fellow over the bank. He pushed the dead guys' bikes over the same bank. I heard them crash so the bikes must have fallen off a cliff. Then Robbins headed on up the path alone."

This is the same story Arnold told, only Dizzy did all of the things he said Charles did, Bonnie thought.

"Did you follow Mr. Robbins?" Frulik asked.

"Yeah, but I had to push my motorcycle and couldn't keep up with him. In places, it was all I could do to get my bike through the mud. When I got to the top, I saw someone move toward the house. From under the big old weeping willow, I could see him, but he couldn't see me because those branches touched the ground," Dizzy said and cleared his throat.

"Is the man you saw in the courtroom?"

"Yes! I saw Charles Robbins slip out of the shadows. He sneaked across the yard, and I saw him kick the door in. I heard a shot, then a man yelled, 'What do you want?'

"As long as Robbins was inside, I moved onto the porch and peeked in the doorway. Robbins was yelling 'give me all your money,' but old man Wilms was saying that he didn't have any money in the house."

"How did Mr. Robbins react?" Frulik asked.

"Robbins grabbed Wilms and forced him across the kitchen. Robbins yelled, 'Give me your money.' The old man raised his head and again said he had no money. Robbins forced Wilms to put his right arm over the top of a chair. Then he hit Wilms' arm so hard it snapped like a ginger snap. And then he yelled 'give me your money' again and he pushed Wilms into the living room," Dizzy said.

Until now, he's telling the same story Arnold Rigby did. Arnold had to see Dizzy abuse Donald, Bonnie thought.

"Could you see what Mr. Robbins did to Mr. Wilms in the other room?" Frulik asked.

"Just inside the door, Wilms tripped and fell. Robbins kicked the old man on the right leg then yelled for him to get up. The old man tried two or three times to get up."

I know that's wrong, because Donald had a bruise on his left leg, Bonnie thought.

"How could Mr. Wilms get on his feet with a broken arm?"

"I don't know how he did it. All this time, Robbins had his gun on Wilms. Robbins motioned for Wilms to sit in the big rocker. As Wilms fell into the chair, his broken arm hung over the arm of the chair," Dizzy said and paused. "What happened then?" Frulik asked.

Dizzy hesitated, apparently not knowing what to say next or which direction to go.

"Please continue, Mr. Welch. What happened then?" Frulik asked.

"Robbins slapped the old man around the face and head. Soon, he doubled up his fist and hit Wilms in the back of the neck. I heard the old fellow moan. The old man told him again that all the money he had at the house was in his billfold on the dresser in the front bedroom," Dizzy said.

"This is the guy on the motorcycle. I saw him fly down the wet path and a cross the railroad tracks. He had blood on his white shirt," Charles whispered.

Bonnie handed Charles a note pad and a pencil. "If you think of anything else, please make a note of it." She noticed Charles sat more erect than before. He appeared to listen to what Dizzy said happened.

"What did Mr. Robbins do next?" Frulik asked.

"The little guy doubled up his fist and smacked Wilms in the mouth as hard as he could. The blood ran out of Wilms' mouth onto his white shirt. Wilms tried to talk. Robbins yelled, 'Well, old man, are you ready to talk now?' Wilms tried but couldn't make a sound.

"Robbins ran over and grabbed a vase off the table. He swung it at Wilms a couple of times. Then he hit Wilms on the right side of the head. Wilms' head fell forward. I figured he was unconscious or Robbins had killed him. I didn't know which," Dizzy said.

"Objection, the witness is speculating. I move that his last remark be stricken from the record," Bonnie said.

"So ordered," Judge Rowland said.

"What did Mr. Robbins do after that?" Frulik asked.

"He went into the bedroom. You should have seen that room when he got through. Then Robbins rode down the hill on Wilms' motorcycle."

"Your witness." Frulik returned to his chair.

"No question at this time, your honor," Bonnie said.

"Call your next witness," Judge Rowland said.

"The prosecution rests," Frulik said.

The judge looked at the big clock on the wall. "Court will adjourn until Friday, at 10:00 a.m. at which time the defense will present their case."

Bonnie watched Judge Rowland scan the court. Then he rose from his chair and quickly departed.

"Hey lady, why didn't you ask Dizzy some questions?" Charles asked.

"When I accuse Dizzy of perjury, I want to be able to prove it," Bonnie said.

Art met Bonnie and Mike in the hall, and they returned to the house. Each had a different view point of Dizzy telling about what happened that day on the mountain.

"I know he tried to cover his tracks. You have to admit he did a good job. If you fellows were in my shoes, how would you force him to tell the truth?" Bonnie asked.

"Not being in your shoes, I can't answer your question," Art said.

Bonnie laid her sandals on the desk. "I'm all ears," she said, as she quietly leaned back in her chair and waited for an answer.

"I'll leave a note in your shoes that will explain what I think you should do," Art said and grinned.

CHAPTER 18

Friday morning, all Bonnie could think about was Dizzy Welch and how he blamed Charles Robbins for killing Donald Wilms. *I've overlooked asking what and where he was Sunday morning. I'll take care of that pronto.* She recalled some of Mike's remarks about Dizzy in the past, and she wondered what he thought of his story to Bob Ingram and Lyle Frulik last Saturday. "Did you believe Dizzy's tale about how Charles murdered Donald?" she asked and watched Mike's expression.

"I think Dizzy lied in the interrogation room and again in the court when he was under oath."

"Thanks. Since we feel he's a liar, I'll put Mr. Gees, the manager of the hardware store where Charles shopped, and Art on the stand before I call Dizzy."

Bonnie and Mike walked leisurely across the lot up the old cracked and worn steps. Mike held the door open.

A couple crowded in ahead of Bonnie and would have knocked her down had Mike not caught her. Bonnie was certain the strangers rudeness irritated Mike when he said, "Take it easy, Mister. Where's your manners?" But the stranger simply threw Mike a dirty look and continued into the courthouse.

Bonnie straightened her clothes a little. She noted that the cool breeze smelled sweet blowing in from the roses outside the open window. As she and Mike moved onto the courtroom floor, the bailiff called out, "All rise."

She was positive, even before his bottom touched the chair, that the judge called out, "Miss Cole, call your first witness."

Bonnie looked at the crowd. "I call Mr. Floyd Gees." She glanced at her notes while a tall, middle-aged fellow came forward. The bailiff swore him in, and he took the stand.

"Mr. Gees, I'm sorry to have to take you away from your work today, but it's necessary. You know Mr. Charles Robbins?"

"Yes, I do. Mr. Robbins comes in the hardware store where I work," Gees said.

"Did you see Mr. Robbins on Sunday morning May 3rd?"

"Yes, I stopped at the coffee shop for some breakfast. Mr. Robbins was sitting at the counter reading the paper. I joined him and bought him a cup of coffee and a doughnut."

"What time?" Bonnie got that far when suddenly the lights flickered a couple of times then went out. She looked at the ceiling just as the lights came on again. Bonnie repeated her question. "What time was this?"

"It was 7:30 a.m. I was on my way to work. I had to open the store at 8:00 a.m."

"Did you notice what time Mr. Robbins left the coffee shop?"

"It must have been around 7:40 a.m. because I left at 7:50 a.m."

"That will be all," Bonnie said. "Your witness."

Frulik jumped up and asked, "Mr. Gees, you opened the store at 8:00 a.m.?"

"Five minutes to eight," Floyd said.

"You didn't see the defendant after 7:45 a.m.?"

"No."

"Mr. Robbins could have easily gone up the river, down the path, and killed the Ryan brothers. He could do it before 9:30 a.m., which was the time the coroner said the two men died. Nothing further," Frulik said.

"I call Mr. Art Wilms," Bonnie said. She noticed a surprised expression on Art's face as he moved passed her.

"You have been sworn in Mr. Wilms. Please take the stand," Judge Rowland said.

Bonnie watched Art as he moved slowly to the chair. "Mr. Wilms, can you tell us how far it is from the coffee shop to the path that runs up the north side of the Snake River?" Bonnie asked.

"The shortest way from the coffee shop is almost one mile to the path that goes up the river," Art said.

"You have traveled the trail up the Snake River to the path that leads to Mr. Donald Wilms' house?"

"For more than 40 years," Art said.

"How far does one have to travel up the path along the river before you turn up the hill to the Wilms' house?"

"It's a good five miles. The path is crooked. In places it runs so close to the bank, one must be very careful not to slide off into the Snake."

"How far is it up the steep path to the house, then down the east side of the mountain where someone shot the Ryan brothers?" Bonnie crossed over in front of the jury.

"That's at least a quarter of a mile to the house then another quarter down the steep deer lane toward the creek," Art said.

"Mr. Robbins had to ride his motorcycle from the coffee shop to your father's house. In order to shoot the Ryan Brothers in the back of the head, he had to figure a way to get through the thick timber and sneak up on them," Bonnie said. She hesitated. "Mr. Wilms, would Mr. Robbins have time to do all this in an hour and a half?"

Art stared at Bonnie. He was finally ready to accept Bonnie's belief that Charles didn't kill anyone. He leaned forward and laid his arms on the front of the witness stand. "No! No way could Mr. Robbins have done all that in so short a time."

"Thank you, Mr. Wilms," She turned to Frulik. "Your witness."

When Bonnie got to her seat, she noticed Frulik start to stand. He looked at Art. Slowly, he dropped back onto his chair and said, "No questions."

"That will be all," Judge Rowland said. "It's 11:30 a.m. Since I have to render a decision on another case, court will adjourn until Monday, September 14th, at 10:00 a.m."

The officer came for Charles. Bonnie asked if she could talk with her client for a few minutes. Bonnie turned to Charles. "What did you do that Sunday morning between 9:00 a.m. and noon?"

Charles took so long to answer she was afraid the officer wouldn't wait. Finally, he said, "I tried to remember what the fellow at the bar said. I crossed the bridge and made a left turn and followed the path along the river. Finally, I got to a path up the mountain. It was narrow and curved around almost every tree. Sometimes I had to get off my bike and wiggle it around the bend in the path. I dunno how far I'd gone when I runned into a fellow that had a gun. He wanted to know what the hell I thought I was doin? When I told him, I was lookin for Wilms Mountain, he said, go back to the bridge and go east. We're west of Wilms Mountain. When I saw that gun, I coulden wait to get off that mountain. It took me a long time to come down that path and back to the river. That's why I didden get to the path to Wilms Mountain until almost noon," Charles said.

"Thank you, officer," Bonnie said as the uniformed guard took Charles away. Bonnie joined Art and Mike and the three drove to the house. Bonnie spoke, "Do you gentlemen have time to lend me your ears?"

Both men nodded, and Art pushed the button to turn on the coffee pot. Bonnie hustled to her room, gathered up every tape and note she felt was appropriate. With her notes and recorder in place, she was ready to begin when Mike spoke first. "I don't think Charles killed anyone."

"I believe Art would agree, but it's a good thing he didn't hear what Charles told me," Bonnie said. She peered over her glasses just as Art entered the office.

"Good thing I didn't hear what?" Art asked, as he relaxed in his chair on the other side of the desk.

Bonnie's eyes met Mike's. How she hoped he'd help her. Instead he showed he didn't intend to get involved. At that moment, as she watched Art, how she wished she could take back her words.

"Might as well get it out in the open," Art said.

Twice Bonnie tried to speak, but she was unable to get her voice to respond. Her sad eyes watched Art's face when she whispered, "Perhaps it would be better if you didn't hear this." She glanced at Mike and then back to Art and continued. "The first day of court, Charles said when he walked in the living room and saw Donald, he was still alive. Charles went ahead and robbed him of his wrist watch and rings." Bonnie couldn't go on.

"How did he know?" Art asked in a loud strained voice.

"Donald moaned and tried to ask for help," she said.

"Oh, my God!" Art said, as he leaped about three feet in the air and ran from the room.

"You better go to him. He needs your help more than mine," Mike said.

"What on earth will I say?" she asked.

"Maybe just let him know we care," Mike said.

When Bonnie entered the hall, she could hear a loud noise. She ran up the stairs as fast as she could and pushed on the partially open door to his room. His face was pale, and he looked older than the gray-haired man sitting on the corner selling pencils. He pounded the wall with both hands. "I'll kill that son-of-a-bitch."

"You don't really want to kill Charles," she said softly, as she pulled his right arm away from the wall and put hers around his neck. She looked into a pair of tear-filled blue eyes. He didn't make a sound and gently laid his head on her shoulder. She could feel the hot tears trickle down her back.

Soon he raised his head, grabbed his handkerchief, wiped his face, kissed her wet cheek, and said, "Let's go downstairs and find the killer."

Bonnie squeezed his hand, and they joined Mike in the office. She sat in the same chair she had earlier. Art pulled his chair away from the desk, held his head high, and his back was as straight as a steel post. She watched him stir through the stack of papers and tapes. In a voice unfamiliar to Bonnie, he said, "Well, we better settle in for an all-night session." Mike nodded.

"I need your undivided attention," Bonnie said.

"Excuse me," Art said and disappeared through the doorway into the kitchen. In a moment, he returned with three beers and three frosted glasses. "I'm ready. Where do you want to begin?"

"I think we should listen to Arnold's story, then compare it with

Dizzy's," was Bonnie's response.

"Before we get into the deep stuff, please tell me what we're after," Art asked.

"If you hear anything out of the ordinary that we haven't discussed or you feel we should go over, please say so, and I'll rerun it."

"We've listened to these tapes so many times, I think we've wasted enough time," Mike said.

"We have to find a clue to the culprit in what I have here or start over somewhere else and I don't know where that someplace would be." Bonnie ran the last tape she made of Charles. "I know he held back." The grandfather clock in the hall struck 11 times. *I haven't heard a thing that gives me any ideas,* she thought. "How about a rest and some dinner? The treat's on me."

"You never cease to amaze me, but I do agree with you. Let's go eat," Art said and helped her put the tapes and papers in the safe.

Outside, the moon was so bright she felt like she was 16 again. She tipped her head to the man in the moon and threw him a kiss. She wondered what Art thought when he laughed.

"Is he the best man you can find to kiss?"

She grinned at him then said, "As long as I can remember, I've always thrown him a kiss, and I suppose I always will."

CHAPTER 19

Early the next morning, Bonnie crawled out of bed. As she lowered the west window, she yawned, shook her head and blinked. *I'm sure this had to be the shortest night of my life.* She applied her makeup quickly and slipped on a red and white gingham dress and a pair of red earrings.

As she entered the office, she kicked off her red and white sandals with a happy "Good morning," and Art gently pushed her into the chair behind the desk. He sat across from her, and soon Mike took over the chair at the end of the desk.

Bonnie could always tell when Mike had a problem by his expression. "All right, gentlemen, let's have it. Somethings on your mind."

Art shifted his weight in the chair. She was positive he had an idea that he wanted to talk about. Art spoke as he put his feet on the corner of the desk, the position she had come to know indicated he was preparing for a long discussion. "I listened very carefully to Dizzy's testimony. I can't believe Robbins is capable of murder."

"Dizzy gave us a trumped-up story. The truth is somewhere right before our eyes." She wondered why Mike had been so quiet. "How about your nickels worth?" she asked and looked at him.

"I thought about your client. Dizzy said Robbins killed the Ryan brothers and hid their bodies. Art, I have to agree with you." Mike's voice had pity in it when he said, "Robbins is a weakling who could never kill anyone."

"Well, fellows, what do we do?" she asked.

With a frown on his face, Art rubbed his hands together. Then he said, "I thought about how Arnold described Dizzy dragging the Ryan brothers over the path and putting them under a bush." Art paused. "I grew up on Wilms Mountain. It's easy to lose your sense of direction on the way to the creek, and that might have happened to Arnold. Especially since he's mentally deranged, we could have misunderstood him. Suppose we get into some old rags and search the side of the mountain for that gun. I played on that side of the mountain, and Dad cut our wood in that area."

"Let's change," Mike said.

Half an hour later, Mike and Art came into the office. She poured three cups of coffee and noted that Mike looked at her in an odd way.

"Isn't that dress and fancy white sandals a funny outfit to look for a gun on a mountain?" Mike asked. "Aren't you going with us?"

"No, I'll stay here and work on Charles' defense," she said.

"You'll miss seeing all the snakes," Art said with a chuckle.

"Oh Art, you're breaking my heart," she said and pretended to be very sad. "Art, your dad must have worked hard at first."

"He did. The summer before Mother died, a large boulder rolled against Dad, breaking his leg and injuring him below the waist. This happened soon after he built the tracks to the mine. Billy Pile's uncle and Johnny Logan loaded Dad in an ore car and rushed him to a hospital. Dad always felt like Aaron Pile saved his life. Aaron died soon after that, leaving his family very well off. Dad decided the only way he could repay Aaron was to help Henry Pile, Aaron's older brother. That's why Dad paid all of Henry's hospital expenses and helped Billy and his mother," Art said.

"Thanks, Art. I've wondered why Donald helped them so much," she said.

"That's the reason. Dad always said that no man ever existed who was any better than Henry." Art looked at Mike. "We better get started for the mountain." Bonnie waved goodbye to them as they headed out the kitchen door.

Some three hours later, Bonnie was in the office when Art followed Mike in with three beers and glasses on a tray. Art lowered himself into the chair across from Bonnie.

"Did you find the gun?" she asked.

"You bet," Mike said. It was clear from their faces that the mountain hike had been a strenuous one.

"I've ordered dinner. They should deliver it any minute," Art said.

Bonnie excused herself and hurried to her room to freshen up before dinner arrived. It was a restless evening for them all. What a difference the gun would make.

Sunday was a busy day for Bonnie. With the new evidence, she had to revise her approach and put Mike on the stand. She was certain the district attorney would object and try every way he could to prove her wrong.

On Monday, the men seemed in a hurry to get into court. Bonnie found herself again having to hurry to keep up with them.

She rushed into the courtroom just in time to get to her desk before an officer brought Charles in. His eyes showed clearly that he was tired, and that perhaps the seriousness of the situation had finally soaked in. It surprised Bonnie when Charles called her name, turned in his chair, and stared at her. "It was an awful thing for me to leave that old man like I did. He couldn't even help himself. Besides, I stole his jewelry away from him," Charles said.

"Yes, that was a terrible thing to do," Bonnie said, as she watched the judge take his seat on the bench.

"Be seated," the bailiff said.

"Miss Cole, do you want Mr. Welch to take the stand?" Judge Rowland asked.

"Not at this time, your honor. I'd like to call Mr. Mike Dailey," she said.

"Objection, your honor. Mike Dailey is not on the defense witness list," Frulik said.

"That's true, your honor, but new evidence was found on Saturday." The judge barked his decision. "Overruled. Go ahead."

The bailiff swore Mike in. Mike showed being on the witness stand was nothing unusual for him. She wondered how often he had testified. *He moves in such a calm confident manner. It's a pleasure to have him testify.* "Mr. Dailey, where were you and Mr. Art Wilms Saturday?"

"Art Wilms, Jim Rams and I spent the day on Wilms Mountain. We wanted to try and find the gun that killed the Ryan brothers."

Bonnie handed Mike an automatic and asked, "Is this the gun you found?"

Mike examined it and said, "Yes, the serial number matches what I have."

"Your honor, I'd like to enter this 38 automatic into evidence," Bonnie said.

"I have a continuing objection to all of this," Frulik said.

I knew Frulik would doubt us, she thought.

"So noted. The bailiff will enter the gun," Judge Rowland said.

"Mr. Dailey, did you find the gun on the mountain?" Bonnie asked.

"Yes. As a child, Mr. Wilms played on that side of the mountain. I've been in that area before. A person could hide a gun in many places that a stranger would overlook. Mr. Wilms remembered a snake pit about 50 feet from where the Ryan brothers' bodies were hidden. We found the gun caught in a bush on the side of the pit. I gave the gun to Sheriff Ingram."

"Thank you." With a slight nod to Frulik, she said, "Your witness."

Frulik jumped up so quickly he and Bonnie nearly collided. "Sorry," he said and faced Mike. "Mr. Dailey, you want this court to believe the three of you went to Wilms Mountain and produced a gun, which the sheriff's deputies couldn't find?"

"We spent sometime digging around in a foot of leaves and pine needles before we found the pit. The planks that covered the pit had dirt and leaves a foot deep on top of them," Mike said.

"Then how did Mr. Robbins drop the gun in?" Frulik asked.

"Objection, there's no evidence that my client even had the gun, much less dropped it in the pit."

Frulik raised his voice. "I'll rephrase, your honor." Frulik turned to Mike. "How did the killer drop the gun in the pit?"

"I saw small openings along the sides of the planks. He must have tossed the gun aside, and it slid between the plank and the side of the pit. We found the gun on a bush. If it had fallen among the snakes, it probably would have been lost forever," Mike said.

"If you can convince this jury of such a story, you're a better liar than I am, Mr. Dailey," Frulik said in a loud voice.

Bonnie knew Frulik wanted to impress the jury. "Objection, Mr. Frulik is trying to destroy the credibility of my witness."

Mike moved in the witness chair, faced the judge, smiled and said, "Your honor, if you don't mind, I'd like to respond to Mr. Frulik's statement."

Bonnie immediately spoke. "I withdraw my objection."

Mike leaned forward and put a hand on each knee. In a calm and confident manner, he said, "You see, sir, that's the difference between you and me. I'm not here to tell a story. I'm relating exactly what I saw, what I found and what I did."

If Mike were the district attorney's witness, he'd aggravate me to tears, Bonnie thought.

"Your honor, I'd like the witness' last remark stricken from the record and order the jury to disregard," Frulik said.

The judge shook his head. "The witness' statement stands. Mr. Frulik, you asked for it."

Disgusted, Frulik said, "I'm through with this witness." He frowned. At his table, he picked up a pencil and threw it so hard that Bonnie was certain everyone in the room could hear it.

"Miss Cole, any redirect?" Judge Rowland asked.

"No, your honor."

"You may step down," Judge Rowland said. "Miss Cole, call your next witness."

Bonnie glanced at the sheriff on her right and said, "I'd like to call Bob Ingram." She noticed Bob smiled at her as he leisurely took the stand.

"You're still under oath," Judge Rowland said.

Bonnie moved across the courtroom floor to the evidence table and picked up the gun. "Sheriff Ingram, is this the gun Mr. Dailey gave you Saturday afternoon?" She waited patiently while he examined it.

"It is."

"Where did Mr. Dailey tell you he found this gun?"

"On Wilms Mountain in a snake pit, just as he explained to the court."

"Can you tell if this is the gun that killed the Ryan brothers?"

"Yes. Ballistic tests prove this was the weapon used to shoot the Ryan brothers."

"No more questions," Bonnie said.

"Does the prosecution wish to cross?" the judge said.

"Yes I do, your honor." He stared at Bonnie, spun on his heels. "Sheriff Ingram," he blurted out in an angry voice. "If Mr. Dailey and his crew could find that gun, why couldn't your men?"

"Wait a minute, Lyle Frulik. We searched in all the reasonable places. I don't appreciate your smart remarks about my men," Bob shouted in anger.

"Sorry Sheriff Ingram, I didn't intend for my question to put you in a defensive position."

"Mr. Art Wilms said his father covered that pit with planks more than 40 years ago because Art and his friends played in the area. That's how Art remembered it was there," Bob said.

Bonnie noticed the judge's eyes on her as though he expected her to object. *It's hearsay, but I think I'll let Sheriff Ingram's answer stand,* Bonnie thought.

"I've nothing more, your honor," Frulik said.

Bonnie peeked at her watch and said, "Your honor, it's 11:45 a.m. My next witness will take considerable time."

"In that case, court will recess until 2:00 p.m.," Judge Rowland said.

At 2:00 p.m., Bonnie, Art, and Mike were back to the courtroom. When the judge entered, he appeared hurried and rushed.

"Miss Cole, call your next witness," Judge Rowland said.

I've never dreaded to face a witness so much in my life, as I do right now, she thought. She moved around her table into the middle of the floor. In a calm, but firm voice, she said, "I call Mr. Dizzy Welch."

Bonnie observed the way Dizzy sat in the witness chair. She compared him with Mike and Bob. She wondered if Dizzy planned to get smart with her. She remembered Mike's description that he was a cold, heartless killer and could choke her before anyone could get there to help.

"Mr. Welch, you're still under oath," Judge Rowland said.

Bonnie saw Dizzy smirk at her in a snide way. She never let on, but she did feel a cold chill creep over her. Then he grinned in a rude manner. She wondered if he wanted to come onto her in hopes of leniency. Bonnie noticed the judge watched her very closely.

Bonnie never let on. She pulled in her stomach so tight she was positive it could have made a curve in her backbone. Then she studied her notes for a second. With her head high, she asked, "Mr. Welch, you were on Wilms Mountain on May 3rd?"

"Yes," Dizzy said.

"You went up the river the day before with the Ryan brothers."

Before Bonnie could say another word, Dizzy interrupted her. With a snap in his voice that could crack the plaster on the wall, he said, "I went to Wilms Mountain on May 2nd. Don't try to confuse me, lady."

In a businesslike way, Bonnie said, "Mr. Welch, you and the Ryan brothers stopped about a mile up the Snake River. Here, one of the Ryan Brothers found an old can and went down the bank to the river and got some water. The three of you had a drink, then talked for almost 20 minutes about the Pennsylvania prison and how you enjoyed your freedom. That was Saturday morning, May 2nd."

Dizzy choked and coughed. Barely above a whisper, he said, "I told you I was alone."

"One of the Ryan brothers asked you what you went up for. Do you remember your answer?"

Dizzy bent forward and spoke louder. "No, I don't remember my answer, because it never happened."

"Your honor, Miss Cole is badgering the witness," Frulik said.

"I asked Mr. Welch if he were on Wilms Mountain on May 2nd. I'd like to clarify what he did that day," Bonnie said.

"Overruled. Continue," Judge Rowland said.

Out of the corner of her eye, Bonnie saw Frulik drop on his seat and shake his head. She turned to the witness. "Mr. Welch, would you tell this court why you are an escapee from the Harrisburg Prison?" Bonnie was sure of herself on this one because the warden at the Pennsylvania prison had enlightened her on a number of things.

Dizzy wiggled around in the chair and ran his fingers through his hair.

"Do you want me to tell them?"

"No, I'll answer the question. When I escaped from prison the first time, I needed a car. I saw an old man close by in a good one. He got mean about it. I hit him harder than I intended. It killed him."

She noticed Dizzy's voice had changed and his eyes were glassy. "No! Mr. Welch, remember you're under oath. How did you kill the old man and where did you leave his body?"

She didn't like the expression on Dizzy's face, and she knew he was angry when he shouted, "I shot the son-of-a-bitch and threw him out along the road side." Dizzy spoke so fast that Bonnie couldn't understand what he said.

She heard the gavel. "Mr. Welch, no more swearing or shouting in this court. You will repeat your answer and keep the swearing out of it," Judge Rowland said.

"I shot the old boy in the head and left him along a country road."

"Objection. Mr. Welch's past has no bearing on this case," Frulik said.

"Your honor, I'm trying to establish the fact that Mr. Welch has a history of eliminating anyone who gets in his way," she said.

"I think you have done that. Move on," Judge Rowland said.

"Yes sir." In a serious way, Bonnie asked Dizzy. "What did the Ryan brothers tell you they were in for?"

"They held up a small grocery store and tickled an old lady on the belly," Dizzy said and chuckled in a dirty, silly way.

Judge Rowland tapped the gavel again. "Mr. Welch, I demand a respectful response to counsel's questions. Is that clear?"

"Yeah," Dizzy replied.

"According to the court records the jury found the Ryan brothers guilty of armed robbery and rape. Isn't that so?" Bonnie asked.

He slumped in a haphazard way and said, "Well, you could put it that way."

"Thank you." She walked to her table and collected some notes. She reeled around and faced Dizzy. "On the path up the river, what did the three of you do when you came to the steep path up the mountain?"

"The fellow at the bar said there's a creek farther on. I decided to go to the creek and come in that way. I didn't know it was another five miles to the creek. Lady, did you ever try to ride a motorcycle through thick brush?" Dizzy asked.

"Mr. Welch, you're here to answer questions, not ask them," the judge said.

"Where did you spend the night?"

"You must know that, to hear you tell it, you know everything I did."

Bonnie frowned and raised her voice. "Mr. Welch, I asked you where you spent Saturday night?"

"We camped on the creek, and it rained on us."

Bonnie responded quickly. "Mr. Welch, will you please repeat your answer?"

"I didn't mean we. I camped on the creek," Dizzy said.

"Everyone heard you the first time. What did Mr. Robbins supposedly do inside Mr. Wilms' house?" Bonnie asked.

"Lady, you're trying to trip me up with your big words. I know what supposedly means, and damn it, there was nothing supposed about it,"

Dizzy said.

"Please tell the court what you saw and I'll remind you one more time that you're under oath."

"I can remember."

"Your honor, Mr. Welch has already told this court what he saw in Mr. Wilms' house," Frulik said.

Bonnie faced the judge. "This witness has lied, and I'd like to have a chance to prove it." She waited patiently. Oh, how she hoped the judge would let her go on.

Judge Rowland paused for a second, then said, "Proceed."

"Please tell the court what you saw in Mr. Wilms' house," Bonnie said.

Dizzy rolled his eyes toward the ceiling and said, "All right. Robbins shoved Wilms through the door into the front room. Evidently, Robbins pushed Wilms so hard he fell on the floor, because I heard Robbins yell, for Wilms to get up or he'd kill him. How the old man got up with one arm broken is more than I know, but the old devil made it." Dizzy grabbed his glass of water with both hands, raised it to his lips, and emptied it in one gulp.

He's more like an animal than a man, Bonnie thought. She noticed how his hands trembled and realized he was beginning to falter. Dizzy gave the glass to the officer and asked for another. The officer handed it to the bailiff, who picked up the pitcher and filled the glass for Dizzy.

He's stalling, and this I can't afford. "Did you see a dog?" she asked.

"Yes, just inside the back doorway," Dizzy said.

"Was the dog alive or dead?"

"He was dead."

"Mr. Welch, will you please pull up your right pant leg?" Bonnie asked.

Frulik called to the judge. "What does she want now, the witness to dance for us?"

"The forensic team found blood and human flesh on the dog's teeth. I'd like to know if the dog bit Mr. Welch," Bonnie said.

"Move onto the courtroom floor and raise your pant legs," the judge said.

"Your honor, I have a bite on my right leg, but I got it two days after the murder," Dizzy said.

"What type blood do you have?"

"I don't know." Dizzy said.

"I do, your honor. His blood is type 'A,' the same type as the forensic team found on the dog's teeth." In a decisive voice, Bonnie asked, "What did you see after Mr. Wilms was able to get to his feet?"

"Robbins hit the old man in the chest, and Wilms dropped into the chair," Dizzy said.

"What kind of a chair?"

"How the hell do I know, woman. You asked the dumbest questions."

The judge whacked the gavel and said, "Mr. Welch, I've warned you about swearing. I don't want to hear any more of it."

"Was it a straight chair, an overstuffed chair, or perhaps a rocker?" Bonnie asked.

Dizzy paused for a second. Then he said, "It was a rocker, because Robbins hit him and Wilms moved back and forth. I heard Wilms beg Robbins not to tie his wrists so tight cause it shut off the blood to his hands."

"Did Mr. Robbins loosen the ties?"

"No, Robbins just kept yelling, 'Where's the money?' Robbins doubled up his fist and hit that old devil as hard as he could in the right jar. I saw the blood fly every place," Dizzy said. Then he waved his left hand in the air and laughed.

This man is a brutal killer. How will I ever make him tell the truth? Bonnie thought.

"Now that Mr. Robbins had Mr. Wilms in such a painful position, what did he do next?"

"He grabbed a glass vase and swung it at the old man several times. When the old devil didn't tell him where the money was, Robbins let him have it on the right side of his head. The old man's head fell forward, and I knew he was dead," Dizzy said.

Bonnie tossed her note pad toward her table. She grabbed the vase with both hands and swung it through the air several times as though she intended to let Dizzy feel how it would hurt. "Did you hit Mr. Wilms like this?" she screamed.

Dizzy grabbed for the vase, but Bonnie was a little too fast for him. She swung the vase the other way at Dizzy. "Did you hit Mr. Wilms like this?" she yelled.

"Objections," Frulik shouted.

The judge pounded the gavel.

Bonnie swung the vase again, even faster this time, and as close as she dared to Dizzy's head and yelled, "You're dealing with B. A. Cole, and that stands for bad-ace! You hit Mr. Wilms in the head."

Dizzy threw his head back to get out of the way and roared, "I didn't mean to hit him. It was an accident."

"Objection, Miss Cole is badgering her own witness," Frulik called out again.

Bonnie tried not to look at Judge Rowland, who was on his feet still pounding the gavel. "What did you say, Mr. Welch, it was an accident?" she said loudly. "You did or did not mean to hit Mr. Wilms? And remember you're not only under oath but you're talking to B.A. Cole."

The gavel sounded even louder. "Miss Cole, I've never seen such a performance in a court room in my life. What do you think you're doing?" Judge Rowland shouted.

Bonnie smiled at the judge and in a calm, polite voice, she said, "I'm sorry, your honor. I had to get the truth out of this witness someway." She walked to her table, picked up the note pad that had landed on the floor. She didn't like the expression on the judge's face when she approached Dizzy. This time she remembered what Mike had said and she stayed six feet away from the witness stand. "Mr. Welch, I'd like to go back to Sunday morning, May 3rd, when you and the Ryan brothers were hiking up the path to Mr. Wilms' house."

"I've told you over and over that I wasn't on Wilms Mountain with the Ryan brothers," Dizzy yelled.

"What would you say if I told you a witness followed you and the Ryan brothers Saturday and Sunday? He saw you shoot the brothers in the head, hide their bodies and toss the gun away." She noticed an odd expression cross Dizzy's face. She turned her head and saw a large man standing.

"If that fellow said he saw me shoot the Ryans, he's a damn liar," Dizzy said.

The sound of the gavel echoed so loud through the courtroom Bonnie jumped. In a commanding voice, Judge Rowland said, "Mr. Welch, I've warned you before. NO MORE SWEARING!"

Bonnie got the gun off the exhibit table and held it up so Dizzy could see it. Bonnie thought from the expression on his face that he recognized it. "Have you ever seen this weapon before?" she asked.

"No," Dizzy said.

"That's strange, because this is the gun you used to shoot the Ryan brother."

"The hell I did," Dizzy yelled and pounded the witness stand with his left fist. Bonnie could hear the handcuffs hit the stand.

The gavel sounded again and the judge shouted, "Mr. Welch you better calm down, you're trying the court's patience."

"If you've never seen this gun and you didn't shoot the Ryan brothers..."

Dizzy interrupted Bonnie. "That's right," he yelled.

She pulled the clip out of the automatic, held it up to the judge, the jury and Dizzy. Then she said, "Please explain to this court how your thumb and two fingerprints got on the clip of this gun?" She looked at Dizzy's face and eyes then moved farther away from the stand.

"You're the only one who says my prints are on that gun. I don't know why you've accused me of handling a gun that I've never seen." He lowered his head in an odd way, and the whites in his eyes was all she could see. His eyes were much like those of a wild animal's eyes and an angry snarl growled from his mouth, which at times showed his deformed dirty teeth.

"I can bring Sheriff Ingram to the stand. He had the gun examined by a fingerprint expert, or we can bring him in if we have to. What did you have against the Ryan brothers?"

"Not a thing, but I want to talk to my lawyer," Dizzy shouted.

"Good idea. No more questions," Bonnie said. She hurried to her table.

"Any questions, Mr. Frulik?" Judge Rowland asked.

Frulik started to get up. Instead he sat again and said, "No questions."

"Take Mr. Welch away," Judge Rowland said.

Bonnie could hear the chains between Dizzy's legs as they dragged across the floor. The heavy logger heels on his heavy boots pounded the hardwood floor as the officers escorted him out of the courtroom.

"After this last witness, I'm ready to adjourn," the judge said. The lights blinked twice, then went out.

The south side of the courtroom room had tall windows that reached from the ceiling to within four feet of the floor. Bonnie was glad to see the sunshine replace the lights.

The bailiff walked over to Judge Rowland and whispered something to him. The judge nodded his head, then turned back to the crowd and said, "The bailiff just informed me that the electricians will be rewiring this courtroom, which will take two or three days. Therefore, court will adjourn until 10:00 a.m., Monday, September 21st."

Bonnie picked up her note pads and pencils and put them in her briefcase. As the officer pulled Charles away, she said, "I'll see you Monday." As she turned to leave the court, Art and Mike were waiting by the front door. Both had their eyes on her. She took a deep breath and thought, *I might as well get it over with.*

She hurried down the aisle with a smile on her face just as if this were another normal day. "I'd like a bite to eat, how about you fellows?" she asked. Art unlocked the Thunderbird, helped Bonnie in, and stepped aside so Mike could get in.

Bonnie sensed Art couldn't make up his mind what to say. Before he started the motor, he twisted halfway around in the seat. "There's an old saying Bonnie. Fools will go where a saint won't tread, and I saw it all today. I've never been so frightened in my life."

"Are you calling me a fool?" she asked.

"A fool! What I saw today was beyond understanding. It was a wonder that murderer didn't grab that vase and brain you before any of us could get there. What the hell were you thinking?" Mike asked.

"It happened so fast. I knew I had to do something to shock Dizzy into telling the truth. After he admitted he did it, and I got to my desk, it was the first time I remembered what you said about the risk. So don't scold me any more. Besides, it worked!"

"Mission accomplished," Art said. In a moment, he started laughing. "What is this B. A. I heard today?"

"That stands for Bonnie Ann," she said softly.

"That wasn't what I heard in court today," Mike said, and they laughed.

"Sounded like bad something," Art said.

"Oh yes, bad-ace," Mike said.

She could feel her face flushing. She rarely blushed, but today was going to be the exception.

"Bad-ace," Art repeated, at the same time he took hold of her chin and turned her face around toward him.

She put her hands over her face and dropped her head. Just above a whisper she said, "Please take me home." She could feel the hot tears running off her fingers onto her dress.

As soon as Art opened the kitchen door, she darted passed him, ran to her room, and tried to close the door. But before she could do so, they were both beside her.

Mike dropped into the big chair and asked, "When and where did a refined lady like you get such a name?"

Bonnie faced the two men. She knew her cheeks were red and wet with tears. "Okay, when I was 10-years-old, I got into a fight with the neighbor boy. He wrapped a plastic bat around my butt. It made me so mad, I grabbed a metal pipe and hit his hind-end so hard he cried. He stumbled across the yard holding onto himself yelling, 'My ass hurts, bad.' It was then another schoolmate began to laugh and called me bad-ace Cole.

"My father and twin sister, Connie, were waiting in the car. When I closed the door, Dad said, 'Bonnie Ann, you could have hurt him with that pipe.' I told Dad he hit me first. Then Connie said, 'yea right on the ass.' Then she called me bad-ace just as the kid in my class did.

To this day, Connie still calls me B. A. when we're alone."

"I never heard about this before," Mike said.

"I'm not proud of that name. I was so upset it just slipped out. When Connie moved to Portland, I made her promise not to tell anyone."

"I'll keep my lips sealed," Art said.

"I won't tell anyone," Mike said.

"Excuse me, suppose I meet you in the office," Bonnie said and stepped lightly into the bathroom. She touched up her face and hurried to the office.

CHAPTER 20

Art and Mike sat relaxed. Mike had crossed his legs in the usual way, and Art's feet and legs were across the corner of the desk. Dizzy's case seemed to be the main topic of their conversation.

"I must go to the jail. Do the two of you want to go along?" Bonnie asked.

"The jail?" Mike asked with doubt in his voice.

"I must talk with Charles. I'm positive he knows more than he's admitted. The way things are now, Charles is the murderer," she said.

"What about Dizzy?" Art asked.

"Dizzy didn't kill Donald. He did hit Donald on the right-side of the head and beat him terribly, but he didn't kill him." Bonnie shivered when she thought about Donald.

"Do you suppose Arnold Rigby told a lie, and he killed Donald?" Mike asked.

"I don't think so, nor do I think Charles is guilty. There's an unknown in this case, and we have the week to find it," she said.

"Well Bonnie, I'm going along to see that Charles doesn't give you any static."

"All right, you promise not to say a word. I've got to talk to this fellow my own way."

"I'll agree to that, but watch him. If he's the killer, he might try to get rid of you," Mike said.

Bonnie glanced at her watch and frowned. "We must hurry."

Ten minutes later, Mike parked in front of the sheriff's office. Inside the jail, she asked, "May we speak to Charles Robbins?"

"Sure. I know room 15 is empty. I'll have Mr. Robbins there in a few minutes," the officer said.

As they strolled down the hall to the room, Mike said, "You're so tired and upset, please don't make yourself sick."

"I'll admit this day has exhausted me, but I would never forgive myself if I'd have to leave this town and not know who killed Donald Wilms." She usually walked and sat gracefully, but tonight she simply dropped onto the first chair available.

"I've never seen you sit like that before," Mike said.

She glimpsed at him. *His eyes are sad, and he shows he cares. I must help him solve this case.*

The officer and Charles came in, the prisoner wearing the usual prison garb, the officer walked back out the door.

"I ain't never expected to see you tonight," Charles said.

"Sit, Charles. We must have a serious talk."

Mike reached for Bonnie's recorder and turned it on.

"You found Dizzy guilty. Why do we gotta talk?" Charles asked.

"Look here, young man, I said we have to talk. That's exactly what I mean, TALK. This is your last chance. You better tell me WHAT YOU SAW, WHAT YOU DID and WHAT DONALD SAID that Sunday on Wilms Mountain."

Bonnie noticed Charles' hands quiver. *This is the first time I've seen him show any emotions.* He lowered his head, as if he had decided to count his finger nails. "I ain't never telled you what I done in Wilms' house."

"Charles, it's now, or you'll spend the rest of your life in prison. You're the last person we know of who went to Donald's house Sunday. Therefore, the jury will conclude you're the killer."

"You ain't never gonna think I did it. Are you?" Charles asked. His voice showed what Bonnie had said frightened him.

"What else can I think? You don't trust me enough to tell the truth." She raised her hand and pointed a finger at him. "You talk now, or I can't help you."

Charles wiggled in his chair like a baby might when it wanted to get down on the floor. He started digging at his finger nails again.

Bonnie slapped the table with her note pad and shouted, "Stop biting your finger nails and talk. I said TALK, or I'll leave right now."

"I toll you that a man came down the mountain so fast and almost runned into the river."

"Yes, but what's his name?"

"That was Dizzy, he had blood all over his shirt," Charles said.

Bonnie wasn't sure whether Charles was in doubt or afraid. "Go on."

"I wanted to go back to town." Charles rubbed his hands together and repeated. "Something or someone, I just don't know, kept saiden for me to go on." Charles stared at Bonnie.

Bonnie waited patiently for him to collect his thoughts.

"I seed a dog on the floor in the kitchen." Again Charles paused. He frowned and shook his head. Again, he wiggled around in his chair. "When I comed into the livin room, I saw a man sittin in a chair. His lap had teeth and gold and blood in it. I'm sorry I took his rings and watch. I jerked a pen set out of his shirt." Charles shook his head. "Now, I don't know how I could have took his rings and watch."

"I see. Then what happened?"

"He made a funny noise. I damn near yumped out of my hide," Charles said and shivered.

"What kind of noise? Did he ask you to help him, or did he cry out in pain?" Bonnie asked. *I must keep him talking.*

"He kept sayin the same thing. Finally, I knowed he wanted me to help him." Charles raised his head and waved his hands.

This I never expected, she thought. "What did you do?" she asked.

"I coulden move, but when he said, 'Please son help me, cut me loose.' I used my pocket knife and cut the strings around his wrists," Charles said. He rubbed his face with his hands. "If you coulda seed that broken arm floppin around." Charles covered his face with his hands and laid his head on the table.

"Did Donald ask for additional help?"

Charles nodded. "He tried to lift the busted arm. I gotta hold of his arm above the elbow and his hand. He moaned when I put his broken arm on the arm of the chair."

That's how blood got on the arm of the chair, Bonnie thought. She glanced at Mike, he frowned and shook his head. She turned to Charles. "What did you do then?"

"When I lifted his arm, I accidentally kicked the vase. I put it on the table." Charles paused. "I forgot to tell you. I thought cuttin him loose was destroyin proof so I put the strings in my pocket. The old man said, 'Please son, my feet.' He was talkin plainer. I could seed what he was sayin. I cut the strings on his legs and put the strings in my pocket." Charles scratched his head. "He kinda scolded me, I thought. Then he said, 'get outta here, hurry son, get outta here.' No one had ever called me 'son' before, and I kinda hated to leave him." Charles smiled, as if he remembered how it felt for someone to call him 'Son.'

"Donald pointed with his left hand. He told me, 'In the cupboard above the sink is a green mug with some change in it. Take it and get out of here.'"

"Did you find the mug?" Bonnie asked.

"Yes, it had big bills and some change. That's why I had money to pay for the gas at the station in town. As I went out, I looked at the old fellow; he was standin and tryin to walk. Outside, I seed my cycle had runned out of gas. I seed a white one sittin in front of the cellar. I almost got on it, but the black one was a beauty," Charles said.

"Did you notice the number on the license plate of the white one?"

"No," Charles said.

"When you left, which way did you go down the mountain?"

"I remembered what he said, so I rushed down the other side."

"Here's my telephone number, if you should think of something, call me."

Mike shut off the recorder and called an officer.

"Thanks, Charles. I may need more information," she said.

After thanking the officers, Bonnie and Mike departed. Bonnie noticed a new Mike. "After listening to Charles' story about how Donald suffered and how he helped him, I'm glad you insisted on defending Charles," he said.

"He gave me the answers I've needed since this thing started, but how will I ever convince Bob Ingram?"

"Unless we find the murderer, I don't think you will," Mike said.

She noticed Art watching her as she got in the pickup. "Bonnie Cole, if you don't get some rest, you are going to collapse," he said.

"I feel so much better. Charles answered all my questions that I've been needling you guys with."

"Charles answered many things we have wondered about," Mike said.

As Mike opened the kitchen door, Art said, "I have a few questions, but I will wait until you get some rest." Art set a box on the end of the table.

"Do I smell chicken? Will I have time to get out of these street-clothes?"

"Yes and yes."

Bonnie dashed to her room, slipped on a white housecoat and returned to the kitchen. The table held three iced glasses and three bottles
of beer. "What a welcome sight, and I always enjoy a cold beer when I'm tired."

CHAPTER 21

The following morning, Bonnie walked out on the back porch and onto the south end to stand in the warm sunlight. *This is going to be another hot day,* she thought as she watched the red and white roses sway in the cool breeze. She listened to the little bluebird's story about what happened and the gossip of the day before. "You don't say," she said. The little fellow's mouth opened and he finished his story.

She sensed steps behind her and heard Art say, "Good morning."

"You surprised me," she said and leaned against the corner post. "You have a question?"

He sat with one foot on the railing and wrapped his left arm around his knee. "I know this is a silly thing to ask, and there has to be a logical answer. Yesterday, you had Dizzy going sideways. Why did you end your investigation so suddenly?"

"First, Dizzy asked for a lawyer, and secondly, I got the shock of my life. You see, Dizzy didn't kill Donald."

"We were so sure," he said in amazement.

"I know. Yesterday when I swung that vase at him, I noticed he tried to catch it with his left hand only. He has something seriously wrong with his right arm, and he hides his disability well. You'll never know how I'd like to remove that bandage," she said.

"I've never noticed it."

"I don't know if you've thought about it, but we're in big trouble. Dizzy's in the clear, and I know Charles didn't do it." She stopped briefly and watched the birds dip in their bird bath, then turned and faced Art. "This is a horrible thought and I don't like to admit what I'm thinking, but we've got a mentally-ill murderer running loose in this town."

In a flash, Art rose and gently seized her by the arm. "Let's get in the house. You and Mike could be the next victims."

"I haven't felt like we were in danger."

"In danger?" Mike called out from the office.

"Bonnie's right. We have a madman at large in Windcove," Art said and called Bob Ingram. "I want an officer at both outside doors 24 hours a day."

After Art talked to Bob, he poured three cups of coffee. Bonnie and Art joined Mike in the office. They settled comfortably in their chairs ready for a long day.

"Art, can you think of anyone in this town who is mentally out of balance?"

"Other than Zeeta, I can't," he said.

Mike held out his hand to Bonnie. "May I have the pictures you took the Sunday we were on the mountain?"

Bonnie reached in her briefcase and handed Mike two envelopes of pictures. "This is a handy gadget," she said. At the same time, she gave Mike an old magnifying glass.

Mike fixed his eyes on the glass, laughed, and asked, "Where did you get this queer thing?"

"I found it at a yard sale in Fargo. Please be careful with it, as I paid 68 cents for that valuable gimmick."

Mike moved the floor lamp closer. He put his left leg over the arm of the chair and squared his shoulders in the opposite corner. He held the magnifying glass in one hand and studied picture after picture. Bonnie noticed after he examined the first picture, he raised his eyebrows. His face showed dismay.

Art and Bonnie talked about yesterday's testimony in court. "Mike, please get the snapshot showing the drops of blood on the rug between the rocker and the library table. I'd like you to tell me what you see in that one. Also, you'll find three pictures showing tracks along and behind the cellar."

Art stood behind Mike's chair, while Bonnie waited anxiously for the men to express their opinions. Art looked at Bonnie and she watched his Adams-apple move up and down. In a low voice, he asked, "What do you see that I'm overlooking?"

"Notice the foot tracks Donald made with his left foot, then compare the right." Again, Bonnie waited and hoped Mike would express his viewpoint. She watched him study the photo. He turned it around and tipped the magnifying glass.

"It is obvious Donald was dragging his left leg. The right foot is making deeper tracks in the carpet, as if he couldn't put much weight on his left leg," Mike said.

"Dr. Phillips said Donald's left leg had a bad bruise on it probably caused by the attacker."

"Arnold told us Dizzy kicked Donald, which caused him to fall in the doorway," Mike said.

Bonnie looked up and asked, "How much did Donald weigh?"

"Dad would weigh from a 160 to a 170 pounds."

"Thanks," she said and kept on writing.

"Why did you ask?"

Bonnie watched Art's face. She spoke slow and deliberate. "I listened to the tape we made at the sanitarium. Arnold said Dizzy tied Donald in the rocker, right?"

"Yes, that's right."

Bonnie rose and sauntered to the north window. Her eyes soared to the top of the large tree along the driveway. She spoke slowly, as if she were trying to compose a poem or tell a story. "We know Arnold's voice had an upturn when he described how Donald's teeth and gold fillings were in his lap." She faced the men. "I know now Charles told us the truth when he said he cut the cords around Donald's wrists and ankles. That's how your father's teeth got on the rug in front of him, and he dragged his body to the telephone." She lingered at the window. "What time did you get the call from Donald?"

"I answered the phone at 12:30 p.m."

"Rick, your service station manager, said he saw the black motorcycle at the pump. We saw it go up Main Street." She looked at Art then Mike. The photos and the magnifying glass were on the desk. After a bit, she folded her arms across her chest and stared out the window.

In a gentle, but hopeful voice, Mike said, "Come on. Don't stop now. When you get to the talking stage, you're usually right on."

"I'm with Mike. Don't disappoint us," Art responded.

Bonnie returned to her desk, laid her head against the soft pillow on the chair and shut her eyes. In a voice a teacher might use to ask her students a question, she asked, "How long did it take us," she looked at Art, "from the time you hung up the phone until we were waiting for Jim?"

"We ran to the car. By the time you and Art got in, I had the motor running," Mike said.

"It's a mile from the house to the garage. Let's give ourselves plenty of time. Make it five minutes," Art said.

Bonnie rocked forward. "By the time we got the call from Donald, Charles had to be at the highway, or on the bridge." She jotted down a few words, dropped her pen and lifted her cup of what had once been hot coffee.

Mike and Art waited for her to continue. "We saw the footprints Donald made on his way to the library table." She turned to Mike and asked, "How did Donald get to the phone and back in the rocker with his arms and legs tied?"

Mike raised his hands and shook his head. "I haven't the faintest idea."

"We know Donald and Tom Finch shampooed the rug Friday. The killer must have made those odd tracks along side Donald's chair," Bonnie said. They stared at each other, each trying to pull the picture together.

Finally, Mike asked, "What do you think happened?"

Bonnie picked up the coffee pot and filled their cups, and as she set the pot back, she said, "I truly believe this madman stood behind the cellar early Sunday morning. He expected Dizzy to show. From the tracks in back of the cellar, he must have paced back and forth in the mud until Dizzy left. Then he brought his motorcycle from behind the cellar and parked it in front of the cellar door. Rushed into the house, but he'd no sooner gotten in the house when he heard Charles' old cycle grinding its way up the south path. He ran outside and again hid behind the cellar until Charles left. Remember the pictures show two sets of tracks up and down behind the cellar. Whoever did this is heavier than the average, because the tracks sank much deeper into the wet soil than mine." Bonnie paused for a moment. "I'm positive this person, and I don't think it could have been a woman because the tracks are too large, besides that Donald weighed too much for a woman to carry him from the table. I feel this was someone that was angry at Donald and probably threw him in the rocker. Then he tied his arms and legs the same as Dizzy had. He grabbed the vase and hit Donald on the left side of his head so hard it killed him. He threw the vase on the rug where we found it.

"He then took his pocket knife and stole Donald's ring. Then he got out of sight before we arrived." She noticed Art's face was pale. He had his hands wrapped so tight together that they matched his face. "I'm sorry," she said and reached out to him.

He caught her hand and gave it a squeeze. "Please don't apologize. We must figure this mess out. I think you're on the right path, but where do we go from here?"

"You seem to be right on today, so stay with us," Mike said, with his eyes on her.

"We still have the rest of the week. One day during this time, I must go to the mountain. I feel we'll find the needed information among Donald's things," Bonnie said as she reached for the telephone.

"Is there anyone in this town who will go all to pieces and rave like a maniac if they hear or see anything they disagree with?" Bonnie asked, all this time eyeing Art.

"No one I can think of except Zeeta," Art said.

"Anybody who resented Donald's money, or felt he gave them a bad deal?"

Art swivelled his chair then sat in thoughtful silence for a moment. He dropped the morning paper in the rack and said, "There's no one I can think of at this time. If you could have known and seen the way the local people treated dad, he wasn't 'Mr. Wilms' or 'sir.' The kids called him Donald or Grandpa." And then with a sigh of exhaustion, "Let's have some dinner. We've been here all day."

Bonnie closed her case. *I'm so tired, I'd just as soon go to bed.* She heard Art's voice, sounding like something from a great distance. "What would you like to eat?" he asked, as he put her briefcase in the safe.

Bonnie smiled. "If I tell, you'll make fun of me."

"You know I won't. Whatever you'd like, Mike and I'll go along," he said.

"You ask for it. I'd enjoy a fat hamburger with a thick slice of onion and a large order of brown french fries and then an iced beer to go with it."

An hour later, Bonnie leaned back against the wall and watched Mike and Art finish their sandwich. "We uncovered very little today," she said.

"Maybe you think we had a bad day, but I think you're on the right track, and you must keep on," Mike said.

For the next three days, the three listened to tapes and talked with anybody who might have any thoughts on the killing. By now, Bonnie felt as if she had the necessary information or knew where to get it.

"Is the killer the fellow who hid behind the cellar?" Art asked.

"Yes, I'm positive he's the guy, but who is he?" Art shrugged his shoulders. Bonnie continued, "I have measured footprints by calculating the length of his steps and the depth of his tracks that sank into the mud along the garage and compared them with mine."

"Do you have those figures?" Mike asked.

"Yes, along with the papers he dropped behind the cellar. I'm certain he ate some breakfast while he waited for Dizzy to show."

"May I have those figures? Perhaps with luck, I can make something of it."

In the office, Bonnie laid a pile of worksheets on the desk. Some were single sheets, others had as much as a dozen sheets clipped together. It was one of these tall piles that she handed Mike.

"Excuse me," Mike said, as he took the stack of her worksheets, the pictures of all tracks she had taken, along with her magnifying glass, and departed. As he went through the door into the kitchen, he said, "Please do not disturb."

Bonnie and Art laughed. "Where would you like for us to start?"

"I know you saw many things while we were on the mountain that day on May 3rd. The most horrid thing for me was the coyotes howling. I've thought so many times that if Dad hadn't called when he did, we might have visited longer before we got out of the house and what could have happened." He covered his face with his hands and walked to the north window.

She picked up his cup of coffee and joined him. "Nothing happened. Count your blessings and let's get to work," she said.

About three hours later, Mike came in. "Do you know who these shoes belong to?" he asked and handed Bonnie the picture that she had taken of the funny printed soles.

"I think so," she said.

"If I had looked and listened sooner, I could have saved us a lot of work," Mike said.

The phone rang, as Art answered Bonnie and Mike listened. "Hello Grace…I won't have to ask them. We'll be there…About what time would your loving arms like to greet us?…See you then." Art laughed as he hung up the phone. "Grace wants us to have dinner with them. She said to be there early so we can talk, and we'll eat late. On Friday, late to her means around 6:00 p.m."

He paused briefly and then continued. "From the sound of Grace's voice, I believe she has something important to tell us."

Bonnie started to gather up her papers, but in a soft voice, Art said, "You go ahead, Mike and I will take care of these things."

"Thank you," Bonnie said, as she darted to her room to change into a red and white dress. Her only jewelry was a string of white pearls. She hurried to the kitchen where Art and Mike were waiting. As they left, the clock struck a somber four times.

Grace opened the kitchen door in welcome as Art drove into the alley and parked in front of the garage. The sun glistened on her beautiful long white hair, which she had combed high on her head. Her green and white checked dress and the old-fashioned white apron, starched till it could stand alone, was a lovely sight to see.

Clay must be proud to have such a pretty wife, Bonnie thought as she walked toward Clay sitting in his wheelchair in the dining room. He greeted her with a big smile and an outstretched hand.

"Hello Clay," Bonnie said, as she put her arm around his shoulders. "Gee, dinner smells good."

"She's cooking my favorite, roast beef and mashed potatoes."

"How's walking?" Bonnie asked.

"I'm doing all right. Yesterday I took about a dozen steps," Clay said. Then he changed the subject and waved toward Grace in the kitchen. "We're having a new range installed. It was either today, or we had to wait a month."

After dinner, they moved into the front room and chatted comfortably as only good friends can do. "How long have you folks lived in Windcove?"

Clay smiled as he answered Bonnie's question. "Since 1937. My dad ran a freight line. I attended school in the little white schoolhouse over on seventh." He pointed toward the south window.

Bonnie removed her recorder from her briefcase and set it on the table. "Do you mind if I tape our conversation?"

"Of course not," Clay said. "You know anything we can do to help, we will!"

"When did the Piles move here?" She wasn't sure why she asked that, but she felt she must know. From the puzzled expression on Art's face, Bonnie knew that he, too, wondered why she asked that question.

"Old Henry Pile was here before my folks. Henry worked in the mine for Sandy Loft, who owned what later became Wilms' Mountain. That was before Donald Wilms bought it."

Clay continued, obviously enjoying being in the limelight. "Henry Pile was a likeable fellow and a good worker. He worked for Loft, and then Donald until he became so sick with cancer. Henry died when Billy was around 17."

Billy was only 11 when his father had to quit work. "What was Billy like as a kid?" she asked.

"He was a hot head." Clay said. As he shifted in his wheelchair, he eyed Bonnie. "I heard a rumor years ago about how Sandy Loft promised Henry he could buy the mine and also the mountain when Sandy decided to sell them. After Henry died, we forgot about that. When Donald Wilms came here, Sandy sold the mountain, including all the mineral rights to him."

Bonnie noticed Art and Mike hadn't said a word for a while. *Have I taken over the conversation? Should I take a back seat and let them talk a bit?*

"You know, Clay, lately Billy Pile has been drinking more than he ever did. He always acted a little silly on Friday nights, but he never staggered around. Besides, he never wanted to fight until recently," Grace said.

"A week ago last Friday night, Billy was at our diner. He was swearing and demanding food. But I had cut my hand, and it was as if the sight of that blood turned him on. He asked how I did it, and then he told me about how so much blood had run on the rug from Donald's fractured arm," Clay said.

"It was a pitiful mess," Art said.

"Remember Art, we'll always be here if you need us." Grace hesitated then continued. "Until lately, Billy was always so polite and easy to wait on, even when he had too much to drink."

"I wonder what brought all this on?" Bonnie asked.

"I don't have a clue," Clay said.

"When did you notice such a change in Billy?" Mike asked.

Grace and Clay looked at each other momentarily and then Clay shook his head. Neither of them answered the question directly. "Trouble is, Billy may lose his job unless he changes his attitude."

Clay's eyes moved toward Art. "Donald and Billy got along good. I thought perhaps if you talked to Billy, maybe you could help him," Clay said.

The old clock in the dining room struck nine times. They had spent a pleasant several hours when they all said goodnight. Art, Bonnie and his Mike made their way to the car.

On the way, Bonnie asked, "Were the Wilders giving us a line about Billy? I noticed when they told us about Billy Pile drinking, being so hateful and hard to get along with, they frequently seemed to check each other out."

"I didn't see anything out of the ordinary," Mike said.

"In your business, do you look for clues all the time?" Art asked and turned his head toward her.

Bonnie noticed Art kept his eyes on her longer than she thought he should. She wiggled around in the seat and accidentally bumped him on purpose. Before she answered his question, she said, "Is that a dog on the highway ahead of us?"

Bonnie felt the car slow. "You're right," Art said.

"In answer to your question, I think we get in the habit of watching and analyzing people more than the average person does."

Bonnie awoke early Saturday morning. She thought about what Clay said about a conversation between Loft and Henry Pile years ago. *I got the impression Clay thinks Billy Pile feels he should own Wilms' mountain and the mine. If he is, that's one of the dumbest ideas that ever entered a human's brain.* She got a whiff of coffee. The whiff turned to reality when Art set a steaming cup in front of her. "Thank you," she said and looked into Art's kind blue eyes.

Before he seated himself, he said, "Clay asked me to talk with Billy. Truthfully, I don't know what I could say to a big, fat Irishman that would change his mind."

"Let's listen to Billy's tape the day he was at your house telling about what he heard at the Cross Roads Bar on Friday before the murders. The last thing I heard Billy say was that he hoped you folks find out who did this. "Well, good morning, I didn't hear you come in."

Mike nodded. "I heard you say 'that's the dumbest idea any human ever created.' What idea?" he asked.

"Does Clay think Billy feels he should own Wilms' mountain?" Art asked.

"That's what he said. At the time, I didn't think much about it, but later I've wondered," Mike said.

"If Billy believes such a silly idea, it will come out during the trial," she said.

Mike slowly rolled his chair against the end of the desk. "What gave you the idea or what did you see that convinced you Dizzy didn't kill Donald?" Mike asked.

"The coroner said the blow to the left side of Donald's head killed him. Dizzy is left-handed. His right hand and arm have never developed properly. I realized it when Dizzy had to use his left hand to get his right arm onto the witness stand," Bonnie said.

"His right hand and arm seemed okay to me," Art said.

"Did you fellows notice when I swung that vase at Dizzy?" Bonnie said.

Mike raised his voice when he said, "Notice! You damn near scared me to death."

Art quickly said, "I felt the same way."

"Well, it worked. Dizzy tried to catch the vase with his left hand. If his right hand had been normal, he'd have grabbed the vase with both hands."

"Are you convinced Dizzy hit Dad on the right side of his head, not the left?" Art asked.

Bonnie picked up her cup and had a small sip of coffee. "I was so sure we had our man. Dizzy beat Donald and killed the Ryan brothers. With his powerful strength, he pulled them over the bank with one hand. Honestly, I've wondered if Charles could have dragged those two men down that bank," she said and held up all the photos the police had taken. Art got his large magnifying glass out of the desk. The three studied each picture carefully.

"What's on your mind?" Mike asked.

"I think I know who killed Donald," Bonnie blurted out in one breath.

Art's mouth dropped open. His head fell forward with a questioning look on his face. "Whatever crossed your mind to make you say something like that? We all thought Dizzy killed Donald."

Bonnie hesitated and turned to Art. "I don't think he did. I think I have it." Bonnie lifted the receiver and pushed Bob Ingram's button.

Bob answered with a blunt, "Hello."

"Bob?" Bonnie asked.

"That was my name yesterday, but today I'm not sure," Bob said. "How can I help?"

"If I should need a search warrant tomorrow, will any judge in this town help us?"

"Judge Tillman has helped me in the past. He probably will. Let me call him."

"Are we ready for a warrant?" Mike asked.

"I hope we will be by noon tomorrow. We have so little time. I've considered every thought that's crossed my mind."

The phone rang. "If that's Bob, he got an answer fast."

Before she could say a word, Bob's voice sounded loud. "Judge Tillman will be home all day Sunday. He'll be glad to help us."

"Thanks. The minute I have enough information to need a warrant, I'll call."

Mike shoved away the papers that were on the desk. He rolled his white shirt sleeves above the elbows and rested his arms on the desk. "You've got an idea in that pretty head of yours. I wish you would take the floor and explain it."

"I think we'll find what's missing in the house on the mountain tomorrow."

"Let's drive to the River Inn and have some dinner. Maybe a few hours away from this steady grind will be good for us," Art said.

CHAPTER 22

"You're fresh and chipper this Sunday morning, and what a beautiful day," Art said.

"A perfect day to fly, but for me to expect to find an answer in that house is as far fetched as throwing a bottle in the ocean and expecting the right party in England to find it. We must search that house once more," Bonnie said. She had on a dark pantsuit and oxford's.

Mike strolled in. "Well, I see the big-city lawyer is ready for work."

"If we're going to the mountain, we better get moving. If you know who killed dad, why are we still on the prowl?" Art asked.

As Bonnie climbed in the car, she said, "I don't have the strap that cinches the saddle. It has to be in or around that house."

Art drove to the helicopter hanger. Soon, they flew over the river and up the mountain to the landing. They got out, and Bonnie walked toward the cellar. "Let's see if there are any visible tracks left in the dirt." There were, and they all noted a couple of tracks still very much in sight.

"I thought you were exaggerating when you told me how large these tracks were," Mike said.

"Nope. I don't even think Big Foot wears that large a shoe," she said on her way to Donald's house. Inside, Bonnie stooped and measured the footprints on the kitchen floor. "Those tracks are larger than I thought." She examined the kitchen chair where Dizzy broke Donald's right arm. In the front room, Bonnie noticed blood still remained on the hardwood floor and the edge of the rug where Donald fell. "They said he fell, but I think Dizzy kicked him. That was the reason he dragged his left leg like a club foot." She crossed the room to the large roll-top-desk.

Art whirled the big chair around so she could sit. "Might as well make yourself comfortable," he said.

She pulled open the left top drawer and removed Donald's checkbook. She noticed three checks per page with large stubs attached. Each stub carried a description of the amount and to whom Donald had written the check. "Your father kept a complete record of each check," she said.

"Yes, he did. If we want to take the time and go through the shoe boxes of checks in the closet, we can find the first checks Dad gave the men who worked in the mine."

"Do you mean the closet where Dizzy searched for money?"

Art nodded. "Great Scott," he shouted, "that's how someone started the rumor about shoe boxes full, and they assumed it was money."

"I'll bet you're right. Dizzy saw those boxes the day he ransacked your dad's bedroom," Bonnie said.

She turned more of the check stubs. "Donald cashed a $14,000 check every six months. Could this be blackmail?"

"Not that I know of. If someone was blackmailing him, I suppose I could receive a threat one of these days."

"Could be another reason. If Donald sent your grandmother money, and he paid somebody to forward her a certain amount each month, it would be easy money, if all they did was mail $2,000 a month to your grandmother and kept the balance. If we're right, whoever received the money neglected to notify Donald when she died."

"She died 10 years ago. Let's see, that would be $280,000 of easy money," Art said.

"I haven't seen anything here that benefits us." She moved across the room to the library table. All she found in the drawer was paper, stamps and envelopes. She stared at the rocker. *I've put this off as long as I can.* After she slipped on a pair of gloves, she glanced at Art.

"We have to," he said.

She nodded, slowly walked to the brown and tan velvet rocker and lifted the cushion.

"Please Bonnie, tell me what you want done," Art said, as he took the cushion from her.

"Please tip the chair, I'd like to know if there's anything under it," she said.

While Art had the rocker tipped up, Mike walked in.

"Find anything?" Art asked.

"Nothing we can use," Mike said. He stooped beside the chair Art was holding.

Bonnie noticed Mike squeeze the lining.

"Do you mind if I cut this cloth along the side?" Mike asked and raised questioning eyes to Art.

"Do what you want. Dad kept a pair of scissors in the kitchen drawer," Art said.

Mike returned and cut the lining of the rocker. He reached in and pulled out an unusually large pocket knife with the blade still open. "It has blood on it," he said.

While Art lowered the rocker, Bonnie held an evidence bag for Mike. "How did the forensic team miss that?" she asked.

"I have no idea," Mike said.

"Well, I convinced the jury we found Dizzy's gun. What will they think when I present this?" she asked.

"This is another one for Ripley," Mike said.

Art frowned as he replaced the cushion in the chair. "I guess the closet comes next."

Bonnie's steps were short and progressively slower. *How will I ever get past the boxes of checks Dizzy dragged out?* she thought. "Did he stomp on those boxes?" she asked.

"I think so. If we hadn't interrupted him, he probably would have opened every box with that big foot of his," Art said.

Art handed Bonnie a large box of pictures. She sat on the bed with her magnifying glass and examined every picture. Once in a while, she laid one aside. "Hm," Bonnie said. "I've set aside 20 pictures. Do you know any of these workers?"

"In those days, I didn't know any of the men. I was 10 when Dad showed me the mine. He built the tracks before Mother died."

"I have all I need. Shall we go?"

The three walked back outside. Art and Mike replaced the plywood over the kitchen door, and the three boarded the helicopter. On their way to town, Bonnie asked, "Is there a telephone at the hangar?"

"Sure, help yourself."

The minute the helicopter landed, Bonnie ran for the phone. "Hello Bob, am I too late?"

"No, tell Mike to meet me at the office," Bob said.

Art, Bonnie and Mike took the pickup to the garage where Bonnie and Art got out and Mike left for Bob's office.

"Shall we take the demonstrator or the motorcycle?"

"I'd like to go home and change before we go to The Diner," she said.

"Ah, come on. You'd look good no matter what you wear, and that outfit looks especially great," Art said and held out his hand to her.

In a few minutes, they were on the big white motorcycle headed to The Diner for dinner. The cool air felt good. It seems as if every car they met honked. "Do you know everyone around here?" she asked.

"Not exactly, but this is the only white motorcycle like this in the area."

After dinner, they returned to Art's house. "It surprised me," Bonnie said, "when Grace and Clay didn't know some of the men who worked at the mine."

"Usually, Grace can tell the name and what kind of work anybody does in this town. I don't think she remembers as well as she used to. I've noticed she makes more mistakes counting change."

"I wonder how Mike and Bob got along with Judge Tillman."

"I expected Mike to be here by this time," Art said.

"So did I. If things go right, tomorrow could be the last day of court," she said with a sigh.

"I'd hoped a stranger committed this murder and not someone Dad considered his friend."

"That will make a difference, especially in so small a town." She looked at Art's face and sad eyes. *I hadn't noticed how much weight he's lost. He's skin and bones.* She carefully packed her briefcase to make sure all of her notes were in order and set it out for morning.

The next morning, the grandfather clock in the hall struck six times as Art and Mike entered and waived the warrant at her. Mike greeted her with a smile. "We're all set."

"Since I have so little to go on, with two hours to fill before court adjourns, you better tie the gas pedal to the floor."

Mike smiled. "Goodbye and give him 'el.'"

Bonnie kept busy until it was time to leave for court. Art picked up the keys to the thunderbird. As he backed out of the driveway, she said, "I feel something is wrong, or I'm in for a shock." She walked briskly through the courtroom until she came to the swinging gate onto the courtroom floor. Here, Lyle Frulik overtook her. She noticed he looked so happy. His steps were shorter and faster than usual, as if he had a white velvet carpet under his feet. He appeared to be overflowing with energy.

The officer came in with Charles. His color reminded Bonnie of Swiss cheese and he sat on the edge of his chair digging at his fingernails.

The bailiff called out. "All rise. The Honorable Judge Rowland presiding."

Bonnie watched Charles, sadly. *How will I feel if I can't produce enough evidence to free this young man. He knows so little about real life. In many ways, he's only 14 or 15-years-old.*

The District Attorney stood and surprised all by asking, "May we approach the bench?"

As the judge waived them forward, Bonnie put her shoulders back and walked proudly to the bench. No way on earth would she appear anything other than confident and satisfied.

"Your honor, a new witness has come to my attention," said the district attorney.

"Your honor, the district attorney didn't notify me about a new witness. Besides, he's rested his case."

"Ordinarily, I'm against any surprise witnesses, but I'll allow it," Judge Rowland said.

On her way to her table, she cringed. *This morning I felt something wasn't right. For him to have a witness that will explain all that has happened in this case and perhaps solve it today is beyond reason.* As the jury took their seats, some slouched along, while others smiled and seemed happy to be there.

Judge Rowland said, "Mr. Frulik, call your witness."

Bonnie watched Lyle Frulik stand. As he turned to face the side door, he called out, "Mrs. Zeeta Cockran."

"What's going on?" Art whispered.

Bonnie looked around and shook her head. She pretended she was making notes. Her heart felt like it would explode. She reached for the ever ready glass of ice water.

Bonnie whispered to Charles. "Have you ever seen this woman?"

"I ain't never seen her before," he said.

She whispered, "Whatever happens, you keep your mouth shut," and gave Charles a pencil and pad.

Zeeta was sworn in. As she took the stand, Frulik grinned at Bonnie, as if he had the moon attached to his kite string. He stood in the middle of the floor. "Mrs. Cockran, how long have you lived in Windcove, Idaho?"

"Twenty months."

"When did you meet Mr. Charles Robbins?" Frulik asked.

Zeeta hesitated. From the expression on her face, Bonnie felt she was about to tell a lie.

"It was about 10-years-ago. He came to my hometown, which is Indenville, Georgia, quite often. He murders people for money," Zeeta said.

Bonnie turned to Charles. "You better tell me the truth. Use that pad and pencil as we go along," she whispered.

"Your honor, will the court instruct this witness to only answer my questions?" Frulik asked.

"Mrs. Cockran, you only answer the direct question, nothing more," the judge said.

"Okay," she said and frowned at Bonnie.

"Who came to your house wanting a hitman?"

"Mr. Art Wilms," she shouted. "He's right behind that city lawyer." She pointed her finger at Art.

"How much did Mr. Wilms tell you he'd pay?"

In a loud harsh tone of fury, she said, "$250,000."

Frulik stood in front of his table. "How long did Mr. Wilms stay at your house the evening he said he would pay for a hitman?"

"I'd say he stayed two or three hours," she said with a glow in her eyes.

"Did you have sex?"

"Yes, and I'm pregnant," she shouted.

"How far along are you?" Frulik asked.

"Dr. Crugar says I'm more than five months along."

"Has Mr. Wilms paid the $250,000?"

"No. I haven't seen a cent of the $250,000" Zeeta said and shouted, "I need it."

"That type of bill isn't collectable, so no one will get a cent," Frulik said.

"I know. That's why I threatened that big city lawyer. She told Art Wilms not to pay me," Zeeta said.

Bonnie came to her feet in a hurry. "Your honor, I object to these unfounded allegations."

"Mr. Frulik, do you have proof of Miss Cole's involvement?" the judge asked.

The district attorney had the grace to hesitate and duck his head. "This is the first time I've heard of it."

"Mrs. Cockran, we have your word only. How do you know Miss Cole is involved?" the judge asked.

Her voice had a hateful twang. "Art never paid me. She must have talked him out of it because she's sweet on him."

"Your h-o-n-o-r," Bonnie said and lingered on the last word.

The judge held up his hand. "Mrs. Cockran, unless you can offer some proof, I want no more snide remarks." He focused his eyes on the court reporter. "I order all remarks this witness has made about Miss Cole stricken from the record. Mr. Frulik, you may continue."

"Your honor, I have nothing further." He quietly placed himself behind his table and picked up his note pad.

"Miss Cole, in order for you to prepare your cross-examination, court will adjourn until 10:00 a.m. on Tuesday." Judge Rowland said.

"Thank you."

He nodded to Bonnie, closed the book in front of him, and departed.

Bonnie studied the eager-to-leave reporters. She wondered if the local papers could make this mess any worse. The crowd inched its way to the exit. Many grinned; some just nodded. She smiled as she waved to the crowd. Bonnie dropped her pen and pad in her briefcase and snapped the lock.

"Things aren't so bad," Art said softly and picked up her briefcase.

"By the time I get through with that witch, she'll wish someone had taped her mouth shut," Bonnie said in an angry voice.

Art grinned. "I've never seen you in a mood like this. Where do we start?"

"We start with Mike's report about her. Eventually, his trips out of town always pay. I'll bet Frulik will wish he had never put her on the stand."

In the hall, a reporter asked, "Miss Cole," as the other reporters charged at her from all sides, "are you in love with Mr. Wilms?"

"No!"

"Did you help Art Wilms arrange to kill his father?" one reporter asked.

"That's an insult. Who do you work for?" she asked.

Several more reporters shouted questions.

"Be in court tomorrow and you will get your answers," she said.

Art helped her through the crowd as the reporters shouted. Bonnie thanked Art. On their way out of the courthouse, John and Effie Weeks, the owners of Week's Grocery, met them and both were smiling broadly.

John Weeks, with a sound of bitter hatred in his voice, said, "Someone has to stop Zeeta or run her out of town. Bonnie, we're depending on you."

"Mrs. Cockran has caused more hard feelings than you can imagine. Not to mention the food she steals and destroys," Effie said.

"I understand. Come to court tomorrow, you may find it interesting."

"We'll be there. Know we're right behind you," John Weeks said.

"It's wonderful to have the support of friends like that," Bonnie said and smiled as they left.

Bonnie got in the pickup beside Mike and Art climbed in along side of Bonnie. Art's blue eyes blazed with anger and he hit the dash with his fist. "That Zeeta." Bonnie interrupted. "Don't say a word, Art. We know you didn't do it. We've dealt with her kind in the past. Before we go to the house, I must talk to Charles."

Mike parked the truck in the lot, and they hurried inside. As Bonnie, Art and Mike waited in line to speak to the officer at the city jail, Julie Foster stopped.

"Bonnie Cole, what are you doing here?"

"I must see Charles Robbins." She looked at Art. "Mike and I better talk to Charles alone."

"I'll wait here by the door."

"Come this way. I can help you," Julie Foster said, as they hurried down the hall. "On Tuesday morning, I think you better hold court in the main street of the town. Everyone will want to be there."

"I hope not," Bonnie said and smiled.

"Wait in here," Julie said. "The officer will bring Robbins."

"Thanks. Will you be in court tomorrow?" Bonnie asked.

"Yes, I'm looking forward to it," she said.

"I'll do the talking. One way or another, I've got to get this fellow to answer my questions," Bonnie said.

After the officer left, Charles started talking before he sat. "I ain't never been so scared in my life."

"Charles, I begged you to tell me everything in the beginning. You were so sure of yourself and look at the trouble we're in now. I'll ask you again. Have you ever seen Zeeta Cockran before today?"

"I ain't never seen her."

"Have you ever been in Georgia?"

"I ain't never seen the Mississippi River," Charles said. He paused temporarily. "I sat in the dirty Phoenix jail for 60-days, cause I got sick and threw up on a cop."

Bonnie noticed Mike leave. "Do you remember the date you were in jail?" she asked.

"I'd been in Phoenix about a month when I got arrested the first of March."

"You were in jail March and April?"

"Got out April 26th."

"When did you arrive in Windcove?"

"Friday evening, before someone killed Donald Wilms."

"Where did you sleep Friday night?"

"The fat man took me to his house on wheels. He only had a little bed, so I slept on the floor," he said.

"How long did you stay with him?"

At first, Charles avoided her question. Then he said, "He paid me a dollar to scrub up his house. I ain't done much scrubbin. He didn't like the job and booted me out."

"What about Saturday."

"I stole a can of beans and slept in the park," he said.

"Did you talk with anyone about Mr. Wilms or the old man on the mountain?"

"Nope."

"Good, I'll see you tomorrow."

She thanked the officers and got in Art's truck. "I've half a day to find the answers. Let's have some lunch. I haven't had a bite since last evening."

After lunch, Mike said, "I suggest we go home, lock the kitchen door so no one can disturb us and get to work."

"Good idea. Thank goodness you made a trip to Zeeta's hometown," Bonnie said. After hours of work, she looked at the clock and realized it was after 2:00 a.m. "We have enough information to make that woman wish she had never heard of Windcove." She yawned as she packed everything ready for court.

Bonnie blinked several time. The face on the little alarm clock showed 6:00 a.m. She lowered the two large windows and pulled the shades. While she showered and dressed, her thoughts were on Zeeta Cockran. *I hope I make a better impression than Lyle Frulik did Monday. That woman needs a lesson in honesty and humility.*

In the hall, Bonnie smelled what she calls the staff of life. Someone had beat her to the kitchen. She pushed the swinging door quietly and Art jumped when Bonnie picked up a cup and saucer off the tray. "Please let me," he said, as he held the coffee pot.

"Thank you." She noticed dark circles under his eyes.

"A man could kill a woman for embarrassing him like Zeeta did me," he said angrily.

"What! Art Wilms, don't ever say anything like that again. What if something happened to her last night?"

"You're right. I've always tried to show utmost respect for women. It's hard to show her any respect." He stopped, and his eyes lingered on Bonnie.

"I have put off asking this question as long as I can."

He gave a slight nod along with half a smile. "I know what your question is. Have I ever touched that woman sexually?"

"I must have the truth."

He faced Bonnie, his eyes met hers. "No way, I've never so much as kissed her on the lips."

"I'm glad. Don't let what I might say or do in court today surprise you."

Mike ran in. "We better go."

The three drove to the courthouse. The courtroom already had standing room only. Bonnie had the very irreverent thought that if one fell over, the rest would all drop like dominos! At 10:00 a.m. the officer had Charles in court. Judge Rowland hurried to the bench, looking nervous and obviously wanting to get the show on the road.

"Miss Cole, do you wish Mrs. Cockran returned to the stand?"

"Yes, but her real name is Mrs. Leta Corkie, alias Mrs. Zeeta Cockran."

Lyle Frulik's feet hit the floor. "Your honor, I object. Mrs. Cockran's name has nothing to do with this case."

"Miss Cole, can you substantiate your remark?" the judge asked.

"I can, your honor."

"Very well. Proceed," the judge said.

An officer brought Zeeta to the stand.

"Mrs. Cockran, you're still under oath," the judge said.

"Good morning, Mrs. Zeeta Cockran or is it Mrs. Leta Corkie?" Bonnie asked.

"Your honor, I object to this kind of cross-examination," Frulik said.

Judge Rowland looked at Bonnie. "Your honor, you asked if I could substantiate my first remark."

"I did. Proceed," the judge said.

Bonnie noticed an almost-hidden smile on his face and a twinkle in his eye. Frulik seated himself and pulled the table closer.

"Mrs. Cockran, when did you remarry? After you and Mr. Albert Corkie divorced?" she asked.

"I'm using the name Cockran to hide from my ex," she said.

"Are you referring to Mr. Albert Corkie?" Bonnie asked.

"Yes, I am," she said angrily.

"Why, he's happily married. I understand he and his wife are expecting their first baby next month."

Bonnie's quick steps were light as she approached the jury, and she placed her right arm on the railing. "You assumed the name of Cockran when you moved to Windcove. You used the name of Ryanberg in Atlantic City, and also the name of Ryerson at the gambling tables. Would you like me to go on?" Bonnie asked and glanced at the jury.

"Your honor, I believe our new attorney is having a reverie," Frulik said.

"Will counsel approach to bench?" the judge asked.

Bonnie softly stepped in front of the bench.

"I've never heard such carrying on in a courtroom in my life," Frulik said.

The judge grinned. "You're pouring it on a little strong, Miss Cole. Can you prove this?" Judge Rowland asked.

"Your honor, this information came from her folks. I can bring them on to testify if the court wishes?"

"That won't be necessary," the judge said.

"Your honor, this woman owes one bookie $200,000. That's why he's looking for her, and also the reason she's hiding in Windcove under the name of Cockran."

"Mr. Frulik, did you know about this?" the judge asked.

"No. I didn't," Frulik said sheepishly.

"I see! Miss Cole, let's move on," the judge said.

"I'll be glad to," she said and returned to the courtroom floor.

"Mrs. Cockran, what date and time of day did Mr. Wilms get to your house and asked you to find him a hitman?" Bonnie asked.

"That was the 25th of April," Zeeta said.

"Are you sure? Could it have been a day or two before or after?"

"I'm positive. I marked it on my calendar," Zeeta said and pointed her finger at Bonnie.

Bonnie glanced at the judge then Frulik. "This is unusual." She paused a second. "This is really odd, because Art Wilms, Donald Wilms, Jim Rams and Rick Iverson were in Detroit for the Ford celebration. The four men spent five days there and returned April 27th," Bonnie said.

"Maybe I made a mistake," Zeeta said.

"Yes, I think you did. You know as well as I do that Art Wilms never came to your house," Bonnie said.

Zeeta began to stir in her chair. She glanced at the judge, then Lyle Frulik.

"Answer the question," Judge Rowland said.

"I'm pregnant and it has to be..."

That was as far as Zeeta got when a gray-haired man in the crowd jumped up and yelled, "That's my baby. She was living with me at that time."

The judge rapped the gavel. "Sit down or I'll have you ejected from the court room."

"But, your honor," he shouted.

"Sit or I'll find you in contempt of court," the judge ordered. "Miss Cole, get on with it."

"Mrs. Cockran, how long have you known Charles Robbins?" Bonnie asked.

"I met Charles Robbins about 10 years ago in my hometown. He used to spend a lot of time there," Zeeta said.

Bonnie glanced at Charles. His mouth was open. *I hope he doesn't make a fool of himself. I told him to be quiet.*

"Are you sure it was 10 years ago?"

"Asked and answered," Frulik said.

"Sustained," the judge said.

"Ten years ago, was Charles Robbins earning money as a hitman?" Bonnie asked.

"Oh yes, he asked me to let him know if I ever heard of anyone who needed an eliminator."

"I see," Bonnie said, as she stalled.

"Your honor, how long are we going to let Miss Cole take to make up her mind if she has seen enough?" Frulik asked.

"Please move it along," the judge said.

"Sorry, your honor." She whirled back facing the witness. "Mrs. Cockran, just how old do you think Mr. Robbins is?"

"He's over 35-years-old," she said.

"According to his California drivers license, dated last March, Mr. Robbins is 24-years-old. This means he was 14-years-old when Mrs. Cockran insisted he told her he was a hitman," Bonnie said in a strong voice.

"What?" Frulik shouted.

Bonnie hastened to her table. "I have a copy of his driver's license here." She handed the copy to the judge.

"I'd like to have this entered as defense exhibit number seven," Bonnie said.

"So ordered," the judge said.

"Your honor, I submit every word of testimony this witness has given this court is a lie," Bonnie said.

"I'm inclined to agree. Mr. Frulik, I want this woman held for investigation on possible charges of perjury," the judge said. "It's now 11:45 a.m. Court will adjourn until 2:00 p.m." He stood. Before closing the door behind him, he glanced at the courtroom.

Bonnie and Art could hardly wait to share their morning with Mike. "Judge Rowland held her on possible perjury charges. Honestly, I felt sorry for Lyle Frulik; he had such good intentions and she made him look like a fool," Bonnie said.

"You would have enjoyed court this morning. Bonnie made Zeeta look like an idiot," Art said.

CHAPTER 23

When they returned after lunch, Bonnie scrutinized the old oak furniture in the courtroom. Each piece showed marks of wear and abuse. She listened to the crowd as it gathered. Some were discussing Zeeta's testimony. The reporters were milling around. Apparently each one believed his competition had somehow gotten a better seat.

The officer brought Charles in just before the bailiff called out, "All rise. The Honorable Judge Rowland presiding." After the judge had seated himself, the bailiff said, "You may be seated."

She noticed before the judge spoke that he watched her for a moment. He lowered his head slightly, before he said, "Miss Cole, call your next witness."

Bonnie stood, glanced over the courtroom. "I call Billy Pile," she said.

No one came forward.

"Mr. Pile, will you take the stand," the judge said in a louder voice. Still, no Billy. "Did anyone serve Mr. Pile with a subpoena?"

"I did," Bob said. He started to leave when Bonnie heard him say, "Mr. Pile just entered the room."

As Billy Pile came through the swinging gate, Bonnie got a strong smell of whiskey. *I hope he hasn't over indulged to cause the judge to postpone court until tomorrow.*

"You may take the stand." As Billy sauntered across the floor, the judge said, "You're still under oath."

Bonnie noticed every hair in place. His large Irish face was cranberry red and his eyes tried hard to match the color. Billy's 300 pounds of blubber made the witness chair moan. She glanced at her notes one last time and stepped forward. "Good afternoon, Mr. Pile," she said.

Billy nodded.

"Mr. Pile, you have to answer, so the court reporter can make a record," the judge said.

"Okay," Billy said.

"Mr. Pile, when did you meet Mr. Wilms the first time?" she asked.

"I was 12-years-old," he replied.

"How long did your father work for Mr. Wilms in the mine?"

"Only six months. My father had to quit because he got sick," Billy said.

"How old were you when your mother moved to Boise?"

"I was 13 in my last year of grade school," Billy said.

"After a couple of years in Boise, your folks had spent their savings. From then on, how did your mother manage?"

"Dad's illness cost a lot. We received help from Mr. Wilms," Billy said.

"Who paid your father's funeral expenses?"

"Mr. Wilms."

"Mr. Wilms didn't stop with the Boise expenses, did he?" Bonnie asked. She quickly stepped in front of the jury and faced Billy.

"No, he paid off the mortgage on the farm and paid our living costs until Mother got a job," Billy said.

"At which time your mother thanked Mr. Donald Wilms for past favors. Isn't that true?"

"Yes, if anybody needed help, we did," Billy said.

"Why didn't you get a job like so many other young men your age?" she asked.

"I tried, but no one would hire me."

"Billy, do you really know why Mr. Wilms helped your family?"

"He helped a lot of people in Windcove," Billy said.

"Yes he did. When Mr. Donald Wilms had a serious accident in the mine, your Uncle Aaron saved his life. Three years later, Aaron died very suddenly. He left his family well-to-do. To show his appreciation for Aaron's kindness, Mr. Wilms decided to help Henry's family," Bonnie said.

"I've never heard that before. Donald Wilms owed us because he took the mine away from us," Billy shouted.

"Are you telling this court that Donald stole the mine from your father?"

"That's right."

"Sorry, Mr. Pile. Mr. Donald Wilms saw an ad offering a mine for sale in the Phoenix News. If the mine belonged to your father, how could Mr. Loft sell it?" she asked, then moved closer to the witness stand.

"Mr. Loft promised my dad if and when he sold the mine, Dad could have first chance at it," he said.

"Did he put that in writing?"

"Not that I know of."

"Unless your father had something in writing, he had no claim on the mine," Bonnie said.

"Miss Cole, you're as dumb as my mother. I couldn't make her understand that we should own that mine," Billy said.

"Mr. Pile, no more smart remarks," the judge said.

For a moment, Bonnie felt sorry for Billy. *He's spent his entire life grieving over an idea. It's so imbedded in his mind, no one could convince him otherwise.*

"Miss Cole, let's get on with it," the judge said.

"Yes, your honor," Bonnie said, as she studied the man in the witness chair. "Do you own a white motorcycle?"

"Your honor, what does Mr. Pile's motorcycle have to do with this case?" Frulik asked.

Before the judge could answer, Bonnie said, "Your honor, this has more to do with this case than appears on the surface."

"Very well, answer the question," the judge said.

"I do own an old white motorcycle," Billy said and moved nervously in his chair.

"Mr. Pile, I contend that after you listened to the conversation at the Cross Roads Bar that Friday evening, you were positive Dizzy Welch would go to the mountain Sunday morning."

"He did and killed Donald Wilms," Billy said.

Bonnie disregarded Billy. "Mr. Pile, early Sunday morning, you hid your white motorcycle behind the cellar. You waited and watched for Mr. Welch to show. You heard the shots on the east path. Then you saw Mr. Welch push his motorcycle across the lawn. You heard him kick the backdoor in. After Snapper barked and you heard the shot, wasn't it horrible to stand behind the cellar and wonder what had happened?" Bonnie asked.

"No, because I wasn't there," Billy said.

"Your honor, she's accusing this man of a crime he knows nothing about," Frulik said.

"Miss Cole, can you prove this?" Judge Rowland asked.

While Bonnie returned to her table, Frulik stood ready to blast her again with objections.

"Your honor, I believe this picture will answer your question," Bonnie said. She handed the judge a snapshot. "Mr. Pile ate a sandwich, a hard-boiled egg, and drank a cup of coffee, while he waited for Dizzy Welch."

"Continue," the judge said.

Frulik shook his head, stampeded to his desk, and muttered. "Someone could have dropped that sandwich wrapper and styrofoam cup a week ago."

Bonnie returned to her table, got a small plastic bag, and took it to the bench. Frulik ran to the bench a second time. Bonnie felt it took Frulik an hour to figure out what to say.

"Your honor, this is the most far-fetched, ridiculous testimony I've ever heard," Frulik said.

The judge glanced at Bonnie. "Can you substantiate this?" he asked.

"Yes, it rained on the mountain Saturday night before the murders. These papers show no sign of being out in the rain," Bonnie said.

"That doesn't prove a thing, your honor," Frulik said.

Bonnie grinned. "It does, your honor, when Billy Pile's fingerprints are on them."

"Do you wish to enter these as evidence?" the judge asked.

"Please," Bonnie said.

"So ordered," the judge said.

Bonnie switched her attention to Billy. "Mr. Pile, did it surprise you when a man who resembled Mr. Donald Wilms rushed out of the house and ran into the timber?"

Billy answered without thinking. "I almost fainted." He paused, raised his left hand, and scratched his head. "Really, Miss Cole, I've no idea what you're talking about?"

"You will in a minute. Mr. Welch rushed out of the house with blood on his white clothes, jumped on his motorcycle, and raced down the south path. You rolled your motorcycle from behind the cellar and parked it in front of the cellar door. I have pictures of your tracks in the mud along the side and behind the cellar, along with the tire tracks," Bonnie said.

"I did nothing of the kind," Billy said.

"Then you ran into the house."

"Miss Cole, can you prove your statement?" the judge asked.

"I can." Her steps were light but fast. She gave the judge three enlarged snapshots of Billy's tracks along the cellar.

Again Frulik's wooden heels reminded Bonnie of a shod horse running on pavement as he approached the bench. "Your honor, how long do we have to put up with such nonsense?" he asked.

"I can prove this, your honor."

"Proceed," Judge Rowland said.

"Mr. Pile, in the front room you found Donald Wilms tied in a rocker, his teeth in his lap, and blood running out of his mouth. Donald asked you for help. What did you do?" she asked. *Since I have this figured out, it's easy to ask questions*, she thought.

Billy's bloodshot eyes glared at Bonnie.

"Answer the question, remember you're under oath," the judge said.

Billy looked at the judge. "Your honor, honestly, I have no idea what this woman is talking about."

"Oh, yes you do. Before you had time to attack Mr. Donald Wilms, you heard a motorcycle on the path to the house. You ran outside and again hid behind the cellar," Bonnie said.

"I didn't, Miss Cole, I swear I didn't."

"To your surprise, Charles Robbins appeared on the scene. He spent about 30 minutes in the house. After he left, you returned to the house," Bonnie said. She looked at Billy. His once red face was a grayish white, and his eyes had a frightened look.

"Mr. Pile, are you all right?" the judge asked.

"I'd like a glass of water," Billy said.

The bailiff handed Billy a glass of ice water. She glanced at the jury to see their reactions. They were sitting rigidly in their seats. Some had their eyes on her while others watched Billy.

"Proceed," the judge said.

"Mr. Pile, as soon as Mr. Robbins left, you returned to the house. You heard Donald Wilms talking on the telephone. When he said, 'Hurry son, please hurry. I'm hurting.' I submit you slammed the receiver."

Billy asked for another glass of water. He gulped it down, looked at the judge, then the floor.

"Answer the question," the judge said.

"She's blaming me for what Dizzy did," Billy said.

"Mr. Pile, you know that's a lie. You lifted Donald Wilms off the chair by the phone. For revenge, you threw him into the rocking chair, tied his arms and legs exactly like Mr. Welch had," Bonnie said.

"I never, so help me, I never," Billy said.

Bonnie moved quietly to her table and got a large grocery bag. "I'd like to enter these shoes into evidence, number nine." She pulled the largest pair of shoes most of the audience had ever seen, out of the bag. "Will the court please disregard the horse and cow manure?" Bonnie asked as she set the shoes on the judge's bench. It didn't surprise her when the judge pushed as far back in his chair as he could.

"What do you want to do with these?" the judge asked, wrinkling up his nose.

"I'd like for Mr. Pile to put them on," Bonnie said.

The judge motioned for the bailiff to enter the shoes as evidence.

"Mr. Pile, will you remove your shoes and slip these on?" she said.

"Lady, if you keep on, I'll have to undress for this court," Billy bellowed.

Several snickers came from the crowd. The judge tapped the gavel. "Silence in the courtroom," he said. Then he turned to the witness. "Mr. Pile, I've had enough of your remarks. Remove your shoes."

"Mr. Pile, please slip these on," Bonnie said, as she held out the exhibit.

"Your honor, do I have to wear someone's old shoes?" Billy asked.

"Put on the shoes," the judge said with a stern tone.

"Those are too small for me," Billy said.

"They will fit because the sheriff found those shoes in your closet yesterday morning," Bonnie said.

After Billy put on the shoes, Bonnie said, "Please step onto the courtroom floor so we can see how they fit."

"You had no right to go through my house," Billy said.

"Everything we've done is legal. We had a search warrant," Bonnie said.

She turned and faced Judge Rowland. "Your honor, please notice the soles on these shoes," she said and pointed at Billy's feet.

The two2 officers holding Billy returned him to the witness stand.

"Would you please give me Billy's right shoe?" Bonnie asked one of the officers. "Your honor, please note the sole in exhibit number eight." She handed the picture to the judge.

"They look alike," the judge said.

"This picture, Your honor, shows blood spots on the kitchen floor leading to the outside door of Donald Wilms' home," Bonnie said.

"Proceed," the judge said.

"Mr. Pile, how did Mr. Wilms' blood get on your glove?" Bonnie asked.

Billy leaned back in his chair. Quickly, he said, "Oh, that's right, I did go to the mountain Saturday afternoon before the murder. Mr. Wilms' hand that he had cut earlier in the day started bleeding again. I helped him wrap it."

While Bonnie asked Billy the last question, she moved toward her desk. She picked up another plastic bag and returned to the bench. She removed the pocket knife from the bag, showed it to the judge, and said, "Your honor, the defense would like to enter this knife into evidence."

The district attorney rushed up to Bonnie. She handed him the knife.

"Objection. No foundation," Frulik said. He handed the knife to Bonnie. She heard Frulik when he whispered something under his breath on the way to his table.

"I can bring in the man who engraved the knife," Bonnie said.

Bonnie noticed Frulik as he started to rise. She looked at the judge, who was holding up his hand. "The bailiff will enter the knife," Judge Rowland said.

The bailiff gave Bonnie the knife. In front of the witness, she held up the knife. "Mr. Pile, do you recognize this pocket knife?"

she asked.

"No!" Billy snapped.

Bonnie thought he was shaking worse than before, and by now, Billy's face reminded her of cold lard.

"Please read the initials on the knife," Bonnie said.

"B.P.," Billy whispered again staring at the floor.

"Louder, Mr. Pile so the court can hear you," the judge said.

"B.P.," Billy screamed. "Are you satisfied?"

"B.P. stands for Billy Pile. After you killed Mr. Wilms, you wanted his valuable ring so much you used this knife to cut off his little finger and part of his left-hand. The ring that Mrs. Wilms gave Mr. Wilms just before she died."

In a sharp disgusted tone, Billy said, "That's sick, sick, sick. I couldn't do such a thing. Your client stole his jewelry. That sounds like something he would do."

"Then how did your knife with Mr. Wilms' blood and flesh on the blade get in the rocking chair at the murder scene?" Bonnie asked.

"Either someone stole that knife, or I lost it over a month before the murder. Miss Cole, I took an oath today to tell the truth. That's what happened, and so help me I can't remember. But that's the truth," Billy said and held up his right hand.

Bonnie heard a loud cough. As she turned, she saw Mike when he turned his head slightly and raised his chin. "May I have a moment, your honor?" Bonnie asked.

"One only," the judge said.

She walked over to her table and slowly leaned forward. "Ask for a recess," Mike whispered.

"Why?"

"Just do it. Trust me."

Bonnie turned to the judge. She knew from the tone of Mike's voice that it was a must. "It's almost 3:00 p.m. I'd like to recess until tomorrow," she said.

The judge glanced at his watch. "It's a little early, but court will adjourn until 10:00 a.m. on Wednesday." He hurried out of the room.

Bonnie turned to Mike. "Why did I do that?" she asked.

"Art knows where he saw the knife."

Bonnie got her briefcase. Out in the parking lot, she slid across the car seat next to Art, and Mike joined them. After Art explained how and where he saw that knife, Bonnie knew she must reorganize her defense.

"Will we search and subpoena everyone in the town before we settle this case?" she asked.

"I know, you hate to do this, but remember Art and I will be with you," Mike said.

"Hate to do this. If I don't break down in the courtroom and go to bawling, it'll surprise me." She shook her head.

CHAPTER 24

Wednesday morning, Bonnie dropped onto her chair and dreaded for court to begin. *How can I ever do this? How, oh how, can I do this?*

The officer came in with Charles, and the bailiff said, "All rise."

The judge took the bench. Bonnie noticed him watching her. "Miss Cole, are you all right?"

"Yes, your honor. Before you recall Mr. Pile, I'd like to call another witness."

"I object," Frulik said. "She has called one witness after another. How long will this go on?"

"Miss Cole, you wish to call a new witness, for what reason?" the judge asked.

"New evidence, your honor. THIS IS IMPERATIVE," Bonnie said with a pleading tone in her voice.

The judge paused, shrugged his shoulders and stared at her for a moment. "Call your witness."

Bonnie returned to her table and hesitated for a second to gather her self-control. She smiled at the judge. "Thank you," she said softly, turned and looked into the crowd. "I call Mr. Clay Wilder." She heard a lot of murmuring and whispering and could feel the number of eyes glaring at her.

"Objection, Mr. Wilder isn't on the defense list. Besides, we've wasted so much time on this case already," Frulik said.

"Mr. Frulik, I let you throw in a ringer, it's Miss Cole's turn. Mr. Wilder, take the stand," Judge Rowland said.

With a smile on his face, Clay Wilder rolled onto the court floor in a wheelchair. *I don't think he has any idea why I have called him.* Then the thought hit her. *He probably thinks I'm going to ask questions about Billy.* The bailiff swore Clay in and then pushed his chair so it sat in front of the witness stand.

"Proceed, Miss Cole," the judge said.

She slowly got to her feet and picked up the pad she had scribbled some notes on. Ready to face the judge and Clay Wilder, "Mr. Wilder, when did you first meet Donald and Mrs. Wilms?"

"A long time ago. I was delivering groceries for Week's grocery, and Grace worked at the Silver Inn. Mr. and Mrs. Wilms ate there quite often," he said.

Quickly, she added. "How long have you and Mrs. Wilder been married?"

"Over 52 years." His eyes roamed over the room until he saw his wife, and he smiled at her.

I hate to do this. They're such a lovely couple. She's going to be hurt so terribly! "How and when did you have your accident?" Bonnie asked.

"It was more than 40 years ago. Cook's Hardware sign fell on me and I was in the hospital for two months," he said.

"After you were able to get around, I understand Mr. Donald Wilms gave you and Mrs. Wilder The Diner?" Bonnie said. At that moment, she saw Clay flinch. She knew from his face that she had touched a sore spot.

"Yes. You see, Grace and I took care of Mrs. Wilms before she died. Later, we looked out for Art while Donald was at the mine. He said The Diner was a token of his appreciation for us taking such good care of his wife and Art."

"Your honor, this is most interesting, but what's the point?" Frulik asked.

"I'm wondering the same thing," the judge said.

"If the court will bear with me a little longer, I'll prove the point," Bonnie said.

"Very well, proceed," the judge said.

Bonnie focused her attention on Clay. "That was a kind thing for Mr. Wilms to do. I hear Mr. Wilms did many things for the people of Windcove?"

"Yes, he did," Clay said.

The hallway door swung open. Bonnie saw Mike and Bob Ingram, and the grin on Mike's face told her what she wanted to know.

"Your honor, may I have a moment?" Bonnie asked.

"Make it snappy," the judge said.

"Thank you."

As Mike touched the gate onto the courtroom floor, he handed Bonnie a plastic bag. Mike whispered, "We found it in his workshop."

Bonnie turned to the witness. "Mr. Wilder, you said you married 52 years ago?" she asked.

"Your honor, we're in the same old rut," Frulik complained.

The judge raised his voice. "Move on, Miss Cole."

"Yes sir. Mr. Wilder were you ever jealous of your wife?" Bonnie asked.

"I'll admit I was before we married, but I got over it."

Clay had hardly stopped talking when Bonnie asked, "How about Mr. Donald Wilms. Were you ever jealous of him?"

Clay glared at her with an angry glint in his eyes, which she didn't like to see. "Of course not, he was happily married."

"Mr. Wilms' wife died about the same time you got hurt. Many things changed after the accident." She noticed Clay's hands also had changed, and he was gripping them so tightly that his fist had turned white. *He didn't expect these questions, but that certainly doesn't make this any easier.* "Recently, your wife had a bad bruise on her right arm. How did that happen?" Bonnie asked and looked at Grace. Her eyes were red, and she was holding a handkerchief in her right hand. *Dear God,* Bonnie thought. *Grace has been covering all this time. She has known Clay is mad, and she has stayed with him. Could she love him that much?*

"Grace came through the swing-doors at the restaurant. One of our waitresses ran into her," he said.

"That's not the story Mr. Williams, one of your customer at The Diner, told," Bonnie said. Clay disregarded her, so she continued. "Mr. Williams told a joke to your wife. You squeezed her right arm so hard she cried out. In a rude way, you told her the cook needed her in the kitchen."

"All couples have troubles from time to time," Clay said.

Bonnie noticed his fists would relax then he'd grip them tighter than before. "After the accident, you weren't the same and that old jealousy began to grow again," she said.

Clay frowned and he looked away.

"Did you ever see your wife joking with Mr. Donald Wilms?" Bonnie asked.

"Yeah, but I never thought a thing about it," Clay said.

"Isn't it true you ordered Mr. Donald Wilms out of the restaurant because you thought he'd made a pass at her?"

"No!" Clay said, loud and hateful.

"Let's ask Mrs. Wilder," Bonnie said and turned toward the crowd.

"I did, but I had a bad day," Clay said.

"Mr. Wilder, it seems to me you've had a lot of bad days lately. You're jealous of every man who looks at your wife especially Donald Wilms," Bonnie said in a forceful voice.

"I saw him kiss her the week before he died," Clay shouted.

"You jumped out of that wheelchair and yelled that you would kill him if he ever did that again," Bonnie said. When Clay took hold of the arm of the wheelchair, Bonnie saw the large rolls of muscles in his arms. The way he grabbed the arms on the wheelchair scared her. "The truth is that you can walk better than I can."

"Your honor, she's badgering her own witness," Frulik said.

"Sustained," the judge said.

"Mr. Wilder, I submit Billy Pile told you about the conversation at the Cross Roads Bar the Friday night before Mr. Wilms died. You gave a flimsy excuse why you couldn't be at the restaurant on Sunday, the day someone killed Mr. Wilms. You were in a jealous rage, hiked up the west side of the mountain, and confronted Mr. Wilms," Bonnie said.

"That's a lie, how could I hike up that mountain?" he asked.

"When you saw Mr. Wilms tied in that chair, you got the vase off the table and smashed the left side of his head in," Bonnie said in a loud voice.

"Your honor, where's the proof?" Frulik shouted.

"It's right here," Bonnie said, on her way to get the plastic bag that Mike had given her earlier. She handed the bag to Judge Rowland. "Your honor, this is the ring Mr. Wilms wore for more than 40 years, and no one ever saw him without it.

"Mr. Mike Dailey and Sheriff Ingram found this ring in Clay Wilder's workshop in his home this morning. Tests prove it has Mr. Wilms' blood on it. I'd like to enter this ring as defense exhibit next in order," Bonnie said.

Judge Rowland stared at Bonnie. "Well I'll be. The bailiff will enter the ring. Please continue."

She whirled around with the plastic bag in her left hand and faced Clay Wilder. "You planned to use Billy Piles' pocket knife, which you have kept in your house since the day Billy Pile made willow whistles for the kids at the restaurant. You hoped to send Billy Pile to prison for the murder of Donald Wilms. You cut off Donald Wilms' little finger and part of his left hand to get this ring." She held up the plastic bag.

"Donald Wilms had been having an affair with my wife for years. They denied it, but I knew what was going on. I decided to put a stop to it." Clay hit the arm of his wheelchair. "On our 53rd anniversary, I intend to throw that ring in her face," Clay shouted and shook his fist at Bonnie.

"Oh! Mr. Wilder, you're so wrong, oh so wrong," Bonnie said. She knew she had to get control of her emotions. "Mr. Wilms couldn't have an affair with your wife. Forty some years ago, Donald Wilms had an accident in the mine and lost his manhood."

"You're a liar," Clay shouted.

"Ask his doctor," Bonnie said.

"He's a liar too," Clay screamed. He leaped out of his wheelchair and ran across the floor. He grabbed the bag and drew his right-hand back intending to hit Bonnie in the face. As Clay's hand came at her, she grabbed his arm, gave it a quick twist, and tossed him onto the courtroom floor. Clay landed hard on his back and howled like a cornered pup. *It was five years ago that I took all those Kung Fu classes. I've always wondered if I could do that if I had to!* Several officers as well as Bob and Mike ran to help Bonnie. Judge Rowland stood, leaned over the bench, and stared at Clay. At the same time, Grace screamed and ran from the courtroom.

"I can't believe it," the judge said.

Art escorted Bonnie to her table. "Are you all right?" he whispered.

"Yes, I'm fine."

The rest seemed almost routine. The sheriff handcuffed Clay and got him to his feet.

"I order Mr. Wilder held for further investigation," the judge said.

Bonnie watched as the sheriff and the bailiff took the now weeping Clay from the room. The door closed quietly behind them. She stepped quietly to the bench and placed the bag containing the gold ring on the evidence table. "Your honor, in view of these developments, I request the dismissal of all charges against my client, Charles Robbins," Bonnie said.

"I agree," Frulik said.

"All charges are dismissed. The defendant is free to go," Judge Rowland said. "Court is adjourned." He walked away shaking his head.

As she had expected, Bonnie saw Sheriff Ingram coming on a run, and watched him put handcuffs on Charles. "I'm arresting you for the theft of the jewelry and the motorcycle that belonged to Donald Wilms." Then Bob advised Charles of his rights.

From the expression on Charles' face, Bonnie realized he had figured he was free. "Miss Cole, will you help me get out of this?" he asked.

"Sorry, Charles, I'm packed and ready to leave immediately. I'm sure a public defender will represent you. Goodbye Charles, and good luck."

She watched Bob take Charles away, but as she pushed on the swinging door, it surprised her to find that it wouldn't open. Surprisingly, Billy Pile stood holding it, with a big smile on his face. "Miss Cole, I can't thank you enough for forcing me to realize I had no claim on the Wilms' mine. From now on, I can have peace of mind," he said.

"I'm sorry for the embarrassing questions, but I had to know," Bonnie said.

"Please don't feel bad, I'm most grateful, and I wish you the best."

Bonnie smiled. "The same to you. One thing I'd like to know, did you hide in Donald's hall closet?"

"Yes, when I heard someone coming, I ran in there and closed the door."

"Thanks Billy. I've wondered how mud got on that carpet." He turned and walked away.

Bonnie glanced at the seat where Grace sat. Did she stay with Clay for 53 years out of fear, love or pity? she wondered.

As Bonnie left the courtroom, she saw Mike and Art by the door. Before she could get to them, Frulik stopped her. "I'd like the name of the witness that saw Dizzy kill the Ryan brothers."

"Do you mean the man who stood in court today?" Bonnie asked.

"Yes, I need his name."

"He wasn't my witness."

"Who was he?"

"Arnold Rigby," Bonnie said.

"Arnold Rigby," Frulik shouted. Then his voice softened. "He's crazy. I can't put him on the witness stand."

"I know. I couldn't either," Bonnie said. As she approached Art and Mike, she said, "Art, if you hadn't remembered seeing Billy's pocket knife in Clay's workshop, I'd have sent an innocent man to prison."

"Billy wasn't completely innocent," Art said. He took a deep breath. "Were there three killers on the mountain that Sunday?"

"Actually, the count was four. Within two hours, Arnold Rigby wanted Marie back; Dizzy was after money; Billy Pile wanted revenge; and Clay Wilder was going to stop the affair between Grace and Donald."

Art's mouth dropped open. "That's incredible! Arnold lost Marie 50 years ago. Dad never kept money in the house. Billy was wrong, and Dad never had an affair with Grace. Thanks for everything. As much as this hurts, I'm still glad I know who did it," he said.

She nodded to Art and gazed at the big double doors as they swung open. As they closed, she sighed sadly but in relief: *This will be the last time those doors will close behind me.*

Outside, Mike opened the car door on the passenger side and walked around to get in under the wheel.

Art took Bonnie in his arms and she leaned willingly against him. She responded to his kiss, knowing it would never be repeated. His eyes filled with compassion and appreciation and with love he whispered,

"TILL WE MEET AGAIN."